UNNATURAL ACTS

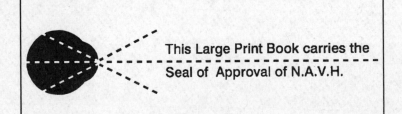

A STONE BARRINGTON NOVEL

UNNATURAL ACTS

STUART WOODS

THORNDIKE PRESS
A part of Gale, Cengage Learning

GALE
CENGAGE Learning®

Detroit • New York • San Francisco • New Haven, Conn • Waterville, Maine • London

GALE
CENGAGE Learning·

Thorndike Press® Large Print Basic.
The text of this Large Print edition is unabridged.
Other aspects of the book may vary from the original edition.
Set in 16 pt. Plantin.

LIBRARY OF CONGRESS CATALOGING-IN-PUBLICATION DATA

Unnatural acts / by Stuart Woods.
    pages ; cm. — (Thorndike Press large print basic) (A Stone Barrington novel)
    ISBN 978-1-4104-4721-0 (hardcover) — ISBN 1-4104-4721-9 (hardcover)
1. Barrington, Stone (Fictitious character)—Fiction. 2. Large type books.
PS3573.O642U56 2012b
813'.54—dc23   2012005142

Published in 2012 by arrangement with G. P. Putnam's Sons, a member of Penguin Group (USA), Inc.

Printed in the United States of America
1 2 3 4 5 6 7 16 15 14 13 12

This book is for Carole Casseus

1

Elaine's, late.

It was as late as it was ever going to get at Elaine's. Elaine had died nearly six months earlier, and the restaurant couldn't make it without her. This was its last night.

"You know," Dino said, gazing at the mob jammed into the place, "if half these people had had dinner here once a week after she died, this joint would still be thriving."

"You're right," Stone said, "but I guess the place could never be the same without Elaine to hold it together."

"I feel sorry for the writers," Dino said. "There isn't another joint in town that gives the best tables to writers. They'll be wandering up and down Second Avenue, looking for someplace to eat."

"And think of all the book deals that won't get made here," Stone said. "Where else do writers and publishers mingle?"

All the tables had temporary tops that

seated ten people, and Stone and Dino were jammed against the wall, so close to the next table that if they wanted to get to the men's room, they would have to stand on their chairs and walk across the table. There were two hundred people lined up on Second Avenue, waiting to get in.

Bill Eggers, the managing partner of Stone's law firm, Woodman & Weld, spoke up from across the table. "Never mind the writers," he said, "where are you two guys going to eat?"

"I have no idea," Stone said. "There just isn't another place in the city that has what Elaine's had. Forty-eight years she was here."

Somebody with a video cam elbowed his way up to the table and panned around the group. Herbie Fisher and his girl and Bob Cantor and his wife were there. Holly Barker had flown up from Washington for the occasion and was staying with Stone. The cameraman moved on. Stone looked around and saw plenty of regulars: Gay Talese, Frederic Morton, David Black, Nick Taylor, Carol Higgins Clark — all writers; photographers Harry Benson and Jessica Burstein were taking pictures; Alec Baldwin, with shaggy hair and a full beard, had found a video cam somewhere and was using it; Josh

8

Gaspero, retired publisher, and his Thursday-night regulars were at their regular table. Gianni and Frank, the headwaiters, and all the waiters, were still there; none had left for another job before the end.

It was just like every other night at Elaine's, except for the three hundred extra people.

Stone had ordered the most expensive wines, because he knew Elaine would have loved that. She had liked nothing better than flogging a few bottles of Dom Pérignon of an evening.

Holly hugged Stone's arm. "I'm sorry, Stone, I know how you loved Elaine and her joint."

"That's what she always called it," Stone said, "her joint."

Dino poured himself another Johnnie Walker Black from the bottle on the table.

"Can I get you a straw for that?" Stone asked.

Dino handed him a bottle of Knob Creek. "And for this?"

A good-looking redhead Stone didn't recognize struggled past his table, heading for either the bar or the front door. Stone was still watching her a moment later when she was stopped by a man who had planted himself in her path. He leaned over and shouted above the din into her ear. She drew back her right hand and punched him squarely in the face. He fell, scattering drinkers, and Stone could have sworn she stepped on him as she continued out the door.

The man was helped to his feet, swearing, his nose bloody, shouting unpleasant descriptions of the redhead to anyone who would listen.

"Did you see that?" Holly asked.

"I did."

"She looked familiar. Do you know her?"

Stone shook his head. "Nope, I don't know any redheads."

"Maybe she wasn't always a redhead," Holly said.

"Who knows? I don't know three-quarters of the people in here."

"I didn't get a look at her face," Dino said, "but I know the guy she knocked down, name of Billy Gaston, ex-cop, now a PI. Nasty piece of work."

"Never heard of him," Stone said.

"He was a street cop, made detective after you left. He was on the take from all sorts of people. The brass couldn't prove it, but everybody knew it. He was told he might be happier in civilian life, and he took the hint."

"She really slugged him, didn't she?"

Stone laughed.

"And I really enjoyed it," Dino said.

Stone and Holly staggered into his house in Turtle Bay and took the elevator upstairs, necking all the way. Leaving a trail of clothing, they made their way into the bedroom to be greeted by a persistently ringing telephone. Stone looked at the instrument. His third line was ringing, the one that the answering machine didn't pick up. Stone pressed the speaker button and fell into bed beside Holly.

"Yeah?"

"It's Dino."

"You son of a bitch," Stone said, "you knew I'd have to pick up line three."

"Of course," Dino said. "I want you to listen to something. It's important."

"*Listen* to something? What are you talking about?"

"Just shut up and listen." There were noises, then Stone could clearly hear a female voice.

"Hey, Dino," she said, "it's Shelley. Well, not anymore, but you wouldn't recognize my new name. I saw you at Elaine's tonight. Sad, isn't it? The first time I was ever in the place, and it was the last night. You and Stone and Holly seemed to be having a good time, but I could tell you were a little depressed. Who were all the other people at your table? Regulars, I guess. Well, it's late, and I'd better let you get to bed. I may be in town for a little while, so I'll call again. Maybe we can actually talk." There was a click.

"That's it," Dino said.

Stone, Dino, and Holly had spent a lot of time in Washington, D.C., the previous summer while Dino and Stone investigated a year-old murder and a suicide, which turned into a string of five murders, all women. Turned out, the murderer had been in their midst all along.

"Holy shit!" Holly said. "Shelley is in New York?"

"What are you going to do about it, Dino?" Stone asked.

"What the hell can I do about it?" Dino asked.

"The woman is a serial killer," Stone reminded him. "You can't ignore this."

"What do you suggest?"

"You might keep that recording for later," Stone said.

"Okay, I'll do that. What else?"

"You're right, I'm stumped, too. If I were you, I'd give Kerry Smith at the FBI a call tomorrow morning and tell him about this."

"Okay, I'll do that, then I'll forget about it."

"Sleep tight," Stone said, then pushed the speaker button again to disconnect.

"So she's still out there?"

"Shhhhh," Stone said, kissing her, then he moved on to other things.

2

Stone woke at his usual seven A.M., but worse than usual for the wear. "Groan," he said.

Holly stirred beside him. "Groan here, too. What were we drinking last night?"

"Bourbon and Dom Pérignon," Stone said, "and I think there was some red wine in between."

"My head remembers them all," Holly said. "Aspirin?"

"In your medicine cabinet," he replied, and Holly padded across the bedroom to her bathroom. "Bring me three," Stone called out. "And some water."

Holly returned with the aspirin bottle and a glass of water, and they both partook.

"A good breakfast will chase away the hangover," Stone said, picking up the phone and buzzing Helene, his housekeeper. He ordered eggs scrambled with cheese, bacon, English muffins, orange juice, and coffee, then hung up.

"Thank God we don't have to fix breakfast," Holly said.

"Or go out for it. Dino does that every day — goes to some diner near his apartment."

"Couldn't face it." Holly pulled the covers over her head.

"Didn't we have some sort of conversation with Dino last night? Something about Shelley Bach?"

"Groan again," Holly said, her voice muffled. "Don't want to know."

"There's been a nationwide APB out for her for what — nine, ten months? How can she elude law enforcement for that long in this day and age?"

"Can't be done," Holly said, still muffled.

Stone pulled down the covers far enough to expose her lips, then kissed her. "Tell me how you'd do that, if you were Shelley."

"Well," Holly said, "she was an assistant director of the FBI, after all. That means she knows how law enforcement finds fleeing felons. Also, she had access to equipment and computers that would allow her to make fake IDs, driver's licenses, et cetera — probably even passports. We know she switched cars early in the chase — she probably bought a car under a false name — and

15

she must have had some sort of hideout ready, something out of the way and quiet. She's got to be calling Dino from a throwaway cell phone — the greatest aid to criminal conduct since the blackjack. The FBI would have to be very lucky indeed to catch her."

"You have a point," Stone said.

"I have many points."

"She's such a striking woman that it's a wonder she could move around in public without being spotted by some citizen. After all, her face was all over TV last summer and fall."

"Yeah, but the only photo they had was the one on her FBI ID," Holly said, "just a straight-on, washed-out black-and-white shot, no better than a mug shot, really, and her hair was short when that picture was taken. Hair dye and makeup can work wonders for a girl these days." She held up a strand of her auburn hair. "Look at this."

The bell on the dumbwaiter rang, and Stone got out of bed and brought back the big breakfast tray, complete with the *New York Times* and the *Wall Street Journal*. Stone took the front page of the *Times* and handed the rest to Holly.

"I can't face the news without something

16

in my stomach besides champagne," she said.

Stone went to the bar fridge, came back with a half bottle of Schramsberg Blanc de Blanc, and popped the cork. "Hair of the dog," he said, pouring half a glass and adding orange juice.

"A mimosa," she said. "Just the thing."

"A Buck's Fizz, the Brits call it. I like that better."

Holly took a long draft. "Whatever you call it, it hits the spot."

They dug into breakfast.

Dino finished breakfast at his local diner then got out his cell phone and speed-dialed FBI headquarters, in Washington.

"Deputy Director Kerry Smith," he said to the operator. "Lieutenant Dino Bacchetti, NYPD, calling."

"Deputy Director Smith's office," a secretary said. "Lieutenant Bacchetti?"

"Right here."

"He's . . . no, wait, he just got off the line."

There was a click, then Kerry Smith said, "Dino?"

"One and the same."

"How are you?"

"A little hungover," Dino admitted. "We closed Elaine's last night, for the last time."

"You know, I never made it there," Kerry replied.

"Too late now," Dino said. "You know who else was there?"

"Who?"

"Your former assistant director, Ms. Bach."

"You *saw* her? Did you call it in?"

"No, she saw me. There was a message from her on my answering machine when I got in. You want to hear it?"

"Yes, please."

Dino held the phone next to the machine and pressed the button. When she had finished talking he put the phone back to his ear. "Could you hear that?"

"Yes, and I recorded it, so I don't have to send two agents over there to rip out your phone and take the tape."

"That's kind of you, Kerry. What now?"

"I'll alert the New York field office, and they'll take it from there."

"You want me to put out an APB with my department? Your guys don't know anything about finding a fugitive in New York."

"I don't accept that contention, but I accept your offer of an APB. What do you think your chances are of finding her?"

"About the same as yours," Dino said. "Zip, pretty much. She's a smart girl, you

18

should forgive the expression, and if you haven't run her down so far, you're not likely to get her now. There are eight million stories in the city, and hers is only one of them."

"You're probably right," Kerry said, "but I'll deny I ever said that. There's more bad news on that front: Shelley had substantial inheritances from her grandfather and her mother, and she moved her capital out of the country, through a series of offshore banks. She worked on capital-tracing cases earlier in her career, so she knows how to do that."

"So she's well financed?"

"Extremely."

"I could never get her to talk much about her background," Dino said. "What do you know about her?"

"Born in Philadelphia, where her grandfather owned a large department store. Her father died in a riding accident when she was seven, fell off a horse and broke his neck. She and her mother moved in with the grandparents, and she had a happy life. College at Mount Holyoke and Harvard Law School, where she edited the *Law Review.* Joined a New York firm after school, lasted a couple of years. Hated it. Joined the

Bureau for excitement, I guess, and she did well."

"Suppose she shows up. What do you want me to do?"

"Are you nuts? Arrest her!"

"I'd feel bad about that," Dino said. "We got close when I was in D.C."

"Yeah, well, she and I were close for a couple of years, too, but I wouldn't hesitate to clap irons on her."

"Yes, you would," Dino said.

"Well, maybe for a second or two," Kerry admitted. "She was really something."

"Yeah," Dino said, "she was. See you, Kerry." He hung up and waved at a waitress for another cup of coffee.

3

Stone got a call from Bill Eggers at ten.

"Stone, we've got a client who needs the sort of attention that you've given our clients in the past."

"What's his problem?" Stone asked.

"We're having lunch with him at the Four Seasons at one o'clock. He'll explain it to you then."

"Fine, Bill, see you there." Stone hung up and reflected on the kind of help he had given to clients of Woodman & Weld in the past. His specialty had been to handle the kind of cases the firm did not wish to be seen handling in-house. Now that he was a partner, Stone did not particularly wish to be seen handling those cases himself. However, he could not refuse such a request from Bill Eggers out of hand. There was an etiquette involved here. Stone would have to listen to the client's problem, then find a way to tell Eggers that he would not handle it. He felt in a strong enough position, now, to tell him to go fuck himself, if necessary. He was responsible for three major additions to the Woodman & Weld client list, one of them his late wife's estate, as well as himself and Peter. He made a decision: if he didn't want to do it, then the hell with it.

Stone arrived at the Four Seasons, which occupied the ground floor of the iconic Mies van der Rohe design, the Seagram Building, which also housed Woodman & Weld. He walked up the stairs, past the bar, and into the Grill Room, where Eggers's permanently reserved table sat. Bill was already there, and they shook hands.

Stone needed to keep his wits about him, so he ordered San Pellegrino mineral water. "So, Bill, who's the client and what's his problem?"

"The client is Marshall Brennan," he said, "of the Brennan Group."

Stone didn't need the firm name; everybody on the planet with a room-temperature IQ knew who Marshall Brennan was and, apparently, was anxious to invest in his hedge fund, which controlled a growing list of diversified companies, everything from hotel and restaurant chains to industrial and high-tech companies. Stone had seen the man across crowded rooms but had never met him. "And what's his problem?"

"Ah," Eggers said, "here he is now." He stood up to greet his client. "Good afternoon, Marshall. I'd like you to meet our partner, Stone Barrington."

Stone shook the man's hand and observed that he was wearing a faded, wash-and-wear suit and a bad necktie and was carrying a cheap plastic briefcase, this from a multibillionaire.

"I hope you've been well," Eggers said. "And Ethel, too."

"Yes, we're both well, Bill. And, Stone, it's a pleasure to meet you. I've been following with interest your progress with the new hotel in Bel-Air."

Stone's son had inherited from his mother an eighteen-acre property in Bel-Air, Los Angeles, and Stone was a lead investor in the project to build a new, ultra-luxury-class hotel there.

"Thank you, Marshall, it seems to be going well. We broke ground last fall, and the old Vance Calder house is being turned into the reception area, with an addition for offices. Construction has begun on the cottages and rooms, too."

"What's your grand opening date?" Brennan asked.

"Probably early next year. I don't think we can make Christmas, unless things go faster than planned."

"My people have had a lot of experience in hotels, so let me know if I can be of any help."

"Thank you, Marshall, that's kind of you." They ordered lunch, then Eggers sat back in his chair. "Stone, Marshall's youngest son, Dink, has gotten himself into a bit of a mess."

"Oh?" Stone couldn't wait to hear this.

"He's at Yale — in Peter's class — and he has acquired a bit of a gambling problem."

"How much of a problem?" Stone asked.

"About two hundred thousand dollars' worth," Brennan interjected, "to a bookie and loan shark."

"Is he able to pay it?" Stone asked.

"Of course not," Brennan replied, "but the bookie knows *I* can pay it."

"Do you intend to pay it?" Stone asked.

"That depends a lot on the advice I get from you. Bill tells me you've dealt with people like this in the past."

"I was a police officer for fourteen years," Stone replied. "I dealt with all sorts of people, some of whom were unable or unwilling to pay their gambling and loan debts."

24

"What happened to those who couldn't or wouldn't pay?"

"Unpleasant things," Stone said. "I've rarely known a bookie or a loan shark to kill people, because the dead can't pay their debts, but quite often such people required medical attention after negotiations failed."

"So, these things are negotiable?"

"Only when the lender is convinced that the borrower can't pay it all. In your case, as you say, he already knows that you're Dink's father."

"That's what I've been told."

"Then I should think that the bookie/lender has every intention of collecting every penny, and the total goes up daily, at the rate of about ten percent a week, so time is of the essence."

"Can I have him arrested?"

"Such activities are certainly against the law, but I don't think you want to get into a legal wrangle with a criminal. First of all, such action would not necessarily protect your son or even you from retribution, and second, there might be an unwanted level of public attention brought to bear on everyone involved. The tabloids would love the story."

"So I should pay up and end it?"

"Paying up is probably necessary, but that

25

might not end it."

Brennan looked alarmed. "Why not?"

"Because paying the money won't deal with your son's gambling problem. Indeed, if you get him off the hook this time, he might take that to mean that you always will. And the paid-off bookie will certainly be willing to extend him more credit."

"So how do I fix this?"

"Marshall, may I ask, what is your relationship like with your son, apart from the gambling?"

"Sometimes good, sometimes bad," Brennan said.

"Good when he gets what he wants, bad when he doesn't?"

"That's about the size of it."

"Then I can only tell you what I would do if it were my son."

"And what is that?"

"How old is he?"

"Twenty."

"That precludes an involuntary commitment to an institution."

"Yes, it does. I thought of that."

"Does he have means of his own?"

"No."

"Then I would sit him down and force him to close his bank and credit card accounts and destroy his credit cards. I would

26

leave him no option but to leave Yale and voluntarily enter an intense, residential treatment program, and by 'residential' I mean a place with a high fence around it and bars on the windows."

"And what if he refuses to cooperate?"

"Then leave him to the tender mercies of his bookie. After a couple of large men have beaten him to a pulp, he may take a different view of things."

To Stone's discomfort, Marshall Brennan began to cry.

Eggers comforted him while Stone waited quietly for him to continue.

Finally, Brennan was able to speak. "I don't think I can confront my son in that fashion."

"Then have someone else confront him."

"Do you have someone in mind?" Eggers asked, obviously hoping that Stone would volunteer.

"I think Herbert Fisher would be well suited to the task," Stone replied.

"Who is Herbert Fisher?" Brennan asked.

"He's a young attorney with Woodman and Weld," Stone replied. "He has a history of such problems in his own past, from which he has recovered."

"He's one of the firm's outstanding associates," Eggers added.

Brennan took a deep breath and let it out. "All right," he said. "Do it."

"Do what?" Stone asked.

"Exactly what you just said. Have your young man deal with it: pay the bookie, recommend a treatment facility, and confront Dink."

Stone took a jotter and a pen from his pocket and handed them to Brennan. "His full name, address at Yale, cell and phone numbers. And a list of his bank accounts and credit cards. And the name of the bookie/loan shark."

Brennan wrote it all down. "There's a briefcase under the table with two hundred thousand dollars in it." He handed Stone a business card. "Call me on the cell number if you need any further information." Then Marshall Brennan got up and left.

Eggers produced a cell phone and pressed a button. "Herbert Fisher, please. It's Eggers. Hello, Herbie? You're invited to lunch downstairs, my table, now." He closed the phone. "Do you need me here for this?"

"Yes," Stone said. "I want Herbie to know this comes from you, and anyway, you haven't eaten yet."

4

Herbie Fisher arrived just as his lunch did. "Good afternoon, gentlemen," he said as he sat down.

"We ordered for you," Eggers said.

Stone reflected that Herbie dressed better these days than many of the partners at Woodman & Weld, and that he had grown up a lot in other ways, helped along by his recent, newfound lottery wealth.

"What are you working on?" Eggers asked him.

"Whatever the partner throws my way," Herbie replied, "and she's thrown me a very mixed bag."

"Tell her that you're going to be dealing with the problem of one of my clients for a few days," Eggers said.

"Yessir."

"We've chosen you for this assignment," Eggers said, "because, among the partners and associates, you are uniquely qualified to handle it."

Herbie shoved a bite of Dover sole into his mouth. "I think that means the client's problem has, shall we say, unsavory aspects."

"You are correct," Eggers said. "Not that we feel there's anything unsavory about you, Herbie, just that you have experience with the kind of people who are a big part of the problem."

"I understand, I think."

"Stone, explain things to Herbie."

Stone explained things to Herbie. "Now, how would you handle the situation?"

"First," Herbie said, "I'd visit the young man and impress upon him that either his life is about to change drastically for the better, or it will change drastically for the worse."

"Good. What if he doesn't buy what you're selling?"

"Is the boy's father willing for his son to take a beating by professionals?"

"Yes," Eggers said. "By professionals, I take it you mean people who can make an impression on the young man without killing or permanently disabling him."

"That is correct," Herbie replied. "What is the boy's involvement with drugs?"

"We neglected to inquire about that," Stone said.

"Well, his kind of behavior is nearly always associated with either booze or drugs or both. Probably cocaine, in this case, so he may owe a dealer, too. Is more money available for that?"

Eggers addressed this. "I believe I can convince our client to come up with whatever is necessary, if he feels that he has a chance to rescue his son."

"All right," Herbie said, "I'll take it on, but I'm going to need some things from you gentlemen."

"Name them," Eggers said.

"Bill, I'm going to need the name and address of a facility that can protect the boy both from harm and from himself."

"I can find out," Eggers agreed.

"And a voluntary commitment form for the kid to sign. I can notarize it."

"In one hour," Eggers said.

"I'm going to need two large men from the facility to be parked outside the boy's residence while I'm talking to him, which means he has to be preregistered."

"I can do that, too."

"Stone, I'm going to need those two guys, the brothers, who work for Bob Cantor."

"Willie and Jimmy Leahy." The brothers were large ex-cops.

"Right. I'll want to take them with me up

31

to Yale and to talk to the bookie."

Stone handed Herbie the list that Brennan had written down.

"Carlo Contini," Herbie said. "I know him. He was my bookie" — he looked at Eggers — "some years ago."

"Good," Stone said. "It's nice that you two are acquainted."

"What's this Carlo like?" Eggers asked.

"Easygoing when a client is paid up, mean when he's in arrears."

"I was afraid of that."

"How much am I authorized to pay Carlo?"

"There's a briefcase next to your right foot containing two hundred grand," Stone said. "Try and get by on that."

"How much does the kid owe?"

"His father says two hundred grand."

"Including vigorish?"

"Apparently."

Herbie reached down and picked up the briefcase. "In hundreds? That's what it feels like."

"Does it matter?"

"Hundreds count faster, takes half as long as fifties."

"Herbie, for all I know it's in pennies."

"Nah, pennies would fill a couple of trunks."

"Deal with it."

"I'll do that," Herbie said, looking at his Cartier Tank wristwatch. "If you can get the Leahys for me first thing tomorrow morning, I can make New Haven by noon." He looked at the paper again. "Dink? What's the kid's real name?"

"Denton," Eggers said. "Exactly what are you going to say to the boy, Herbie? I mean, you've got to convince him to take the deal."

"Bill, I don't think you need to know that, or want to," Herbie replied.

"You're probably right," Eggers said, looking at his watch. "I'd better get upstairs and get you the name of a clinic and the commitment form." He signed the check and left.

"So, Stone," Herbie said, polishing off the Dover sole, "how did my name come up?"

"Your qualifications were obvious," Stone replied.

"Am I the firm's new Stone Barrington?"

"Herbie, think of this as an opportunity to impress Eggers and a very, very important client. If you can pull this off smoothly, nice things will happen."

"And if it doesn't go smoothly?"

"Failure is never attractive, Herbie." Stone clapped him on the back and left.

33

Herbie waved at a waiter. "May I see the dessert menu, please?"

5

Herbie Fisher was up early the next morning. He ordered his car from the garage for
nine A.M., then he showered, shaved, and
returned to his bedroom, where he made
love to Allison, Stone's associate and Herbie's girlfriend for the past few months.

He was dressed and ready to go when
Willie and Jimmy Leahy arrived. They
renewed their acquaintance, then Herbie
gave them coffee and sat them down. "Did
Stone tell you anything about what we're
doing today?"

"Not much," Willie said. Willie usually did
all the talking for his brother. "He said you
wanted us to talk to some people."

"Not exactly," Herbie said. "I'm going to
do the talking. Your job will be to stand
there and look just a tiny bit menacing."

"We can do that," Willie replied.

"Okay," Herbie said, "we're off to New
Haven." He led them to the elevator and

down to the garage.

"What is *that?*" Willie asked, pointing. "It looks like an overgrown Mercedes."

"It *is* an overgrown Mercedes," Herbie replied. "But it's called a Maybach. One of you drive, I'll sit in the back." Herbie settled into the backseat and called out directions to Jimmy, who was at the wheel. Then he put on a headset and tuned in WQXR, the classical station. Herbie loved sitting in the backseat. No one at Woodman & Weld knew that he owned this car. He felt it was not good policy to outdo the partners.

They stopped in front of Dink Brennan's dormitory at the stroke of eleven.

"What if our boy is in class?" Willie asked.

"My guess," Herbie said, "is that our boy didn't make it to class this morning, or on many other days. Let's go." He hopped out of the car and walked over to a van parked close by, which bore the name Winwood Farm on its door. He rapped on the passenger window, and it slid down. Two men in green hospital garb sat inside.

"Are you Mr. Fisher?" one of them asked.

"That's right," Herbie replied. "We're going upstairs to speak with the young man. Give me your cell number." Herbie tapped it into his iPhone. "I'll call if we need you," he said. "Did you bring a straitjacket, as requested?"

"In the back," the driver said.

"I'll also let you know if we'll need it." The window slid back up.

Herbie led the Leahys into the dorm and looked up Dink Brennan in the directory, then they took the elevator to the fourth floor and found the boy's suite. Herbie knocked on the door and got no answer. He tried the door, but it was locked. "Anybody know how to get this open without breaking it down?"

Willie produced a credit-card-sized sheet of plastic and, in a flash, had the door open. They walked into the sitting room, which looked as though a hurricane had swept through it.

"Ugh," Jimmy Leahy said, uttering his first sound of the morning.

Herbie opened the bedroom door and walked in. Both beds were disheveled, and one contained a large lump. Herbie drew back the sheet. "Hey, Dink?" he yelled, close to the young man's ear.

"Huh?" the boy said, lifting his head from the pillow. "Yeah? Who are you guys?" He sat up. "Oh, I get it; you're from Carlo. Tell him I'll have his money in a few days."

"Get on your feet, Dink," Herbie said, and

the boy obediently got out of bed and stood there, awkwardly.

"Have a seat at your desk," Herbie said. Dink did so. Herbie produced two documents and a pen. "Sign these."

"What are they?"

Herbie slapped him smartly on the back of the head. "Questions later. Sign them."

Dink signed his name.

"Willie, Jimmy, witness, please, in the spaces provided."

The Leahys did so while Dink looked nervously at Herbie.

Herbie tucked the documents into his pocket, walked over to a leather club chair, swept it free of dirty clothes, and sat down.

"If you're not from Carlo, who are you?" Dink asked.

"We're not from Carlo," he said. "We're the good guys. The bad guys come later, if you and I don't have a satisfactory conversation."

"I don't get it," Dink said, now fully awake.

"I'm your new attorney," Herbie said. "Don't worry, your father is paying."

"Paying for what?"

"For my getting you out of this terrible fix you're in."

Dink shook his head. "I'm not in any kind

of fix. All I have to do is pay the bookie."

"How much do you owe him?" Herbie asked.

"I don't know, exactly," Dink said, "but I can handle it."

"How will you handle it, Dink? Are you dealing drugs?"

"Of course not," Dink replied.

"Do you have any other source of income? Other than your father, I mean."

"Ah, no. Why do I need a lawyer?"

"To get you out of the treatment center."

"What treatment center?"

"It's called Winwood Farm. I understand it's a lovely place."

"Treatment for what?"

"For an addiction to gambling and the drug of your choice, which is cocaine, isn't it?"

"I snort a little now and then," Dink said.

"Yeah, sure. Let's cut to the chase, Dink. Your father loves you, and he's very concerned about you. That's why we're here, instead of the bookie. He's going to pay off the bookie, and — Oh, by the way, how much do you owe your dealer?"

"Not a dime," Dink said. "He insists on cash."

"That makes it simpler," Herbie replied. "Now, the two documents you just signed are these: a durable power of attorney, giving me control over all your affairs, including your relationship with Yale, and a self-commitment form, making you a residential patient at Winwood Farm, which is only a few miles from here."

"I'm not going to any loony bin," the boy said.

"Jimmy," Herbie said, "pack Dink a small bag — just some underwear, a change of clothes, and his slippers. That's all he'll need."

Jimmy went to a closet, found a small duffel, and rifled a chest of drawers. "Got it all," he said, zipping the bag shut.

"Now, Dink," Herbie said, "I want you to write a nice letter to the dean of students of this establishment, apologizing for your record at Yale and telling him that you are leaving school at this time to get some help, but that you expect to return for the fall semester."

"I'm not writing that," Dink said, "and I'm not going to the funny farm."

"There are two strong men downstairs with a straitjacket, waiting for my call," Herbie said. "You want to do this the easy way or the hard way?"

Dink looked nervously at Willie and Jimmy. "I don't want any trouble."

"Good. Now get dressed, and we'll be on our way. Don't worry about the letter to the dean; I'll write that later."

Herbie found a pair of scissors in a desk drawer, extracted four credit cards from Dink's wallet, and cut them in half. He produced a plastic bag and put Dink's money, wallet, and keys into it, then he led the boy downstairs and surrendered him to the two gentlemen from the funny farm.

"Dink," Herbie said, handing him his card, "in a few weeks, you're going to be feeling a lot better about yourself, and when that finally happens, give me a call and we'll talk about your future. In the meantime, if there's anything I can do for you, besides getting you released, just let me know."

Dink got into the van, and Herbie gave the driver the contents of Dink's pockets. The van pulled away, and Herbie and the Leahys got back into Herbie's car.

"That was easy," Willie said.

"It's about to get harder," Herbie replied. "Now, let's get back to New York, to Little Italy."

6

Herbie's Maybach slid to a halt in front of the La Bohème coffeehouse, an institution that, improbably, was the headquarters of a large criminal enterprise. From three or four of the dozen tables inside transactions took place more quickly than if a mainframe computer had been running the numbers. Carlo Contini, heir to the empire of Carmine Dattila, aka Dattila the Hun, sat out his days there doing mental calculations that gave lie to his outward appearance, which was that of an Italian-American gentleman who operated a fruit stand. No fancy suits for Carlo, just a short-sleeved shirt and a pair of baggy gray trousers. When he took his wife out to dinner, a suit appeared, laid out on his bed with an appropriate shirt and tie, and Carlo had no objection to wearing it, but here, at La Bohème, he was camouflaged as one of the layabouts who alternated drinking grappa with playing bocce in the back garden.

Herbie's appearance at La Bohème caused everyone present to freeze in position, except for a few who inserted a hand into a jacket, just in case. Herbie commanded this sort of attention because, a few years before, distraught over Dattila the Hun's attempts to have him murdered, he had walked into the place and put two Federal hollow-point .45 slugs into Dattila's head. No one had even moved, because the feds had been there a moment before and relieved people of all artillery. Now Herbie was back, and the patrons found this disturbing.

Herbie walked over to Carlo Contini's table, where he sat with his younger brother and consigliere, Gino, and pulled up a chair. "Hi, Carlo," Herbie said.

"You want to place a bet, Herbie, there are guys for that," Carlo said, then feigned ignoring him.

"Nothing like that, Carlo," Herbie replied. "I'm here on bigger business."

Carlo regarded him coolly. "A loan? Talk to Gino."

"No, Carlo, I'm here to settle a large debt."

"You don't owe me, Herbie."

"No, but a young man named Brennan does."

"Fink?"

"Dink. There's a difference."

"So, what are you to do with it?"

"I'm the boy's representative, and I'm here to settle his debt, as I've already mentioned."

"Kid owes me two hundred and thirty K," Carlo said, not bothering to consult a ledger. "You good for that?"

"I said 'settle,' Carlo, not get rolled."

"With the vig, it's two hundred and thirty K," Carlo said.

"I propose that we settle the entire debt, including the vigorish, for two hundred even," Herbie replied. He set the cheap plastic briefcase on the table. "It's right here."

"It's two hundred and thirty K," Carlo said, with conviction.

"Carlo, let me put this in the form of a proposition," Herbie said. "I give you two hundred K right now, in clean Benjamins, and you agree never to take another bet from the Brennan kid and to forget his name."

"From what I hear, his old man can afford two hundred and thirty K," Carlo said.

"Carlo, his old man can buy and sell you before breakfast and not even dent his bank balance, but he's a serious person, and he's

44

making you a serious offer. There is an alternative, though."

"Yeah? What's the alternative?"

"Use your imagination, Carlo. Imagine the NYPD, the FBI, and the IRS crawling over your life like an army of ants, while Dink's old man files a civil suit against you that will take ten years and ten million in legal fees to settle. All these things can happen within twenty-four hours."

Carlo took a deep breath and let it out. "I'm not an unreasonable man," he said, placing a hand on the briefcase.

Herbie pulled the briefcase a little out of his reach, then produced a one-page document and pushed it across the table. "Sign this, and we're done," Herbie said.

"I don't sign stuff," Carlo said.

Herbie pulled the briefcase a little farther away.

"What's it say?" Carlo asked, taking a pair of reading glasses from his shirt pocket. He began to read to himself while moving his lips.

"It says that you are accepting two hundred thousand dollars in payment of all gambling or any other debt owed you by Dink Brennan, and that you agree never to accept another bet from him or contact him ever again."

"You expect me to admit to gambling in writing?"

"It's the way people like Mr. Brennan do business, Carlo. Since the two of you are not acquainted, Mr. Brennan won't take your word. Come on, what's the harm? The paper will reside in his safe and will never see the light of day." Herbie pushed the case back to where Carlo could reach it but did not let go of the handle.

Carlo sighed and signed the document, and Herbie released the briefcase, which vanished under the table.

"Never see the light of day, unless you violate the terms of the agreement," Herbie said, standing. "Take care of yourself, Carlo." Herbie turned and walked out, trailed by the Leahys, one of whom left La Bohème walking backward.

Herbie situated himself in the backseat of the Maybach. "Drop me at the Seagram Building, Willie," he said, "and put the car back in the garage, if you will."

"Sure, Herbie," Willie said. "And by the way, nicely done."

"Thank you, Willie, and the same to you and Jimmy." Herbie picked up the rear-seat phone and pressed a speed dial button.

"Woodman and Weld," Joan said, "Stone Barrington's office."

"Hey, Joan."

"Hey, Herbie, how you doing?"

"Couldn't be better. Is he available?"

"Sure." There was a click.

"Herbie?"

"Hey, Stone."

"How'd it go?"

"It went like this: Dink is now housed in the funny farm, having committed himself and signed a durable power of attorney, naming me, and Carlo Contini is a happy man. I have his signature on a well-worded receipt that will keep him forever away from Dink."

"Well done," Stone said.

"Will you convey that to Bill Eggers?"

"No, I think you should convey it to him yourself, and bask in the warmth of his gratitude."

"I like the sound of that," Herbie said. "See ya." He hung up as the Maybach glided to the curb at the Seagram Building.

Three minutes later, Herbie was entering Bill Eggers's corner office. "Good afternoon, Bill."

"Is it?" Eggers replied.

"Dink Brennan now resides at Winwood Farm," Herbie said, taking documents from his pocket and handing them to Eggers, "and Carlo Contini has accepted our offer. It's all there."

Eggers tossed the documents on his desk without looking at them. "I just had a call, Herbie," he said. "Dink Brennan escaped from the vehicle transporting him to Winwood Farm and is abroad in the land."

Herbie felt as if he had been struck in the chest. "Well, Bill, I did as I was asked. I'm not in the escaped lunatic business."

"You are now, Herbert," Eggers replied.

7

Stone looked up from his desk to find Herbie Fisher standing in his doorway, breathing hard.

"Good afternoon, Herbie," Stone said. "Have you taken up jogging?"

"I walked over here."

"Sit down and catch your breath."

The look on Herbie's face made Stone wonder if the young man was going to explode or just cry.

"I got it all done, Stone, I told you that."

"You did. Did you tell Bill?"

"Yes. He is unhappy."

"Why?"

"Because Dink escaped from the funny farm van and is loose. I told Eggers I wasn't in charge of escaped lunatics, and he told me I am now."

"So you have a new assignment," Stone said. "Be optimistic — it gives you another opportunity to impress Eggers and Marshall

Brennan."

"I don't want to impress them anymore," Herbie said. "They have no gratitude."

"Herbie, you were asked to deliver Dink to Winwood Farm, and you failed."

"I didn't fail — his keepers failed!"

"You entrusted him to them, and they failed you. But you failed Eggers."

"That's warped," Herbie said.

"Tell me something, Herbie, did you enjoy your tasks?"

"Well, yeah, but then everything went to hell."

"Find a way to enjoy tracking down Dink. You'll feel better."

"I have no experience in the field of missing persons," Herbie wailed. "I wouldn't know where to start."

"Herbie, imagine that Dink owes you two hundred grand and that he is trying to avoid you."

"I wouldn't let him get away with that," Herbie said.

"Exactly. What Dink actually owes you is his carcass at Winwood Farm. Find him and make him pay."

"Where do I start?"

"Ask yourself, 'If I were Dink Brennan and I wanted to avoid Herbie Fisher, where would I go?' "

50

Herbie regarded his well-buffed shoes morosely. "I don't know where he would go."

"Well, you know that he would probably not go back to the one place you already know about: his dorm room. Right?"

"Well, yeah."

"Who are his friends? Who is his girlfriend? Where does he drink? Those are all pertinent questions. Start finding out the answers."

"Can I hire a PI? Those guys know how this is done."

Stone sighed. "All right, I will authorize you to hire a skip tracer for three days at the expense of Woodman and Weld."

"Eggers would go nuts if I spent that money."

"No, Eggers would simply bill Marshall Brennan."

"Oh. I hadn't thought of that."

"Suck it up, Herbie. Get it in gear, move your ass."

Herbie got up and slouched toward the door.

"Herbie?"

"Yeah?"

"Do you know a skip tracer?"

Herbie thought for a minute. "No," he admitted.

"Sit down. I'm going to help you out."

Stone pressed a button on his phone. "Joan, please get me Mike Freeman at Strategic Services." He waited a moment.

"Mr. Freeman on one."

Stone picked up the phone. "Mike?"

"Hello, Stone, welcome back from our nation's capital. I read of your exploits in some of our worst newspapers."

"Put it out of your mind, Mike. I have."

"If you say so."

"Mike, you've met a Woodman and Weld associate named Herbie Fisher, have you not?"

"I have. Nice young fellow."

"And you know Marshall Brennan?"

"I do. I invest with him."

"Good. Herbie was sent up to Yale to assist Marshall's son, Dink, into a bucolic establishment in Connecticut where he was to receive attention for his gambling and drug problem."

"Sounds like Winwood Farm."

"One and the same. Unfortunately, in spite of Herbie's stellar work, young Dink managed to extricate himself from the transportation provided and is now wild in the country."

"Uh-oh."

"Herbie is a bright fellow, but he has no

experience in the tracing of missing persons. I thought, perhaps, that you might provide him with some assistance."

"Who's buying? Herbie?"

"Woodman and Weld, until they can bill Marshall Brennan."

"I can do that," Mike said. "Is Herbie with you?"

"Yes, he is."

"Put him on the phone."

"Of course." Stone pointed at Herbie, then at the phone on the coffee table before the sofa in his office.

Herbie went to the sofa and picked up the phone. "Mr. Freeman? Yes, sir. No, sir, I cut up his credit cards and gave his cash to the driver of the Winwood Farm van. He was wearing jeans and a polo shirt and a brown leather jacket and sneakers. I picked him up at his Yale dorm room. No, sir, I don't know the name of his roommate or his friends, and I don't know if he has a girlfriend. Yes, sir, I'll be there in an hour." Herbie hung up, and turned toward Stone. "Mr. Freeman is on it, and I'm to go to his office."

"Herbie, you're about to have a very valuable learning experience. Watch how Mike and his people work and remember everything."

"Okay, Stone," Herbie said, getting to his feet.

"And don't walk, Herbie, it makes you pant and sweat. Take a cab."

Herbie took his leave.

Joan buzzed.

"Yes?"

"Dino on one."

Stone pressed the button. "Hey, Dino."

"We need to talk," Dino said. "Elaine's, eight-thirty?"

"Dino," Stone said sadly, "take a deep breath. Elaine's is no more, remember?" Stone could hear the sound of Dino smiting his forehead.

"Jesus, I've got to get my head on straight."

"Where shall we go?" Stone asked.

"I have no idea," Dino said.

"I know how you feel. How about P.J. Clarke's?"

"Right," Dino said, sounding relieved. "Eight-thirty."

"You book," Stone replied. "They don't hold a table for us at Clarke's."

"Not yet," Dino said, then hung up.

8

Herbie Fisher arrived at Mike Freeman's Strategic Services office in exactly fifteen minutes and was shown in.

"Good afternoon, Herbie," Mike said, shaking his hand and waving him to a seat.

"Good afternoon, Mr. Freeman."

"Please call me Mike."

"Yessir, Mike."

Freeman consulted a computer monitor on his desk. "Well, let's see: Dink Brennan managed to steal back his wallet and cash before departing the Winwood Farm van, by the simple device of opening a rear door and jumping out when the van stopped for a light. Dink, it seems, is fleet of foot.

"His roommate, Parker Mosely, who was returning to the dorm as Dink was driven away, followed the van and has confessed to picking him up upon his escape from the van.

"Dink's most likely destination is his

girlfriend's parents' country house in Washington, Connecticut. Mr. Mosely did not give us that information, but his mien on being asked about it gave my people to understand that that is where he might be. The girlfriend's name is Carson Cullers, and her parents are Robert and Louise Cullers, of Ten-Ten Fifth Avenue, New York. They were apparently not aware of this spontaneous use of their country place."

Herbie was in awe. "Jesus, you found out all that in fifteen minutes?"

"When you have good people in appropriate places it is remarkable what they can learn in fifteen minutes," Freeman said. "Incidentally, Dink has already reported the loss of his credit cards to the various companies, and replacements have been overnighted to him. We were unable to ascertain the address to which they were sent — that would take us another day, at least — but it seems likely they went to the Kirby Road house in Washington. Two of my people are en route there from Hartford and should arrive in another hour or so."

"There doesn't seem to be much left for me to do, does there?"

"I suppose not. If my people find him in Washington, you may be sure that he will have been returned to Winwood Farm by dinnertime."

"That's great."

"Herbie, judging from what I have learned, you did a very fine job today. Dink's being returned to Winwood Farm is entirely due to the self-commitment letter you required him to sign. That was a very smart move, as was your obtaining a durable power of attorney. I'll see that Bill Eggers is aware of that."

"Thank you, Mike, that would be a load off my mind."

"I should tell you," Freeman said, "that since our phone conversation I have been able to learn a great deal about you. I was appalled at the mess you made of your existence early on, but I'm very impressed with the turnaround you've made in your life. Because I'm impressed, I'm going to do you a favor, with your permission."

"You have my permission," Herbie said, "whatever the favor is."

"You will recall that when Stone handled your divorce he got your former wife to cede to you her investment account at her father's firm, amounting to some three million dollars."

"Yes, I recall that, but she and her brother stole so much from the firm's clients that I don't see how those funds can ever be released to me."

"That would be the case if any of the victims had bothered to sue the young woman, but although there was a suit against the firm, their insurance company has made good most of their losses, so a request made to the United States attorney can be made to release the funds to you." Freeman slid a sheet of paper across the table. "If the wording of this request seems satisfactory to you, sign it and we'll go to work to get your money. The trick is to get the funds released before the firm realizes that they should have sued the daughter."

Herbie read the document and signed it. "Thank you, Mike, I'm very grateful to you."

Freeman typed a short e-mail and sent it. "You'll be pleased to learn that, since your divorce, the funds have grown to about three million, six hundred thousand dollars, due to a very successful IPO of a company in which your former wife owned shares."

"Wow."

"Herbie, you're a very impressive young man, and I'm always looking for impressive young men to join Strategic Services. Perhaps you've found an interesting and rewarding career at Woodman and Weld, but I suspect that, in time, you might well be considering a career path that offers you more latitude for personal growth."

"You suspect correctly, Mike," Herbie said. "The truth is, I'm already finding the law something of a grind, because of the sort of work assigned to associates."

"You mean work that no one else wishes to do?"

"Exactly. I mean, getting Dink Brennan into treatment and settling his gambling debt was fun, in its way, but not something that helps build a career."

"Don't be too sure about that," Freeman said. "I'll see that Marshall Brennan knows of your role, and you may be sure that he will express his gratitude, and not just to Bill Eggers."

"That's kind of you, Mike."

"Has it occurred to you that Eggers is probably considering you for the role of the new Stone Barrington at Woodman and Weld?"

"It has occurred to me."

"Stone had a fair deal there, one that paid him a very good income, but one that did not improve his status in the firm. That did not occur until Stone gained us as a client, and further, the Steele Companies, an insurance conglomerate I was able to introduce him to. After that, when he brought his late wife, Arrington Calder, into the firm, a partnership became possible for Stone."

"I had a sort of general idea about that," Herbie said.

"But it took him a long time to accomplish that, and if the firm sidetracked you into the kind of services Stone provided them for so long, you might not get as lucky as he did. Strategic Services offers extremely interesting work and much more rapid advancement for the right young people. I suspect that you might be one of those people."

"I appreciate that, Mike," Herbie said.

"But go on and work at Woodman and Weld for a little while longer. See if you can gain a promotion to senior associate. That would look very good on your résumé. Then, when you feel the time is right, give me a call, and we'll see what we can do for you."

"Thank you, Mike, I'll give that a lot of thought."

A little chime rang, and Freeman turned to look at his computer monitor. "Aha," he said, "young Mr. Brennan is, as we speak, en route to Winwood Farm, and this time, you may be sure he will arrive there."

Herbie felt enormously relieved. "I can't

thank you enough, Mike."

"Tell you what, Herbie," Freeman said, "since we were able to wrap this up so quickly, I won't bill Woodman and Weld for our services. Why don't you call Bill Eggers and give him the good news? Use the phone over there." He pointed to a coffee table.

Herbie went to the phone and called Eggers.

"Hello, Herbert," Eggers said. "This had better be good news."

"Bill," Herbie replied, "Dink Brennan is on his way back to Winwood Farm."

"Well, that *is* good news! How did you manage it?"

"I don't think I need to go into the details, Bill. Suffice it to say that everything you asked me to do has been done, and in very short order. And I have to tell you, I don't appreciate the threat implicit in your earlier statement."

There was dead silence at the other end of the line.

"Goodbye, Bill. I won't be coming back to the office today." Herbie hung up.

Mike Freeman was laughing. "Something else I like about you, Herbie — you have an enormous set of brass balls."

9

Stone and Dino met at P.J. Clarke's bar and had their usual drinks, Knob Creek bourbon for Stone and Johnnie Walker Black Label scotch for Dino. Dino looked troubled.

"What's the matter, pal, are you still grieving for Elaine's?"

"Well, yes," Dino replied, "but that's not what's bothering me now."

"What is?"

"I've had another call from Shelley Bach," Dino said.

"What did she have to say for herself?"

"She has nothing to say for herself," Dino replied. "That's the problem. She doesn't seem to think she's done anything wrong."

"Even after murdering five people?"

"Even after that."

"There's a word for that: sociopath. Someone without a conscience."

"I know that," Dino said testily.

"Next time, just hang up on her."

"Trouble is, I didn't," Dino said.

"How long did you talk?"

"Not long. She wanted to come over to my place."

"She may be a sociopath, but she's not crazy. Why would she want to risk that?"

"Maybe because she believed I wouldn't turn her in."

Stone cleared his throat of the bourbon he had nearly inhaled. "Why would she believe that?"

"Because I didn't turn her in."

"Wait a minute, Dino, are you saying that she came to your apartment?"

Dino just nodded.

"And you didn't call anybody? Nine-one-one, the FBI, anybody?"

Dino shook his head.

"Listen to me, pal, you need to take a hike to the nearest post office and take a look at the ten-most-wanted list. You won't have any trouble finding her there, she's right at the top."

"You think I don't know that, Stone?"

"I know you, Dino, and I know that you are all cop, that you would turn in your mother if she was wanted for five murders."

Dino shrugged. "I wasn't all that crazy about my mother."

"But you're crazy about Shelley Bach?"

"That's about the size of it," Dino said disconsolately.

"Funny, I never noticed that when we met her in Washington."

"You didn't notice, because you were in your room screwing Holly Barker while Shelley and I were in my room, fucking our brains out. We didn't have all that much opportunity to talk."

"I suppose that's so," Stone agreed. "We were both pretty busy at the time."

"Busier than I've ever been in my whole life," Dino said. "We were fucking at least twice a day every day we were there."

"That's a tough schedule, Dino. You're in better shape than I thought."

The headwaiter summoned them for their table, and they followed him into the back room, where they were seated.

"Tell me," Stone said, "in the moments when you weren't raping each other, what did you talk about? Did Shelley even mention the murders?"

"Nope. It's like they never happened. I asked her how she got away so clean, and she said that she had started making arrangements not long after we arrived in D.C. She's a very smart woman. You know that guy from Boston, Whitey Bulger, that the FBI caught not long ago?"

"Sure, it was all over the TV and the papers."

"The FBI spent sixteen years hunting him, and she worked on the case for the last couple of years. I think she learned a lot about how fugitives disappear."

"I guess getting lost is an art," Stone said.

"You bet your ass it is. Just think about all the ways there are to get caught these days, what with cell phone tracing and security cameras everywhere and the Internet. It doesn't seem possible that somebody could just get lost, but that's what she's done."

"But now she's made a mistake," Stone pointed out. "She's contacted you."

Dino shook his head slowly.

"Dino, do I need to point out that abetting a fugitive can end your career and get you some serious time? What are you going to do if she kills somebody else? Then you're in deep shit."

"I don't think she will," Dino said. "She killed the first one in a rage and the others to cover it up. She doesn't have to cover up anything anymore."

"Dino, you're playing a very dangerous game here."

"You think I don't know that?"

"How about this: the next time she contacts you, tell her not to get in touch again, because you'll have to turn her in. That would put you pretty much in the clear."

"That's a good idea, Stone. When I get home tonight, I'll tell her just that."

"You mean she's in your apartment right now?"

"I told her I was going out with you, so she ordered a pizza."

"Dino, promise me you'll drop-kick her right into the street, first thing in the morning."

"I will," Dino said. "If I can."

10

Herbie was in his cubicle at Woodman & Weld at seven-thirty the following morning. He emptied his briefcase of the files he had worked on at home until midnight the night before, then walked up one level to one of the two partners' floors, to Karla Martin's office. Karla had a well-deserved reputation as the toughest partner in the firm where the treatment of associates was concerned.

With the knowledge of Mike Freeman's offer bolstering his courage, Herbie walked into Karla's office and dumped the stack of files on her desk. "Good morning, and there you are," he said. "There's a memo in each file listing the relevant precedents and case law. That makes you and me entirely up to date." He walked over to a table in a corner where a coffee thermos sat and poured himself a cup, then sat down opposite her.

Karla stared at him, unblinking, a glare that any associate would have recognized in a flash as preceding heavy weather. "I don't believe I invited you in for coffee," she said acidly.

"That's just one of the many mistakes you make with associates, Karla," Herbie replied, "especially with me."

"What?"

"I've spent two years shoring up your reputation in this firm, and I'm all done now. I'd like you to recommend me to Bill Eggers for senior associate." This was a step toward partnership, and the appointments were handed out stingily. In fact, he thought, no one could remember Karla ever recommending anyone for senior associate.

"You must be out of your mind, Herbert," she spat, "coming in here and making yourself at home and thinking I would promote you."

"You can't promote me, Karla, I know that, but if you sign this letter, it might help a bit with Eggers." He removed a letter, neatly typed on the firm's letterhead, and slid it across the desk.

Karla picked up the letter and read it.

"I don't think the praise is overdone, do you? I tried to frame it in your own inimitable, grudging style."

Karla was trembling with anger. "You little twerp," she said through clenched teeth.

"You get out of my office!"

"Just as soon as you sign the letter," Herbie said. "Oh, and a phone call to Bill would be nice, too."

"Why do you think I would ever do such a thing?" she demanded.

"Because if you don't, I'm going to start making people around here aware of what a lousy lawyer you are."

"What?"

"You've been kept afloat for years in this firm by smart associates who've done your work for you and kept their mouths shut about it, but I'm not going to keep my mouth shut. I'm in a very strong position in this firm. I have an excellent reputation here, and you don't." Herbie saw a flicker of something in her face that might have been fear. He pounced.

"You know that as well as I do, don't you? You know you couldn't count on the support of a single associate here and not more than one or two partners. You've lost two accounts in the past year, and you haven't brought anything in. You've been on the edge at Woodman and Weld, and all you need is a nudge to tumble into the abyss of unemployment."

"Then why would you want the support in the firm of someone as weak as you think

69

I am?" She smirked, as if she had won the argument.

"Because you never praise anyone for anything, Karla, and the shock just might get Bill Eggers's attention. That's the only reason, believe me." He stood up. "I'll be going now, and I'd like to take the signed letter with me." He held out a hand.

She tried the glare again, saw that it wasn't working, and signed the letter. "Now you can go to hell," she said.

Herbie put the letter into his pocket. "You first," he said, then walked out. He was quivering with excitement and exultation. He had nailed Karla Martin, and he had it in writing. She could never retract that letter.

Herbie walked up another flight of stairs and down the wide hallway that housed the senior partners, then walked into Eggers's secretary's office. "Good morning, Jane," he said, giving her his best smile. He had cultivated her carefully since the day he arrived at Woodman & Weld.

"Good morning, Herbert," she said.

"Do you think he might have a moment?"

She picked up the phone and buzzed Eggers. "Herbert Fisher would like a moment." She hung up. "He'll see you."

"Thanks, sweetheart." Herbie walked into

the big corner office. "Good morning, Bill," he said.

"Herbert," Eggers said. "I got your message about leaving early yesterday."

"Yes, I had a lot of work to get done for Karla, and I didn't want her interrupting me, as she is prone to do, so I took it home and finished it there."

"I see."

"It was the last work I'll be doing for Karla," Herbie said, matter-of-factly.

Eggers looked surprised. "Are you resigning from the firm, Herbert?"

"No, Bill, just from Karla. I won't work for her another minute."

A flicker of a smile crossed Eggers's face. "And how did Karla take that?" he asked.

"Oh, we parted on good terms," Herbie said, handing Eggers the letter.

Eggers picked up the letter and read it, looking more and more amazed. "Herbert, did you forge this?"

"Certainly not, Bill."

Eggers pressed the speaker button on his phone and dialed an extension.

"Karla Martin."

"Karla, it's Bill."

"Good morning, Bill."

"Good morning. I've just read the letter you sent me, recommending Herbert Fisher for senior associate. Do you stand by it?"

There was the briefest of pauses, causing Herbie to begin to sweat, then she said, sweetly for Karla, "Of course, Bill. He's a very bright young man, and he's done fine work for me."

"Thank you, Karla," Eggers said, then hung up. His gaze had never left Herbie's face. "I'm having a little trouble digesting this," he said. "Do you have photographs of Karla in bed with a donkey?"

Herbie laughed heartily. "Karla? I can't imagine her in bed with man or beast."

"Neither can I," Eggers said, "but before you walked in here I could never have imagined her writing this letter, either."

"Hard shell, soft heart," Herbie said, shrugging. "Who knew?"

"Certainly not I," Eggers said. "So you're making a formal request to be promoted to senior associate?"

"Karla was kind enough to do that for me," Herbie said.

"But you do want it, don't you?"

"Of course, Bill. I think I could be more useful to the firm in that position. And not having to slave away for Karla or another partner would give me time to make some rain around here."

"You think you could do that?" Eggers asked.

"Let's find out. My guess is that Marshall Brennan might be disposed to giving us some new business, and I'd like to handle it."

"What else do you want, Herbert?"

"A substantial raise, a real office with a window, my own secretary, and a full-time associate to do everything I don't want to do myself."

"Is that all?"

"For the time being."

"And what will you do if I don't give it to you?"

Herbie took a deep breath and prepared to threaten to resign, but he stopped himself. "I think this is in the firm's best interests, Bill, and you always do what's in the firm's best interests."

"Nobody's ever made senior associate around here in under three years," Eggers said.

Herbie observed that Eggers had not fired him yet, and he pressed his luck just a bit. "I've heard that," he said, "and I think this might give a lot of the associates new hope — even make them work harder."

Eggers pressed a button on his phone.

"Yes, Mr. Eggers?" Jane asked.

"Come in, please."

"We moved George Howard to a bigger office yesterday, didn't we?"

"Yessir."

"Give his old office to Herbert, and find him a decent secretary. Herbert is our newest senior associate. Send out the memo, and send a release to the papers and the law journals."

"Yessir."

"And who is our newest, greenest, most forlorn associate?"

Jane squinted at the ceiling for a moment. "That would be young Bobby Bentley," she said.

"Tell him he works for Herbert now."

"Yessir. Anything else?"

"Yes, type up a memo to payroll for my signature, giving Herbert a fifteen percent raise."

Herbie made a loud coughing noise.

"All right, twenty-five percent."

"Yessir!" Jane sped back to her desk.

Eggers looked at Herbie. "Why are you still here?"

"Thank you, Bill." Herbie tried to leave without appearing to hurry.

11

Dino woke from a sound sleep with the sudden knowledge that his penis was in someone's mouth, and that long, red hair was tickling his belly. He stuffed an extra pillow behind his head and watched, with growing excitement that ended in a veritable explosion. "Oh, God," he moaned.

Shelley Bach moved up the bed to share his pillow. "Well," she said, "I do know what you like."

"I can't deny that," Dino said. He took a deep breath and said what he had to say. "Shelley, you can't be here — it's too dangerous for both of us."

"You're afraid that you'll lose your job if you're found consorting with a fugitive, right?"

"More than that, Shelley, I'm afraid that you'll be in prison soon and that I will be, too. Can't you understand that that is too high a price to pay for a good blow job?"

"A sublime blow job," she pointed out.

"I agree, but they won't put us in the same cell, and I can't afford the tab when the FBI finally closes in on you."

"They won't," she said. "Would you like to know the steps I've taken to prevent that from ever happening?"

"Good God, no! I don't want to know a thing!"

"Listen, Dino, if it's war between the FBI and me, it's a fair fight."

"I don't doubt that for a minute, but we have to end this and right now."

"Oh, Dino," she breathed, "you wouldn't want to disappoint me, would you? You know how I behave when people disappoint me."

Dino got out of bed and reached for a robe. "Shelley, I wish you luck, I really do, but you have to go now."

"You want me to walk brazenly through your lobby and past the doorman?"

"You can take the elevator to the basement, turn right at the laundry room, and go out the service entrance."

"Slink out, you mean, as if I'm ashamed of being with you?"

"That's your call, Shelley, but you have to go."

"But no one knows about us, Dino."

"Stone Barrington knows," Dino replied, regretting immediately having said so.

Shelley sat up in bed, exposing a magnificent pair of breasts. "You told Stone?"

Dino fumbled for a way out. "He saw you come into the building," he said, "and he recognized you. I didn't have to tell him."

"Well now," she said, looking thoughtful. "I'm going to have to see that he doesn't drop any hints to law enforcement."

"Shelley, don't talk like that. Stone would never do that — he would want to protect me."

"I suppose," she said, getting out of bed and taking some underwear from her suitcase.

"I've got to get to the precinct, so I'm going to shave and shower," Dino said, "and I'd appreciate it very much if you would be gone when I'm done. I wish you well, Shelley."

"Yeah, sure," Shelley said, turning her back and stepping into a pair of panties.

Dino went into his bathroom, showered and shaved, then he walked back into his bedroom, looking carefully around. Shelley's suitcase was gone, and his bed was neatly made. He had to search the rest of the apartment before he could feel relieved.

■ ■ ■ ■

Dino arrived at the precinct and went to his office. A pile of mail on his desk greeted him.

"Morning, Lieutenant," a voice said, and he looked up to find his newest detective, an attractive brunette named Viv DeCarlo, standing in his doorway.

"Morning, DeCarlo," he said brusquely. "What do you need?"

"The DNA came back in the Bronson murder," she said. "It's a match for the boyfriend. I need an APB."

"Have you been to his house?" Dino asked. "It would save a lot of departmental bother if you could make the collar without the trouble of an APB."

"No, sir, I haven't," she said. "I'll need an arrest warrant and a SWAT team for that. Would that be less trouble than an APB?"

"It's a toss-up," Dino said, "but call the DA and get the warrant. Type up an authorization for the SWAT team, and I'll sign it." Dino opened the top piece of mail on his desk, a large brown envelope with an FBI return address. He shook it, and a wanted poster featuring a becoming photograph of Shelley Bach spilled onto his desktop.

"Hey," DeCarlo said, "that's the chick from D.C. who offed all those people, isn't it?"

"Yeah," Dino said. "Is there anything else preventing you from getting back to work?"

"No, no, Lieutenant. Thanks for your help."

Dino sat down and looked at the poster, then he called Stone.

"You're up early today," Stone said.

"I'm up early every day, unlike you."

"I don't have to get in early to make the morning shift think I work for a living," Stone replied.

"Well, there is that," Dino said. "Listen, pal, I've got some good news and some bad news."

"Give me the good news first."

"Okay, I threw what's-her-name out first thing this morning."

"Right after you screwed her, right?"

"The point is, she's gone and out of my life."

"What's the bad news?"

"She's not necessarily out of *your* life."

There was a long silence. "Dino," Stone said, "I'm failing to figure out what that means."

"It means she knows you know."

79

"You told her you told me?"

"Oh, no, nothing like that. I told her you saw her coming into my building and recognized her."

"So, you managed to convey my knowledge of her presence in New York while covering your own ass?"

"Well, yeah, I thought that was best."

"Best for you."

"Listen, Stone, it was an accident. We were arguing, and I spilled that you knew, but I couldn't let her think I told you. She might have offed me on the spot."

"So now she'll off me slightly later," Stone pointed out.

"I did my best to convince her that you would never rat her out because you would protect me."

"So, I come out of this dead, but a hero in her eyes?"

"Look, pal, I'm sorry, I really am, but she had me against the wall, and I was grasping at straws."

"Next time, grasp at a different straw, will you?"

"Again, I'm sorry. Gotta run." Dino hung up, and he was sweating. What the hell, he thought, the alternative was not to warn him.

80

12

Stone had just come into his office when Joan buzzed him. "Herbie on one."

Stone picked up the phone. "Good morning, Herbie. How did it go with Mike Freeman?"

"Better than I could have hoped," Herbie replied. "Dink is at the funny farm, thanks to Mike's help, and Mike offered me a job at Strategic Services, if I ever want to leave Woodman and Weld."

"Are you thinking of doing that?" Stone asked.

"No, but having that to fall back on gave me the guts to tell Karla Martin to sort of go fuck herself and get her to write a recommendation to Eggers that he promote me to senior associate."

"Herbie, it takes a while for an associate to break through that particular ceiling."

"It's done, Stone. Eggers went for it."

"What have you been smoking?"

"I kid you not. I'm in an office with a window, next to a corner office, with a beautiful view up Park Avenue, and I'm interviewing secretaries this afternoon. I've got myself an associate to abuse, too, name of Bobby Bentley."

"Go easy on him, Herbie, Bobby's dad is an important client."

"Well, that's good news. I need to make some rain around here."

"Good thinking. Congratulations, and have a perfect day."

"How could it get any more perfect?" Herbie hung up.

Half an hour later, Joan buzzed him. "Marshall Brennan on one."

Stone was surprised; he had never received a call from Brennan. "Hello?"

"Stone, Marshall Brennan."

"Good morning, Marshall."

"I'm calling to thank you for the way you dealt with my son's problem. He called me this morning from Winwood Farm, and we made up. He says he's going to make a go of his treatment, then go back to Yale."

"That's wonderful news, Marshall."

"Tell me, who is Herbert Fisher?"

"He's a lawyer at Woodman and Weld and the young man who made all this happen."

"You mean you weren't responsible?"

"Only indirectly. I judged that Herb was the best man for the job, so I brought him in."

"And he's at Woodman and Weld?"

"Yes, a senior associate."

"What does 'senior associate' mean?"

"It's the level at the firm from which partners are selected, and Herb got that promotion faster than any other associate ever has. I'm sure he'd appreciate a call from you, and he'd certainly appreciate any other work you might be able to send his way."

"Why don't you bring him to lunch today? I'd like to meet him."

"We'd both enjoy that, Marshall."

"P.J. Clarke's at one? I'll book."

"See you there, Marshall." Stone hung up and called Herbie. "You and I are having lunch with Marshall Brennan today."

"You're kidding me!"

"Nope. He wants to express his gratitude for your work, and he might even be more appreciative than that. P.J. Clarke's, at one."

"Not the Four Seasons?"

"Marshall's a pretty down-to-earth guy. I think he was uncomfortable at the Four Seasons last time we met."

"I'll be there."

■ ■ ■ ■

Stone and Herbie arrived at the restaurant simultaneously and found Marshall Brennan already seated. "You're not Herbie anymore, you're Herb," Stone whispered. He made the introduction, Marshall thanked Herbie, and they ordered. Marshall had the bacon cheeseburger.

"Herb," Marshall said, "can you ride a horse?"

"Yes," Herbie replied, with a straight face.

"Can you take a couple of weeks off this summer?"

"I have some vacation time coming," Herbie said, looking askance at Stone, who shrugged almost imperceptibly.

"Dink's going to get out of Winwood Farm sometime this summer, and I'm sending him out to my ranch in Montana for a few weeks, before he starts at Yale again this fall. How'd you like to go with him?"

"Mr. Brennan, I'm a reasonably priced lawyer, but an expensive babysitter."

Brennan laughed. "Dink doesn't need a babysitter, he needs a friend. He spoke well of you when we talked this morning, said he'd like to get to know you better."

"In that case I'd be delighted to visit

Montana."

"Good. I'll let you know the dates later. Now, Herb, I understand you're a senior associate and looking for some business of your own."

"Both of those things are true," Herbie said.

"I have a substantial investment in a start-up software company that I have high hopes for. They're smart kids, but they need some adult supervision with legal matters, especially intellectual property. You know anything about that?"

"I do, sir, and by tomorrow morning I'll know a lot more," Herbie said.

Brennan handed Herbie a card. "This is the CEO. They're housed in an old industrial building in SoHo. Drop in and see them, will you?"

Herbie looked at the card. "High Cotton Ideas," he read. "I like the sound of that. Now, Mr. Brennan . . ."

"Please, it's Marshall."

"Marshall, I have some business for you, if you want it — a young lawyer with two million dollars to invest."

"My bottom limit with clients is ten million," Brennan said. "Who's the young man?"

"I am he," Herbie said, "and I'll make it

five million. That's the best I can do."

"Okay," Brennan said. "My secretary will send you the documents, and you send me a check, then we'll set about making you rich."

"Thank you, Marshall. I'll look forward to that."

Brennan turned toward Stone. "How about you, Stone? From what I hear you've got money that needs to be put to work."

Stone had thought about this before but hadn't known how to approach Brennan. Word was, he was almost impossible to hire these days. "I'll send you a check for twenty-five million of mine and ten million of my son's. He's at Yale, in the drama school."

"You have his power of attorney?"

"Yes."

"I'll send you the paperwork this afternoon."

Their food arrived, and they dug in.

After lunch, the three men walked out of the restaurant to find cabs.

"Herb," Brennan said, looking him up and down, "you dress very well."

"Thank you, Marshall."

"I'm aware that I'm pretty much clueless about clothes. Would you take me on as a patient?"

"Of course."

"I'll call you for lunch again, and you can take me shopping."

Stone and Herbie put Brennan into a cab, then hailed one for themselves.

"Man oh man," Herbie said, "I'm investing with Marshall Brennan! I would never have been able to swing that on my own."

"If it's any consolation, Herb, neither would I," Stone said.

13

Dino looked morosely around P.J. Clarke's. "I don't think I can have dinner here every night," he said. "There are too many people I don't know."

"I know how you feel," Stone said, enjoying his second meal of the day at Clarke's. "Maybe after we've been coming here as long as we went to Elaine's, it'll be better."

"Do we have to wait that long?"

"Do you have a better idea?"

"How about '21'?" Dino asked.

"I was in there the other night. Too many of the people were kids in their twenties who shouldn't be able to afford '21.' "

"You put your finger on it," Dino said. "Them and rich people from out of town. I liked it better in the old days."

"Everything was better in the old days," Stone agreed.

"We sound like a couple of codgers," Dino said.

"Speak for yourself, pal. I'm not in codgerdom yet."

"Then why are we talking about the old days?"

"They weren't the old days, until Elaine died. Now, suddenly, they're the old days."

"That's how codgerdom happens," Dino pointed out. "One day, you're just a regular guy, having dinner three times a week at his favorite joint, then the next day the joint closes, and wham! You're a codger. You've got all of Arrington's money now," Dino said. "Why didn't you buy Elaine's?"

"The restaurant business is a kind of hell," Stone replied. "Either you don't have a social life, because you're there all the time, or you aren't there all the time and the employees steal you blind. And even if I had bought it, I'm not Elaine."

"Nobody is," Dino agreed.

The headwaiter brought two attractive women into the back room and seated them next to Stone and Dino. Neither was wearing a wedding ring.

"Did you tip that guy?" Dino whispered.

"No, but I'm going to."

"Evening, ladies," Dino said to the two. "Will you join us for a drink?"

The two women exchanged glances. "Thanks," one of them said, "but we'll stay on our own. We'll buy you a drink, though."

"That's the best offer I've had in this millennium," Dino said. He introduced himself and Stone. The women were named Rita and Marla.

The drinks came, and Dino raised his glass. "To chance meetings," he said. "If you're having dinner, let's pull our tables together."

The women agreed, and they managed to make two tables one.

"What do you gentlemen do?" Rita asked.

"I'm a lieutenant of the NYPD," Dino said. "Stone is only a lawyer."

"I was a detective with the NYPD," Stone said, "when I was too young to know better."

"How does one go from being a detective to being a lawyer?" Marla asked.

"One takes the bar exam," Stone said. "I had gone to NYU Law, but then became a cop."

"For how long?"

"Fourteen years."

"And what law firm do you practice with?" Marla asked.

"Woodman and Weld."

"Ah," she said, looking impressed. "My late father was a client there."

"He sounds like a wonderful human being," Stone said.

She laughed.

"What do you do, Marla?"

"I'm a choreographer and a director in the theater. Rita is starring in one of my shows, opening next week."

"Not exactly starring," Rita said, "but I'm the lead dancer."

"To me," Marla said, "dancers are always the stars. I used to be one myself."

"What made you give it up?" Stone asked.

"You don't give up dancing," she replied. "Dancing gives you up. It shouts in your ear, 'YOU'RE TOO OLD FOR THIS STUFF,' and it's always right. Then it kicks you in the knee, for emphasis."

"I haven't heard that call yet," Rita said.

"That's because you're ten years younger than me," Marla laughed. "You'll hear it soon enough."

They ordered dinner and talked some more. Rita's last name was Cara, and Marla's, Rocker.

"As in 'off one's rocker,' " Marla said.

"So," Rita asked, "what did you two guys do today?"

"I introduced a big client to a young attorney over lunch," Stone said. "They got on beautifully."

"I sent a SWAT team out to arrest a

murderer," Dino said.

The women looked impressed.

"It's not as exciting as Dino makes it sound," Stone said. "He means he signed a piece of paper."

"How long have you two known each other?" Marla asked.

"We were partners when we first made detective," Dino said. "I taught him everything he used to know."

After dinner, they walked out onto Third Avenue.

"Which way are you going?" Stone asked.

"Uptown for me," Rita said.

"I'll drop you," Dino said, "or vice versa."

"Okay." A cab pulled up, then the two drove away.

"Which way are you going?" Stone asked.

"I live in Turtle Bay," she said.

"What a coincidence — so do I."

They discovered that they lived across the garden from each other.

"Will you stop by for a drink?" Stone asked.

"Perhaps another time," Marla replied. She gave him a card, and he gave her his, then he hailed a cab and dropped her off at home.

"May I go out your back door?" Stone asked.

"Sure, as long as you don't tarry," Marla said. "I had a rough day's rehearsal." She let him into the house and led him through the living room, which was adorned with theater posters and photographs, and to the kitchen door. "There you are," she said, opening the door for him.

"I'm right over there," Stone said, pointing.

"Is there a Mrs. Barrington in residence?"

"I'm a widower," he replied.

"I'm sorry for your loss."

"Thank you. What time do you normally finish rehearsals?"

"Six, if I'm lucky. Two A.M., if I'm not."

"On the off chance that you finish fairly early tomorrow night, would you like to come over for dinner?"

"Let me call you late in the afternoon," she said, "when I have a sense of how great the disaster is."

"I'll look forward to hearing from you." He kissed her lightly on the cheek and stepped out into her rear garden, then into the common garden.

It was a perfect night, and Stone had the feeling the following evening might be even better.

14

Herbie was in his new office by eight the following morning, putting away his papers and files and rearranging the furniture. The desk was good, but he decided he needed a really nice oriental rug to make the room better. There was a knock at his door, and Herbie turned to find a young man in a fairly nice suit standing there.

"Good morning, Mr. Fisher," he said. "I'm Robert Bentley."

"Come on in," Herbie said. "It's Bobby, isn't it?"

"That's right."

"I'm Herb. Let's don't stand on ceremony. There's coffee in the pot over there."

"Can I pour you some?" Bobby asked.

"Black, please."

They sat down. "I know you're disappointed not to be assigned to a partner," Herbie said, "but you're going to have more fun with me and learn more, too."

"They damn near assigned me to Karla Martin," Bobby said. "I look upon you as my rescuer, and I don't care if you're a partner or not."

"The advantage of working with me is that I was where you are a couple of years ago, and I had my baptism by fire with Karla."

"How did you get away from her and to a promotion so fast?" Bobby asked.

"I'll tell you when I get to know you better," Herbie said. "Don't get the wrong idea: you're going to have to work as hard for me as you would have for Karla, but nobody's going to be yelling at you or taking credit for your work."

"I can take yelling," Bobby said.

There was another knock at the door, and a very small and pretty young woman stood there.

"Ah, Cookie," Herbie said. "This is Bobby Bentley, our new associate. Bobby, this is Cookie Crosby, my new secretary. Pour yourself some coffee and sit down, Cookie."

Cookie did so.

"Okay, this is the whole team," Herbie said. "What we're going to be about here is making rain. If we can do that, we'll prosper together, although, of course, I'll prosper more than you will — that's just the law everywhere you go. So, if either of you has a second cousin or a great-uncle in a business in this town, talk to him or her about Woodman and Weld. The firm's reputation will get your toe in the door, and I'll do the rest. Right now, we have only one client, gained yesterday from Marshall Brennan."

"The hedge fund Marshall Brennan?" Bobby asked.

"One and the same, and he has many interests. He's given us a start-up software company, a bunch of smart kids who know nothing about intellectual property rights and probably not anything else, so we're all going to become experts in what they need. Bobby, you and I will go down there later this morning and meet these, ah, gentlemen — we will never call them kids, and we'll treat them as if they're Steve Jobs, on the phone and face-to-face. Got that?"

Bobby and Cookie nodded.

"Good." Herbie extracted a tape measure from a drawer and handed Bobby one end. "Take this down there. Let's see how big a carpet we can cram in here."

"Nine by twelve," Cookie said, looking around. "You'll want to leave some floor around it — it's nice parquet."

"Nine by twelve it is," Herbie said. He sat down and put his feet on his desk, then a moment later stood up and rubbed his back.

"This always happens when I put my feet on my desk," he said.

"Then don't use a desk," Cookie said. "Just a comfortable chair, a table, and a couple more chairs."

"That's a thought," Herbie said. "How do you know so much about this?"

"I used to work for a big-time decorator," Cookie replied.

"Why did you leave?"

"The money's better here," she said, "and while I liked choosing things for other people's houses, I didn't much like dealing with the rich women who lived in them."

"Tell you what," Herbie said, extracting a credit card from his wallet and handing it to her. "Make a copy of this and take it down to ABC Carpet and buy a rug for me. You can spend up to twenty-five grand."

"Which means I'll be looking at things with forty-five-grand price tags," Cookie responded. "I know how to bargain. I think a silk carpet with a lot of yellow and green in it. Silk wears better than wool."

"Sounds perfect," Herbie said "Force them to deliver it today. Bobby and I will drop you off on our way downtown."

"You need a floor lamp for that corner, too," Cookie said, pointing, "and maybe a desk lamp and an *objet* or two and some

97

pictures to make you look smart and tasteful, Mr. Fisher."

"You've got the idea," Herbie said. "And
call me Herb. Keep the whole business
under fifty grand."

"I can do that," she said. "Now I have to
get organized."

"Me too," Bobby said.

"The two cubicles across the hall are
yours," Herbie said. "Keep them looking
neat." He handed Cookie a typed list.
"These are people whose calls I will take
immediately," he said. "Others, I will call
back, and I always return my calls, so keep
after me about that."

Cookie left the office reading the list, her
lips moving. She was memorizing them.

"Oh, and Cookie, order me some firm
stationery with my name on it, no title, and
some business cards. Order cards for Bobby,
too."

Herbie returned to situating his belong-
ings in the office.

At eleven o'clock, Herbie and Bobby
dropped Cookie off at ABC, then continued
downtown.

"What are we going to say to these . . .
gentlemen?" Bobby asked.

"Let's play it by ear. Mainly, we want to

give an impression of listening, then doing everything we can to help them, and not limited to the law. The CEO's name is Mark Hayes. I don't know who his partners are."

High Cotton Ideas was situated on the top floor of a shabby-looking industrial building way downtown, in a corner of SoHo that did not appear to have become fashionable yet. They rode up in a freight elevator and walked into a huge, open room with desks and tables scattered about. Each desk had at least three monitors on it, and cables were strung haphazardly everywhere.

Herbie stood still for a moment and waited for someone to notice them: nobody did. "Mark Hayes?" he shouted. He saw a hand go up across the room. The head of the young man never turned from the computer screen. Herbie and Bobby strolled over to the desk and took in its owner. He was, apparently, tall and obviously skinny. He was dressed in very old jeans and a short-sleeved chambray shirt that had not been ironed and may not have been laundered for a while.

"Mark?"

Finally, he looked up at them. "Yes?"

"I'm Herb Fisher, this is Bobby Bentley. Marshall Brennan sent us to see you."

"Oh, yeah, you're our new lawyers."

"Can you give us a few minutes?"

"Sure," Mark said, rising from his chair and taking his eyes reluctantly from the screen. He led them across the room to a beat-up picnic table, swept half a dozen empty foam cups off it, and offered them a bench. "This is our corporate dining room," he said. "What can I tell you? I can't tell you about our software, but anything else."

"Tell us what your ambitions are," Herbie said, "and we'll see if we can help you get there."

"My ambition is to get our software out of beta and on the market," Mark said. "And frankly, I don't have any idea how to do that. At some point after that I want to do an IPO and get impossibly rich, then write lots of new software."

"Okay," Herbie said, looking around the room. "How long have you been in this building?"

"Three weeks," Mark replied.

"And how long have you been associated with Marshall Brennan?"

"Since day before yesterday," Mark said.

"Okay, Mark, let's run through some basics, then you can get back to work."

"Love to," Mark said.

15

Herbie looked around the room. "How'd you find this place?"

Mark Hayes shrugged. "My sister is going out with a guy, and his mother owns the place. His father used to manufacture dresses here."

"What's your rent?"

"Five grand a month for this floor."

"How many floors?"

"Six."

"What's on the ground floor behind the big doors?"

"Used to be loading docks for trucks."

"Would the lady sell the building?"

"Yeah, but she wants six million for it."

"How much have you got in the bank?"

"Eighteen million, give or take, from Marshall's investment."

"Buy the building today. Offer her five million. Then budget another two million to get a couple of floors in shape. I can handle that for you, and I can recommend an archi-tect."

"Is that a good investment?"

"Mark, it's a steal. If this company works, you're going to need all six floors before you know it. And you can use that old load-ing dock area for a parking garage. That will be very attractive to your employees."

"Yeah, I've been parking my car down there."

"What sort of computer security system you got here?"

"The usual firewall. We unplug everything when nobody's here."

"There's no physical security either, is there?"

"A lock on the door."

"You need to get somebody in here fast to secure this place. Think of it as a storage facility for gold bullion. Let me make some calls."

"Sure, I guess that's a good idea."

"The architect needs to design you an of-fice layout, too, and you need to start mak-ing this place look more businesslike. You should all dress better, too. I don't mean you should wear Brooks Brothers suits, just not jeans — and the clothes should be freshly laundered. The media are going to want to talk to you soon, and you should be ready for them. Think Steve Jobs."

"Funny, that's what my girlfriend says — all that stuff about the building, too."

"Give me your landlord's name, and go back to work, then I'll get to work buying the building."

Mark took a card from his wallet. "Mrs. Friedrich," he said, handing Herbie the card. He went back to his desk.

Herbie picked up the phone on the picnic table and called the number.

"Hello?"

"Mrs. Friedrich?"

"Yes."

"Hi, my name is Herbert Fisher. I'm an attorney representing your tenant, Mark Hayes."

"Uh-oh."

"No, nothing like that. Mark has asked me to make you an offer of five million dollars for the building."

"I told him I wanted six."

"He's a young man just getting started, but he can raise five million."

"Oh, all right. When do you want to close?"

"Is the building entailed? Is there a mortgage?"

"No, I own it free and clear."

Herbie gave her his office number and

cell. "Have your attorney call me to set up the closing. I'll get Mark to raise the money, and we can close in a few days."

"All cash?"

"All cash."

"You tell Mark he's got a deal."

"I'll do that. Thanks, Mrs. Friedrich." Herbie hung up and shouted across the room, "Mark, you've got the building!"

Mark gave him a thumbs-up without looking away from his monitor.

Herbie called Mike Freeman at Strategic Services.

"Good morning, Herb."

"Good morning, Mike. I want to thank you for your advice and for your very kind offer. I was promoted to senior associate yesterday, and I got my first client this morning, a software start-up. I've just bought them a building, but it's completely without any kind of security, physical or electronic. Can you get something done about that?"

"Give me the address and the name of the company."

Herbie recited the information.

"I'll have a team down there in two hours, maybe sooner."

"I'll be here to meet them." Herbie thanked him, hung up, and called James

Rutedge, an architect he'd met through Stone Barrington who had left *Architectural Digest* to start his own firm.

"How are you, Herbie?"

"I'm just great, Jim, and from now on, it's Herb. I got promoted, so I need a grown-up name. How's business?"

"I've got a couple of leads — nothing definite yet."

"I've got something definite for you, Jim. Write down this information."

"Got it. What's the job?"

"A six-story industrial building to be transformed into the offices of a new software company, very promising, and very well financed by Marshall Brennan. Can you come over here right now?"

"Gee, let me check my schedule. I see that I'm free. I'll try not to break my neck hurrying over there. Bye." Rutledge hung up.

Herbie hung up, too.

"Wow," Bobby Bentley said. "That's moving! Does it bother you that a lot of this has nothing to do with practicing law?"

"It all has everything to do with helping a client," Herbie said. "By the end of the day, Mark Hayes won't ever make another move without consulting me. You get back to the office, find the best intellectual property lawyer in the firm, and start making a list of every document we have to generate, every permit we need, and every patent and copyright application we need. But first, ask Eggers's secretary to generate a legal services contract for Mark to sign, and rush messenger it down here. Oh, and get a title search on this building started."

"I'm on it," Bobby said, running for the door.

James Rutledge was there with an assistant in twenty minutes, and the assistant had a laser tape measure. Herbie got them started measuring the space, then his cell rang.

"Herb Fisher."

"This is David Schwartz. I represent Mrs. Friedrich, to whom you made an offer on her building."

"Yes, Mr. Schwartz, and she accepted."

"I can't allow her to do that."

"Why not?"

"This has to be negotiated properly."

"She wanted six million, I offered her five, and she accepted. What's improper about that? She used the words, 'Tell Mark he's got a deal,' and wanted to know how fast we could close. I'm ready to close right now. How about you, Mr. Schwartz?"

The man sighed. "I can do it Friday morning at ten."

"You're on. I've already started the title

106

search. You have our address?"

"Woodman and Weld? Yeah, I know where they are."

"My office at ten. Goodbye." Herbie hung up.

James Rutledge walked over. "This is fabulous space," he said. "I can work wonders with it."

"You know a builder you trust?"

"Yes, and a good one."

"Use this phone and hire him right now. I want him to go to work on Saturday morning, and he's going to need a double crew to get at least part of this place in shape fast."

"All right." James got on the phone.

Half an hour later a group of six men walked in, and the apparent leader introduced himself. "I'm Walt Harris," he said. "Mike Freeman sent me."

"Good to meet you, Walt. I want you to secure this computer layout, then secure this floor of the building and the main entrance. Can you get it done today?"

"Can we work late?"

"As late as you like."

"I can have it done by midnight," Walt said.

"Don't let me slow you down," Herbie replied.

They were done at a quarter to midnight. Mark Hayes was still working at his computer, occasionally interrupted by James Rutledge showing him sketches.

Herbie walked over and stood by Mark's desk. "All right, Mark, nobody can steal you blind now. Here are your new keys and your security system codes." Herbie handed him a sheet of paper.

"Thanks, Herb."

"We close on the building at ten Friday morning. I'm going to need you to transfer five million dollars to Woodman and Weld's trust account the day before."

"I'll call my bank in the morning and have it done. Do I have to be there?"

"Yes. My office at ten." Herbie gave him a card.

"See you then." Mark went back to work.

"Do you ever sleep?" Herbie asked.

"Sometimes," Mark replied.

Herbie chuckled to himself, then went outside and started looking for a cab.

16

While Herbie was transforming High Cotton Ideas and Mark Hayes into an actual business, Stone was shopping for groceries. He had received a call at four o'clock from Marla Rocker, telling him that the chaos was moderate, and she would join him at seven.

Stone left delivery instructions for his groceries and took a cab home. By seven, dinner was under way, and a bottle of vodka gimlets and one of martinis were in the freezer, chilling.

It was seven-thirty before Marla scratched at the kitchen door and was let in.

"Good evening," Stone said. "Would you like a drink?"

"I would kill for a martini," Marla replied, plopping down on the kitchen sofa.

Stone poured her the martini and himself a Knob Creek and sat down beside her. "Cheers," he said. "Is the show coming into shape?"

"It is," she said, "praise God. The structure is intact, and the lines, music, and choreography have been learned by my cast. Now we're just working on not tripping over the scenery."

"Congratulations on not having to panic at this juncture," Stone said, clinking her glass with his.

"Mmmmm," she said, sipping her martini. "Perfection. Don't let me drink more than eight of these or I'll make a fool of myself."

Stone laughed. "I promise — not one more than eight. Now, if you'll excuse me, I'll talk to you from the direction of the stove."

"What are we having?"

"Osso buco," Stone said, "with risotto."

"Doesn't that take hours?"

"Not in the pressure cooker," he replied. "The risotto takes half an hour, though — no way to speed it up."

"It all smells wonderful, and I thank you for not making me dress up to go out to a restaurant." She pulled up a stool to the stove and watched him add stock to the risotto and stir it in. "Let's get this out of the way," she said. "Tell me about your wife."

"She was murdered by a former and

insanely jealous lover," Stone said.

"I hope he got the chair."

"They don't do the chair anymore, it's the needle nowadays," Stone said. "But, in any case, he's still at large, probably in Mexico."

"That must be hard to take."

Stone shrugged and added more stock. "I'm not a vengeful person. He'll be caught, eventually, and will spend the rest of his life in prison."

"Not the death penalty?"

"I'm opposed to the death penalty."

"On what grounds?"

"Religious, moral, and economic."

"I can understand the first two, but economic?"

"The death penalty costs the state several times as much as a prisoner's serving life without parole, what with appeals. And in prison, they can make him earn his keep, until he's too old or sick to work."

"I never thought of that," she said. "I guess I'm more vengeful than you."

"I'll try never to earn your vengeance," Stone said.

"Smart move. I can be a real bitch."

"Or your anger."

Stone turned off the pressure cooker and let it cool, but he kept stirring the risotto and adding the stock. Finally, when all the liquid had been absorbed, he folded in half a container of crème fraîche and a couple of fistfuls of grated Parmesan cheese, then raked the rice into a platter and made a wall of it around the rim. He opened the pressure cooker, spooned out four slabs of the veal, and poured the sauce over it. "Voila," he said, setting the platter on the table. And seating her.

"Why so much?" she asked. "Are we expecting someone else?"

Stone tasted the wine and poured them each a glass. "Nope, but I'll have leftovers for lunch tomorrow and maybe for dinner tomorrow night, too."

"How long ago did your wife die?"

"A year ago Christmas."

"And how long have you been dating?"

"You're the first woman I've asked out in New York," Stone said.

"Are you sure you're ready for this?"

Stone raised his wineglass. "You have convinced me I'm ready."

"I'm flattered."

"I'm flattered that you're flattered. Try your food."

She forked a piece of the veal into her mouth and chewed thoughtfully, then tried the risotto. "You're hired," she said. "Can you come to the theater and make lunch every day?"

"I work every day," he replied, "but I appreciate the offer."

"Your offices are in the Seagram Building, aren't they?"

"That's right, but my office is right through that door and through a couple of rooms. It used to be a dentist's offices, but when I inherited the house, I made it into my workplace. It houses my secretary, an associate, and me."

"You inherited all this?"

"Yes, from a great-aunt, but it wasn't in this good a shape. Took a lot of work."

"I want to see the whole place," she said.

"After dinner. Besides, I haven't heard your life story yet."

"Born in a small town in Georgia called Delano," she said. "Learned to tap dance at four — a regular Shirley Temple — started ballet at six, and danced my way through school and college. Came to New York, auditioned for thirty-seven shows, finally got one, and I haven't been at liberty since."

"That was concise," Stone said.

"Well, I skipped the early husband, who turned out to be gay, and a few unsatisfactory love affairs. Something I don't understand about you: how did you make the leap from the NYPD to Woodman and Weld?"

"I graduated from NYU Law before be-coming a cop. Then I was wounded and in-valided off the force. An old law school friend, who was at Woodman and Weld, took me to lunch and convinced me I should take a cram course for the bar exam and get myself a license. He promised me work."

"So Woodman and Weld was your first job?"

"Not exactly a job. I was 'of counsel,' which meant, in my case, that I handled the cases the firm didn't want to be seen to handle."

"Such as?"

"Oh, a client's wife is involved in a hit-and-run, a client's son is accused of date rape, that sort of thing."

"Sounds sordid."

"Actually, it was very interesting indeed. I had more fun than anybody over at the Sea-gram Building."

"Is that what you still do for them?"

"No, I became a partner last year, after I made some rain."

"What does that mean?"

"It means I brought in some serious busi-ness."

"What sort of business?"

"A large corporate security business called Strategic Services, Centurion Studios, the

Steele insurance group, and a new hotel being built now in Bel-Air, California."

"Sounds like a great list. Did you and your wife have any children?"

"A son, Peter, who's at the Yale School of Drama now."

"Studying acting?"

"Studying everything. He wants to direct. In fact, his first film is being released this fall."

"An indie, of course."

"Yes, but it got picked up by Centurion."

"You have anything to do with that?"

"I introduced Peter to the CEO. He did the rest."

"Sounds like a very bright boy."

"You have no idea."

They lingered over their wine, then he showed her the house. Just before eleven, she made her way back across the garden to her own place, unmolested.

Stone couldn't remember ever having let that happen before.

17

Herbie slept his usual six hours and made it into work at seven-thirty A.M.. He walked into his office, which was oddly dark, and felt for the light switch. He was in the wrong office.

"What do you think?" Cookie asked from behind him.

Herbie looked at her, then turned back to the strange room. It was now lit by lamps in the four corners and one behind an Eames lounge chair, with a matching ottoman, which seemed to have replaced the desk. A glass coffee table sat next to that, and a leather sofa on the opposite side, with matching armchairs on the other two sides of the table. A beautiful oriental rug glowed golden in the light from the lamps. Sunlight was shut out by venetian blinds that matched the wood in the floor.

"Do I work here?" Herbie asked.

"You do, if you want to," Cookie said. "I

can send it all back, if you don't like it."

Herbie went and sat in the beautiful chair and put his feet on the ottoman. His back didn't hurt. "I like it," he said. "No, I *love* it. Where's all my stuff?"

"In the credenza at your right hand," she replied. "There are four file drawers and eight ordinary ones."

Herbie reached to his right and his hand fell on the phone. Next to that was a marble pencil box. He looked around and saw handsomely framed pictures on the walls and a Chinese terra-cotta horse in the center of the coffee table.

"It's T'ang dynasty," she said, "about eleven hundred years old." She handed him a sheet of paper. "Here's the bill for everything."

Herbie looked at it: $54,540. "You're nearly five grand over budget."

"Tell me what you'd like to send back," she said.

Herbie looked around. "Absolutely nothing. How'd you get this done so fast?"

"ABC has people who are accustomed to putting together whole rooms for movies and TV commercials in short order. I know one of them."

"Cookie," Herbie said, "how'd you like to redo my apartment in your spare time?"

"What's my budget?"

"You can go to half a million, if you have to, but that won't include art — I like the art I have."

"My fee is five percent of what I spend," she said.

"You're hired."

She poured him a cup of coffee, and it tasted much better than it had the day before.

"This isn't my usual coffee," he said. "It's a lot better."

"I'm glad you like it," she responded. "Excuse me, I have to get to work on your closing Friday morning."

"We've got a real estate department for that," Herbie said.

"I know how to put a closing together," she said, "and it will take me a third less time than if they do it."

"Then go to work."

Herbie looked around for his phone messages: there were two, one from Stone Barrington and one from Mike Freeman. He called Mike first, and was surprised when he answered his own phone. "Hey, Mike. Don't you have a secretary anymore?"

"She doesn't get in this early," Mike said. "Only the boss does."

"Thank you so much for sending your

team down to High Cotton," Herbie said.

"They're back this morning — they've got the whole building to wire."

"That's great. With your help, I'll turn this little venture into a real business."

"From what Marshall Brennan tells me about their ideas, that will happen very quickly," Mike said. "Tell me, Herbie, how'd you like a new client?"

"I'd like nothing better!"

"I hired a guy yesterday, and he's going to set up a new division for me that will specialize in bodyguard training. We've always done that for our own people, but now we're going to offer the training to our clients' employees. We've bought an old road racing track upstate a ways that we'll turn into a high-performance, defensive-driving school, and there'll be four firing ranges, too — everything from handguns to automatic weapons."

"Sounds terrific, Mike. How can I help?"

"I'd like you to create a corporate framework for the division, set up the accounting and a purchasing system for equipment. Though it's wholly owned, I'd like it to operate like a separate company."

"I can do that."

"The guy I've hired, who'll be the CEO, is called Josh Hook. He's ex-CIA, spent a little over twenty years there, in operations. His experience is broad and deep. I'll have him call you."

"I'll look forward to hearing from him, Mike, and I'll go ahead and set up the company as a client. You have a name yet?"

"Strategic Defense," Mike said.

"Got it."

"You'll hear from Josh later today." Mike said goodbye and hung up.

There was a knock, and Herbie looked up to find Bill Eggers leaning against the doorjamb. "What the hell is this?" Eggers asked.

"Come in, Bill, and have a seat."

"I didn't authorize you to redecorate," Eggers said.

"No, and you didn't pay for it, either," Herbie pointed out.

"In that case, I'll have a seat." He settled into an armchair and looked around. "I didn't know you had taste this good, Herbert."

"I don't," Herbie said, "but I have good taste in secretaries. She's out in her cubicle right now setting up a real estate closing for Friday."

"We have a department for that," Eggers said.

"She'll use their checklist, but she can do

it faster and cheaper. You can bill High Cotton Ideas for your department."

"You only got this piece of business yesterday, didn't you?"

"That's right, but it's not a business yet, just a collection of ill-groomed computer geeks. I'm turning it into a business."

"So I heard. And I hear you've got Strategic Services involved, and an architect, too. Are we going to make any money out of this?"

"I billed fifteen hours yesterday, and my associate as many. By the way — thanks. I like Bobby Bentley."

"Good." Eggers stood up.

"Oh, and I got a new piece of business this morning." Herbie told him about his conversation with Mike Freeman.

Eggers listened, nodding, his face not betraying much. "Herbert," he said, when Herbie had finished. "How much did this new stuff cost?"

Herbie picked up the bill and handed it to him.

Eggers folded the bill and tucked it into his coat pocket. "I'll take care of this," he said.

Herbie smiled. "Thank you, Bill. Oh, and I'd like to give my secretary a fifteen percent raise."

Eggers nodded. "I'll take care of it," he said, then he turned and walked back down the hall.

"Cookie!" Herbie yelled. "Get in here!"

18

Herbie Fisher was sitting in his new office, letting the past two days wash over him, luxuriating in his new status, his new clients, and a new kind of self-regard that had always been out of his reach until this moment. His phone buzzed.

"Mr. Joshua Hook to see you," Cookie said.

"Send him right in," Herbie replied. He got to his feet as his new client entered his office. The man was six-two or -three, two-twenty, thick salt-and-pepper hair, tanned, and very fit-looking. He looked around Herbie's office. "Holy shit!" he muttered, half to himself.

"Josh, I'm Herb Fisher. Please have a seat."

The man gave Herbie a bone-crushing handshake, settled into a big chair, and set his briefcase and a cardboard tube on the coffee table. "This is the first lawyer's office

I've ever felt comfortable in," Josh said.

"Would you like some coffee?"

"If it's very strong," he replied.

Herbie poured him a mug. "Try this."

Josh sipped it. "A man after my own heart," he said. "This stuff would eat its way through the stomach wall of an ordinary human being."

Herbie thought the statement said as much about the man himself as about the coffee. "I'm glad you like it. And congratulations on your new job at Strategic Services."

"I work at Strategic Defense," Josh said. "Strategic Services just owns me."

"I understand you had a career at the CIA," Herbie said.

"I did."

"What did you do there?"

"None of your fucking business," Josh replied, coolly.

Herbie laughed. "No, I guess not. I take it you were on the operational side, though — that's according to Mike Freeman."

"I would have made a poor support man," Josh said, "and an even worse analyst."

Herbie produced a legal pad. "Mike has told me you'll need to set up a corporate structure. I take it you'll be CEO?"

"That's right. Mike will be chairman of

the board. If you do decent work I might ask you to join the board."

Herbie jotted all this down. "I take it there's a piece of property upstate somewhere."

Josh popped the end out of the cardboard tube and shook out a thick sheaf of papers. "There is," he said, "and this is what we're going to put on it." He unrolled the papers and tucked one side under Herbie's T'ang dynasty terra-cotta horse, and Herbie set his marble pencil box on the other end.

"As you can see," Josh said, "we've got a dozen buildings, six of which have just been completed, four outdoor firing ranges, each with a high earthen berm to stop the lead, and two indoor ranges, as well. We've already got a five-thousand-foot runway in place, with two large hangars and a fuel farm. Mike bought a private field intact, along with another six hundred acres."

"You're expecting a lot of executive aircraft, then?"

"It's more secure to fly your students in. We don't want to arouse attention at a commercial airport — Stewart International is the nearest — and a lot of them will be bringing in personal weapons."

"I see."

"You ever fired a weapon, Herb?"

"Yes," Herbie replied, "but in a coffeehouse, not a firing range."

"Did that get you arrested?"

"It did, but I was released after a short time. I had a good lawyer who made a good case to the DA for self-defense."

"Did you hit anybody?"

"Only the man I was aiming at."

"That's the idea, isn't it?"

"I suppose it is," Herbie said.

"I'd like you to come up to our place and do a course with us."

"That would be interesting," Herbie said.

"It will be more than that," Josh said. "It will be educational, in the best sense of the word."

"Then I'll do it," Herbie replied, smiling. "I could use some more education, especially since it's something of a practical nature."

"It's a dangerous world," Josh said. "It's practical to stay alive and unharmed."

"I'm in favor of both of those," Herbie said. "Did you come directly to Mike from the Agency?"

"No, in between I started my own consultancy. That's how Mike found me — we were competitors. It was smart of him to buy me out."

"When do you start getting your first students?"

"Next week, as soon as construction is complete on the barracks and the indoor ranges."

"Can I be in your first class?"

"What sort of shape are you in?" Josh asked.

"Pretty good. I work out five days a week at the gym in my building."

"How far can you run without passing out?"

"I have no idea," Herbie said. "I'm a city boy — we don't do a lot of running, except in Central Park."

"We'll see how you do."

Herbie was beginning to regret volunteering for Josh's first class. "Running until I pass out would be an unnatural act for me."

"We'll see," Josh said.

"Josh, forgive my asking, but what is the point of your boot camp approach? Are your students, in their professional lives, going to be required to run two miles without fainting?"

"Probably not," Josh admitted.

"Do you think you might be requiring all this exertion because you can do it yourself?"

"Maybe."

"My advice is to treat them like professionals, not Marine recruits. You'll use their time better, and they'll leave better equipped to do their work."

"That makes a lot of sense," Josh said.

"Good. Now let me make myself clear. I'm not running *anywhere* for *any distance* while I'm at your facility. I'm there to learn, not faint."

"Okay, Herb, okay," Josh said. "You won't have to run."

"Thanks." Herbie felt that he had drawn a line in his relationship with this guy and that, in the future, he'd get more respect.

"Now," Herbie said, "let's go through the list of what I need to set up for you." He began checking off items, and he got Josh's full attention.

19

Bobby Bentley met his father for dinner at his club, the Brook, on East Fifty-fourth Street in Manhattan, a monthly occurrence. They sat down in the library for drinks. Bobby was his father's only son, a surprise product of his second marriage to a much younger woman, with the result that Robert Eaton Bentley II (Bobby was III) was old enough to be his son's grandfather.

"Well, my boy," II said. "How are things at the venerable firm of Woodman and Weld?" This was an ironic question, since II regarded the firm as a bunch of wild-eyed, liberal arrivistes, mainly because its birth did not predate his own. Still they represented him in some things. "You've been there, what, all of a week?"

"Ten days, Dad," Bobby replied. "And I've had a wonderful break."

"I would be interested to know what you regard as 'a break,'" his father said.

"Instead of being assigned to work for a partner, I've been assigned to the firm's newest senior associate, a young man named Herbert Fisher."

"If you had let me know, I could have made a call and put that right," his father said.

"Although he's thirtyish, Herb Fisher graduated from law school two years ago, and he's the first associate ever to make senior associate in less than three years."

"He sounds green as grass," II said. "Why would any client hire him?"

"He was promoted three days ago, and he's already brought in two important clients."

"What do you mean by 'important'?"

"A hot software start-up, backed by Marshall Brennan, and a new subsidiary of Strategic Services."

II blinked. "Marshall Brennan and Mike Freeman, of Strategic Services, are both members of this club."

"That's what I meant by important," Bobby said. His father did not impress easily, and he was enjoying the moment. "I think this software firm is something you should keep an eye on," he said. "They'll eventually have an IPO, and it could be a big one."

II withdrew an alligator-clad jotter from his pocket and uncapped his fountain pen. "Herbert Fisher, you say?"

"Yes, sir."

"And the name of the software company?"

"High Cotton Ideas."

II displayed a small smile. "I like the name."

"The great thing about working for Herb," Bobby said, "is that instead of learning to be an associate, I'll be learning to be an attorney, and Herb has a broad idea of what that means." He told him about the experience of watching his boss get High Cotton organized.

II regarded his son with an expression of wonder. "I rather thought that you'd be laboring in the law library and logging sixty billable hours a week for five or six years."

"As I said earlier, I got a break."

"I would like to meet Herbert Fisher," II said. "Can you arrange that?"

Bobby glanced at his watch. "I rather thought you would like to meet him. He'll be joining us for a drink about . . ." Bobby looked up to see a retainer showing Herb Fisher into the room. "Now."

II swiveled his head to take in the door. "My goodness," he said, rising to greet his unexpected guest.

Bobby made the introduction, and they sat down again.

The retainer hovered.

"Knob Creek on ice," Herbie said to the man, "if you please."

"That's what I'm drinking," II said to Herbie.

"It's the patriotic thing to do," Herbie replied, echoing what Stone had once said to him. "A fine American whiskey."

"My son has been telling me of your exploits at Woodman and Weld," II said.

" 'Exploits' is a colorful word to describe such a short career," Herbie said.

"There's nothing wrong with a young man's being in a hurry, Mr. Fisher," II said, "as long as he doesn't take too many short-cuts along the way."

Herbie smiled. "Choosing one's shortcuts carefully is always a good idea. I wouldn't like to get caught off base."

"That's a good way of putting it," Bentley said. "I know it's short notice, but do you think you could join Bobby and me for dinner here?"

"Thank you, sir, I'd like that."

Bobby excused himself and went to the men's room.

"Your son is a very bright young man," Herbie said. "He doesn't have to be told twice what to do. I think he's going to do very well."

"It pleases me to hear you say that, Mr. Fisher. I worried when he decided to go into the law. I suppose I had some hopes of his joining the family firm."

"What is the family firm?" Herbie asked.

"The Bentley Company. We manufacture precision machine parts for the oil, aircraft, and aerospace industries."

"Of course," Herbie said. "I think I read something in *Fortune* a few months ago about the company."

"I'm the third generation," II said.

"Perhaps Bobby will be the fourth yet," Herbie said, "but I think he needs to prove himself in an unconnected field first."

"Did he tell you that?"

"No, I surmised it."

"Well, Mr. Fisher, you've given me new hope."

Bobby returned.

"Shall we go in to dinner?" II asked, rising. The two younger men followed him to the dining room, where they were given a corner table.

Herbie noticed that Mr. Bentley took the gunfighter's seat, facing the room. They received menus and ordered, and Bentley chose an expensive French claret for them.

"Tell me, Mr. Fisher," II said, "what would you do if a client of yours found themselves faced with an unjust and potentially dangerous lawsuit? Do you have any experience with commercial litigation?"

"We're a large enough firm to have people experienced in every area of the law," Herbie said. "I think of myself as a generalist. If my client were faced with such a problem I would assemble an expert team from the firm's partners and act as liaison between them and my client."

"That's a very sensible way to proceed for someone in your position," II said.

Their dinner arrived, and II led the discussion from one subject to another for an hour. When coffee arrived, he said, "You know, I had hoped that when Bobby had acquired some experience at his firm, I might ask him to represent the firm in some area or other. I had thought that some years might pass before I had the opportunity to do that, but since he's obviously found a good place to be in the firm, maybe I can make it happen more quickly."

"I would be happy to help in any way I can," Herbie said, "and I'm sure Bobby would, too. We can put the best of Woodman and Weld at your disposal."

"I'm very glad to hear that," II said, then ordered them a fine brandy.

20

Stone was having a sandwich at his desk when the phone rang. Joan had gone to the bank, so he answered.

"Hi, Stone," a silken and very familiar voice said. "It's Tiffany."

Tiffany Baldwin was the United States attorney for the Southern District of New York, and something of an old flame of Stone's. He did not wish to hear from her, but he didn't want to alienate her, either, given her position. "Hi, Tiff," he said, as pleasantly as he could manage.

"Something came across my desk involving a client of yours," she said.

"Oh? Which client?"

"One Herbert Fisher. Seems Mr. Fisher got the funds in a brokerage account as part of a divorce settlement."

"Oh, yes, I remember," Stone said. "I believe I wrote to you about it some months ago."

"Some months ago releasing the funds would have been out of the question, given the criminal history of the former Mrs. Fisher, but things may have changed. Now, discussing the matter is not out of the question."

"I would be very pleased to discuss that at your convenience," Stone said.

"I would find it convenient to have dinner at Daniel tonight, then have a drink at your place."

Stone hoped she didn't hear him grit his teeth. "Of course, Tiff. May we meet at Daniel at eight?"

"We may," she said. "See you there."

Stone hung up and called Daniel immediately. The place was, arguably, the most expensive restaurant in New York and was packed every night, but he managed to get to the maître d' and finagle a table, which would cost him. He hung up, relieved, and wondered what the hell had suddenly moved Tiffany to call him about this now, months after she had ignored his written request.

Stone arrived on time and ordered a drink in the bar. Tiffany, who was reliably late by nature, joined him twenty minutes later, and he had a second drink with her. The bourbon in his veins led him to appreciate her appearance more than he might have when sober. She was a tall woman, slim, with long blond hair and a particularly fetching shape, including impressive breasts, which were on display this evening, barely contained by a tight black dress with a precipitous décolletage.

"How is the fighting of crime going?" Stone asked, trying unsuccessfully to keep his gaze at eye level.

Tiffany leaned in on her elbows, which allowed her breasts to pretty much roam free. "Tough, but we're winning." They sat at a small table, which allowed her to run a fingernail up his inner thigh.

"That's encouraging to hear," Stone replied, crossing his legs in self-defense. This was a voracious woman, and he knew he was not going to make it through the evening without feeding her pleasure.

The maître d' materialized and led them toward the main dining room, pausing long enough to palm the C-note that Stone dangled in his fingers for the man to snag.

"I'm impressed that you could get this table on short notice," Tiffany said, arranging herself so that she could cast an eye over the room for familiar faces.

"So am I," Stone said.

Menus arrived, and they ordered dinner.

"May we have champagne?" Tiffany sort of requested.

"Of course," Stone said, opening the wine list and running an eye over the right-hand column, the one with the prices. He chose one that was only $250.

The next hour and a half were spent in hyper-expensive gorging, and then they stumbled out into the street and lucked into a quick cab. It took less than ten minutes to drive to Stone's house, go upstairs, strip, and dive into the sack.

"I trust there are no cameras present this time," she said from her perch atop him. She alluded to an occasion when, without Stone's knowledge, a bad person had wired his bedroom for both video and audio, then sent a copy of a tryst between himself and Tiffany to Page Six at the *New York Post*. Fortunately, the angle of the camera's view had made it impossible to entirely identify either of them, though some accurate guessing took place.

"We are entirely alone," Stone said, lying back and letting her do the work. He waited until she had come three times and exhausted herself before rolling her off him and sitting up on one elbow. "Now to business," he whispered in her ear.

"I released the account this afternoon,"

she said. "Your client is now three and a half million dollars richer. Oh, and you can thank your friend Mike Freeman, who called the attorney general on your client's behalf."

"Why didn't you tell me that at dinner?" he asked.

"Because if your wish had been granted too early, you might have been less interested in the latter part of the evening," she said. "And I'm staying the night."

"I hope you won't mind if I get some sleep," Stone said, rolling over and pulling up the covers.

"Not at all," Tiffany said. "I'll let you know when you're needed."

And she did.

The following morning, suffering from soreness, Stone called Herbie Fisher.

"Herbert Fisher's office," a female voice said.

"Good morning. It's Stone Barrington."

"Mr. Barrington, this is the receptionist. Mr. Fisher and his secretary are in a real estate closing at the moment. I'll tell him you called."

"Thank you." Stone hung up, wondering what real estate sale Herbie was closing.

An hour later, Herbie called. "Sorry about not taking your call, Stone."

"Not at all, Herbie. What were you closing?"

"A new client of mine, High Cotton Ideas, bought an old building in SoHo for its headquarters."

"Oh, this is Marshall Brennan's software start-up?"

"One and the same. I've already got a construction crew in the building, making it habitable for a shiny new corporation."

"Then you're a full-service attorney."

"You betcha."

"I have good news, Herbie."

"By the way, it's Herb, remember?"

"Of course, negligent of me."

"What's the good news?"

"Mike Freeman called his friend, the attorney general, on your behalf and yesterday the U.S. attorney released your ex's brokerage account. You may now do what you will with the money."

"That's great news, Stone. After what I've seen and heard downtown, I'm going to put it all into High Cotton Ideas. My client is so happy with my services that he has offered me an investment opportunity."

"I won't ask you for details, to avoid having to explain myself to the SEC after the IPO takes place."

"You give yourself good legal advice, Stone."

"I do, thank you. And you owe me a very good dinner for what I had to do last night on your behalf."

"I think I know exactly what that means," Herbie said, "and I take the position that your lack of virtue was its own reward."

Stone hung up, laughing.

21

Herbie oversaw the signing of the last of the closing documents, then invited Mark Hayes back to his office for a cup of coffee.

"How does it feel to own commercial real estate?" Herbie asked.

"It feels just great," Mark said, "and I want to thank you for suggesting that I buy the building personally and lease it back to the company."

"And I want to thank you for your invitation to invest with you," Herbie said.

"I've been thinking about that," Mark said. He took a notebook from his pocket and did some scribbling, then ripped out the page and handed it to Herbie. "That's the number of my shares you'll get for investments of one, two, or three million dollars."

Herbie took a quick look at the numbers and made a quick decision. "I'll do the three million. I'll draw up the documents, move the money today, and have a cashier's check for you tomorrow."

Mark nodded. "I'm impressed that someone your age can come up with that kind of cash on short notice."

Herbie smiled. "I'm impressed that someone your age can start a company that's worth the investment."

"I suppose you're wondering why I'm willing to sell you these shares," Mark said.

"I expect you can use the cash for the renovation of your new building. That way, you won't need to mortgage it."

Mark nodded. "My new architect and builder tell me it's going to cost a million dollars a floor to make the space habitable, and I'm going to reinforce the roof, so that I can build myself a penthouse up there."

"What a great idea! I live in a penthouse, and I can tell you, you're going to love it."

There was a rap on the door and Bill Eggers stepped in.

"Good morning, Bill," Herbie said.

"I understand our new client is here," Eggers said, offering his hand to Mark.

"Mark," Herbie said, "this is our firm's managing partner, Bill Eggers."

"Good to meet you." Mark rose and took Eggers's hand.

"I've wanted to meet you since Marshall

Brennan told me about your start-up," Eggers said. "Are we meeting all your legal needs?"

"More than meeting them," Mark said. "Herb has given me a wealth of good advice in a very short time."

"That's what we're here for," Eggers said.

"If you'll excuse me," Mark said, "I have a computer to get back to. I'm unaccustomed to seeing daylight during the workday."

They said their goodbyes and Mark left. Eggers took a seat, and Herbie handed him a cup of coffee.

"Well, Herbert," Eggers said, "congratulations on making our new client happy."

"Thank you, Bill."

"Now, what have you done for me lately?"

Herbie laughed aloud. "Greedy, aren't you?"

"You'd better know it."

"Well, last night Robert Bentley the Third and I had dinner at the Brook with Robert Bentley the Second."

Eggers's eyebrows went up. "And?"

"And the elder Mr. Bentley says he'd like to give us some new business soon."

"How soon?"

"I'm going to leave that up to him, and I'm not going to rush him. He said something interesting, though."

"What was that?"

"He put this to me hypothetically: how would I handle a major piece of commercial litigation for a client?"

"Tell me what you told him."

"I told him that we are a large enough firm to have specialists in every area of the law, and that I would assemble a team of our best litigators, then act as the firm's liaison with the client."

"Whew!" Eggers said. "I'm relieved to hear it. I'm glad you didn't tell him you'd handle it yourself."

"I'm young, Bill, but I'm not crazy."

"Do you have any idea if he's referring to a real lawsuit?"

"My guess is, yes. He described it as 'dangerous.' "

Eggers frowned. "I'm not aware of anything like that looming in Bentley's future."

"Perhaps it hasn't happened yet. Perhaps he's thinking of suing, not being sued."

"I'm going to have a word with our litigation department and see what we can find out. If Bentley comes to us with this, I want to be ready." Eggers got to his feet and wandered out.

Cookie came in with a brown envelope and handed it to Herbie. "This just came by messenger."

"Thanks, Cookie. You performed brilliantly in putting together that closing."

"Thank you, kind sir."

"You're getting a fifteen percent raise, starting with your next paycheck," Herbie said. "And it is richly deserved."

Cookie smiled broadly, revealing small, beautiful teeth. "Thank you again." She curtsied, then went back to her desk.

Herbie opened the envelope and removed the contents. It was a statement of his ex-wife's brokerage account, with a letter saying that it had been released to him. He flipped through the pages, looking at the investments, then he called Cookie back in and handed her the statement. "Write a reply to the signatory of this letter, to be hand delivered, thanking him and instructing him to immediately liquidate all the shares, except the Apple stock, and to wire the proceeds to my checking account. Then write another letter to my banker, telling him that upon receipt of the funds he is to issue a cashier's check for three million dollars, payable to Mark Hayes, and have it hand delivered to me."

"It will be done," she said.

"And when those are done, I'll dictate a document transferring some of High Cotton

Ideas stock to me, for Mark Hayes's signature."

"I shall return," she said.

Herbie sat back and reflected that things were going very well indeed for him, and that it had been his experience that whenever things were going very well for him he always found a way to screw it up. When he had won sixteen million dollars, net, in the lottery, he managed to blow six million of it in three months, and all he had to show for it was an apartment, a car, and some clothes. He resolved that henceforth he would devote himself to making his fortune grow, instead of blowing it. Now that he had money in Marshall Brennan's hedge fund and an investment in High Cotton Ideas, he was off to a good start.

22

Stone met Dino for dinner at P.J. Clarke's.

"Are we ever going to have dinner anywhere else?" Dino asked.

"I'm game," Stone said. "Suggest somewhere."

"I mean, I've always liked Clarke's, but none of the regulars from Elaine's are ever here."

"That's because, like us, they don't know what else to do with themselves."

"I miss them," Dino said.

"Why? You didn't spend a lot of time with them."

"Yeah, but I miss them anyway."

"Dino, I've got news for you: Elaine is dead, and Elaine's is closed for good. Get used to it."

"I'm trying."

"Are you seeing the dancer, Rita?"

"Oh, yeah, but the hours may be more than I can deal with. Right now, she's available in the evenings, because she rehearses in the daytime, then, after tomorrow night, she'll only be available in the daytime, when I'm working, because she's performing at night. You going to the opening?"

"I think we're sitting together."

"Okay, and there's the party at Sardi's afterward. It may be the last time I see Rita."

"Cheer up, maybe the show will close after the first performance."

"I wouldn't wish that on her. How much have you seen of Marla?"

"Only the once. Fortunately, unlike Rita, she'll be available in the evenings once the show has opened."

"Good for you. If I can't see Rita, then I'm going to start thinking about Shelley again."

"Have you heard from her since you booted her out of your bed?"

"I had a postcard with a picture of the Port Authority bus terminal on it. No signature."

"What did she have to say?"

" 'See you around.' "

"That sounds ominous."

"Tell me about it."

"I hope you burned the postcard. You don't want that lying around the house."

"I've been a cop all these years, and you

think I don't know how to destroy incriminating evidence?"

Stone laughed. "I was getting worried about you."

"I was getting worried about me, too. You know, there's this female detective in my squad named Vivian DeCarlo, nice Italian girl."

"Dino, the next worse thing to fucking Shelley Bach is fucking somebody in your squad."

"Unless we can get away with it," Dino replied.

"Oh, shit," Stone said. "You're determined to destroy your career, one way or the other."

"So what if I do? I've got the money from my divorce settlement, and a pension waiting for me."

"Retirement would be an unnatural act for you. What would you do with yourself?"

"I don't know. What do other retirees do?"

"Play shuffleboard and wait to die."

"I could travel."

"You hate travel, unless I'm there to fly you."

"I could buy a place in Italy and go live there."

"You're a New Yorker, not an Italian."

"With a name like Bacchetti, I'm not Italian?"

"You live and breathe New York. What would you do in Italy? You speak about as much Italian as I do."

"I used to speak Italian, with my grandmother, when I was a kid. It would come back to me."

"You'd end up sitting in some bar in Rome, trying to pick up American tourists, so you could talk to somebody."

"That's pretty much what I do here, except they're not tourists."

"What you do here is be a cop. I hope you're not stupid enough to give that up before they boot you out."

Dino sighed. "Don't worry, I'm not going to quit."

"If you start seeing this DeCarlo girl, you'll end up getting one or both of you transferred, probably to the Bronx or the outer reaches of Brooklyn."

Stone looked toward the door and saw Herbie Fisher standing there.

"There's Herbie," Dino said. "At last, a familiar face."

Stone waved him over. "He wants to be called Herb now — he's growing up."

Herbie sat down and ordered a drink. "What a day!" he said. "What a week!"

152

"Is that good?" Dino asked.

"You bet your ass it is," Herbie said. "I got promoted to senior associate and pulled in two pieces of new business, maybe three."

"What's the third?" Stone asked.

Herbie told them about his dinner with Robert Bentley II.

"Sounds promising," Stone said.

"Eggers is champing at the bit for me to get that."

"I'm sure he is."

"But I'm not going to rush it. I'm going to let him come to me."

"That's wise, if he comes."

"He'll come — his son is my associate."

"How'd you swing that?" Dino asked.

"I didn't swing it. The kid is the newest associate, and I'm the newest senior associate."

"A marriage made in heaven," Dino said.

"Don't laugh, it could turn out that way. If we handle a major litigation for Bentley, it could bring millions into the firm."

"Eggers would like that," Stone said.

"I'm redoing my apartment," Herbie said, apropos of nothing.

"Okay," Stone replied.

"My secretary is doing it. Turns out she has a real gift. You should come and see my office — even Eggers liked it. He picked up the tab for it, too."

"My word," Stone said, "you did have a good week, didn't you?"

"I'm going to make more rain," Herbie said. "My goal is to bring in more business than a senior associate ever has."

"The boy has ambition," Dino said. "Who knew? Herbie —"

"Herb, please."

"Ah, Herb, how'd you go from being a gold-plated fuckup to being a senior associate at Woodman and Weld?"

"Hard work and good luck," Herbie said. "And good friends."

"That's an unbeatable combination," Stone said, clapping him on the back.

Stone looked toward the door and saw Mike Freeman standing there. "Over here!" he yelled.

Mike came over and sat down. "You know, I went to Elaine's automatically, looking for you."

"I have to stop myself from doing the same thing," Stone said.

"Stone, you up for a trip to L.A.?"

"What's up in L.A.?"

"I think it's time we had a look at our hotel's progress."

"Well, the hotel is a Woodman and Weld client, so I guess I can justify the trip."

154

"We'll take the Strategic Services G-550," Mike said.

"That will take the sting out of air travel."

"Can I come?" Herbie asked.

Stone shook his head. "No junkets for you. You have new business to take care of."

"How about me?" Dino asked. "I can take the time."

"You're welcome, Dino," Mike said. He looked around. "Do they serve food here?"

23

The big Gulfstream lined up for takeoff on Runway 1 at Teterboro, and the pilot pushed the throttles forward.

"What happened to the beautiful pilot Suzanne Alley?" Stone asked. "We had dinner in London once."

"She got a better offer," Mike replied.

The pilot rotated and the jet rose and climbed quickly.

"I'll be interested to see if we get cleared all the way to cruising altitude," Stone said.

"Not until we get away from Newark Liberty," Mike said, "but that won't take long."

The airplane leveled off at Flight Level 440. The stewardess unbuckled her seat belt and came aft with a tray of breakfast pastries and a pot of coffee.

Dino accepted a pastry and a cup of coffee. "This is better than flying in your airplane," he said to Stone.

"We have pastries and coffee on my airplane," Stone replied. "If you bring them."

"I believe my point is made," Dino said. "I'd also have to bring my own stewardess."

Later that day they set down at Burbank and got into a waiting rented Mercedes. Mike drove.

"I've booked us into the Bel-Air," he said. "Might as well check out our competition."

"I hope they don't know who we are," Stone said. "We might get mugged."

"They'll know," Mike said. "They knew well before we broke ground. Shall we visit the site now?"

"Sure," Stone said.

Mike drove them to Bel-Air and up to Vance Calder's old property. Cars and pickup trucks were lined up along the road for a quarter of a mile. "I guess they don't have any parking areas finished yet," he said. They turned into the driveway and stopped to identify themselves to the security guard, then they continued up the winding driveway. "There'll be cottages on both sides of the road all the way up," Mike said.

They parked just short of the front door to the old house and got out of the car. A portico wide enough for half a dozen cars was being constructed, and the old garage was being turned into interior space. They looked down the hill to where an enormous pit had been dug. Mike pointed. "Underground parking," he said.

"It looks like a giant anthill," Stone said. "I've never seen so many workmen on a site."

"We've got three construction companies working two shifts," Mike said. "Nobody is going to believe how quickly this hotel is going to open."

"Where is Arrington's house going to be?" Stone asked.

"Follow me," Mike said, and led the way into the house, which was being enlarged to serve as the reception area and main restaurant. They walked down the central hallway and into the back garden, then around the swimming pool, to where a building was being framed.

"Here we are," Mike said.

They walked through the rooms on plywood subflooring. The sound of electric hammers and saws was everywhere.

"This is good," Stone said. In the original deal he had negotiated for Arrington to have her own house on the property. "It's not as big as the old house, but it's plenty big."

"It's your house now," Mike said. "And Peter's."

"And yours, Mike, and yours, too, Dino, whenever you're out here."

"Free?" Dino asked, amazed.

"You can pay your own room service bill," Stone said.

"That's a pretty good deal," Dino said, laughing. "How many bedrooms?"

"Four bedrooms, six baths, and two powder rooms, plus two staff rooms. Also, living room, dining room, kitchen, and a very nice study/library."

"Are you going to let them rent it when you're not here?" Mike asked.

"Maybe. It's arranged so that the master suite can be locked off from paying guests."

"That will help with the cash flow," Mike pointed out. He found the architect and the construction foreman, and they began answering questions.

Later, they checked into a three-bedroom cottage at the Bel-Air Hotel.

"What did you think about how things are going?" Stone asked Mike.

"I was impressed," Mike said. "Everything is on schedule. Frankly, I hadn't expected that."

There was a large bowl of fruit on the entrance hall table, and a note addressed to Stone, from the manager. He read it aloud

159

to Mike and Dino. "The Bel-Air welcomes the competition," it said. "We'll do our best to show you how it's done."

Everybody had a good laugh.

On the living room coffee table was a large flower arrangement, with an envelope. Stone picked it up and handed it to Dino. "It's addressed to you."

"It can't be," Dino said. "Nobody knows I'm here."

"Nevertheless, it has your name on it," Stone replied.

Dino took the envelope and opened it. His face fell.

"What?" Stone asked.

Dino handed him the note inside.

Stone read it: "I hope you had a good trip," it said. "See you when you return." It was signed, simply, "S."

"Uh-oh," Stone said.

"Yeah," Dino agreed.

"What is it?" Mike asked.

"Nothing much," Stone replied, "just a note from a serial killer of Dino's acquaintance."

24

The following morning they visited the building site again and talked more with the architect and construction foremen, then they drove back to Burbank Airport and boarded the G-550. They were back at Teterboro in time for Stone and Dino to make the opening of Marla's new show.

At the final curtain Stone and Dino stood and beat their hands together and cheered, along with the rest of the audience. Marla and Rita took their bows, and finally, the curtain fell again.

They strolled through Shubert Alley over to Sardi's and were seated at a large round table, which gradually began to fill up. Marla and Rita arrived looking freshly scrubbed and excited.

"It was wonderful," Stone said.

"Do you really think so?"

"Everybody in the house thought so, and

the critics will, too. You're looking at a long run."

Dino turned to Rita. "Am I ever going to see you again?"

"I get one night off every week," she said.

The party continued past midnight, then somebody arrived with a stack of newspapers, and the producer stood on his chair and read the reviews aloud, to appreciative applause from the crowd.

Stone looked around the room and saw someone familiar. He turned to Dino. "Hey, remember our final dinner at Elaine's, when a tall redhead clocked some not-so-innocent bystander?"

Dino looked tense. "Yeah. Why?"

"Because I just caught a glimpse of her over there somewhere," Stone replied, pointing.

"Oh, shit," Dino said.

"What's wrong?"

"That's Shelley."

"Who's Shelley?" Rita asked.

"Somebody Dino doesn't want to meet," Stone said.

"Why not?" she asked.

"There was some unpleasantness a while back."

"What kind of unpleasantness?"

162

"Rita," Dino said, "let it go. Please."

"Well, I guess I know what you'll be doing when it's not my night off," she said, digging him in the ribs.

"I will be bereft," Dino said. "I promise."

"Well, if it's a promise, I guess 'bereft' is appropriate."

Stone turned to Marla. "I hope you have more than one night a week off."

"I'll see the next couple of performances and give some notes, but then I'll have to let go and just let it run. Then I'll have plenty of nights off."

"I'll start thinking of ways to use them," Stone said.

Dino excused himself and started across the room in the direction Stone had pointed.

"Uh-oh," Rita said. "Is there going to be trouble?"

"I doubt it," Stone replied. "Don't worry, Dino can handle it."

"He can always call in a SWAT team," Rita said.

Dino made his way through the crowd while the reviews continued to be read. She was tall, so he kept his eyes riveted on the tops of heads. Then he spotted the red hair moving away from him. He pursued, but unless he used his elbows, the crowd kept him from gaining. The redhead pushed through a pair of swinging doors. Dino finally got there and found himself in the kitchen.

"Can I help you, sir?" a waiter asked in an unhelpful way.

"I'll be out of your way in a minute," Dino said. He walked slowly through the busy kitchen, dodging waiters and men with knives, but he didn't see her. Finally he came to the rear door and stepped out into an alley, which contained only garbage cans, lit by the lights from West Forty-fourth Street. He walked all the way down to the street and looked both ways. He thought he saw red hair in the back of a taxi, but then it was gone.

Dino went into Sardi's by the front door and made his way back to the table. The two women were headed toward the ladies' room.

"Any luck?" Stone asked.

Dino shook his head. "She went through the kitchen and out into the alley, then she was gone."

"You're going to have to do something about this, you know."

"I know," Dino replied. "I just don't know what."

■ ■ ■ ■

The women returned from the ladies' room.

"It's getting late," Stone said to Marla. "Come home with me?"

"Oh, I'm exhausted," Marla replied. "Just completely drained."

"Dinner tomorrow?"

"Let me call you after I've seen the show again a couple of times."

Stone sighed. "All right."

She put her hand on his cheek and kissed him. "Just be patient for a little while."

25

Shelley got into a cab. "Carlyle Hotel," she said to the driver. She didn't look over her shoulder. Dino would be back there somewhere, and she wasn't ready to see him face-to-face again. The circumstances would have to be more favorable.

Shelley got out of the cab and walked into the Carlyle, then turned left into the bar. She could use a drink. She settled on a stool, ordered a cognac, and listened to the jazz trio, who filled the room with sound.

She had been there maybe five minutes when a man came into the bar and took a seat two down from her. He took off his hat and laid it on the bar, and she froze. She knew him; he was FBI. Bob something-or-other. He was assigned to the New York field office, and he had driven her around New York once, when she was on an official visit from Washington.

As casually as she could, she turned slightly away from him and checked out the room in the mirror over the bar. If this was a bust, there would be other agents backing him up and watching the doors. Then a woman came through the door from the direction of the ladies' room and sat between Bob and Shelley. Another agent. Was this socializing or a setup?

Shelley drained her glass, put a twenty on the bar, and walked past the jazz group. A man was leaning against the wall beside the door, snapping his fingers to the rhythm of the group, and he gave her a good once-over. She left the hotel and threw herself in front of a passing taxi.

"Lady, you want to watch it," the driver said. "I nearly clipped you."

"I know, my fault. Go up to Seventy-ninth, then left on Fifth, then down to Seventy-sixth and take another left."

The driver stepped on it. "That's a complete circle," he said.

"I know, but on Seventy-sixth, cross Madison and let me out at the other hotel entrance on Seventy-sixth."

"It's your fare," he said.

"And let me know if anyone seems to be following us." She didn't want to look back herself, exposing her face.

"Jealous lover?" the driver asked.

"Jealous ex-husband," she said.

"Yeah, I got an ex like that." He turned left on Seventy-ninth, then again on Fifth Avenue and started downtown, then he made the left on Seventy-sixth, crossed Madison, and stopped at the hotel's side entrance.

"Here you go," he said. "Would you like some company tonight?" He turned and looked at her.

He wasn't bad, she thought: young, good haircut. "You ever been shot by an ex-husband?" she asked.

"Not so far."

"Let's not start tonight." She handed him a ten, got out of the cab, and ran into the hotel, making for the elevator bank. She pressed the button and waited nervously for the car to arrive, forcing herself to look neither to the left nor to the right. Finally, it arrived, and she got in and pressed the button two floors above her room, then she got off and took the fire stairs down two floors and let herself in.

She leaned against the door, breathing hard. Two FBI agents in one evening was too much to take. She hoped to God neither of them had noticed her in the bar. Maybe the hair color would be enough to throw them off.

She undressed, then removed her makeup and checked out her face in the bathroom mirror. She had never liked her nose much; maybe this was the moment to do something about it.

She sat on the bed and picked up a copy of *New York* magazine, remembering an ad she had seen in the back pages. She found it and read it carefully, looking at the before-and-after photos of a woman who had had cosmetic surgery. There was an 800 number and a notation that it was manned at all hours.

"Doctor's office," an answering service operator said.

"I'd like to make an appointment for a consultation," Shelley said. "The sooner, the better."

"I can give you ten tomorrow morning," the woman said.

"Perfect." She gave her traveling name and her cell number.

"Please, how did you hear about the doctor?"

"His ad in *New York* magazine." She hung up and got ready for bed, calming herself the whole time.

Shelley presented herself on time at the

doctor's office, which was only a couple of blocks from the Carlyle. It was in a brownstone, and the reception room was nicely decorated. A nurse came and took her to the doctor's office.

"Good morning," he said, offering his hand. "I'm Dr. Charles."

He looked awfully young, she thought.

"I'm thirty-four," he said, laughing. "That's always the first question. I've been in practice for six years, and I'm board-certified. How can I help you?"

"Well," she said, tapping her nose with a finger, "I've finally decided to do something about this."

He motioned for her to turn her head. "Ah, yes," he said. "Let's photograph you, and then I can give you a very good idea of what changes we might make." He sat her in front of a camera and took shots of her from ahead and both sides, then he tapped a few computer keys, and her image, in right profile, appeared twice on the screen.

"Now," he said, using a laser pointer, "my guess is you'd like this bump to go away."

"Yes," she said.

He tapped a few more keys, and the bump went away on the right-hand photo.

"Wonderful!" Shelley said. "I'd like my nose to be a bit shorter, too." She watched as her nose changed. "That's very good," she said.

"Perhaps, since we're shortening your nose, we should make your nostrils slightly smaller, in scale with the new length." He tapped a few more keys.

"Yes, that's perfect."

"One more suggestion," the doctor said. "We can turn your nose up just a bit. That can be very attractive." He made the change.

"I like it," she said. The upturned nose made her look very different from her old self.

"Now, let's take a look from the left profile and the front."

Two more shots appeared on the screen.

"I think it looks great from every angle," Shelley said. "And I'm very impressed with your equipment."

"Eliminates guesswork, doesn't it?"

"It certainly does."

"How quickly would you like to proceed?"

"As soon as possible," she said.

He opened his diary and flipped through it. "Tomorrow is a surgery day," he said. "How about two P.M. tomorrow?"

"Very good. How long will I be in the hospital?"

"The hospital won't be necessary," he said. "I have a complete operating suite

171

upstairs, and a recovery room where you can spend the night. After that, you can go home, then come back to see me in a week. We'll remove any stitches at that time, and any swelling will have gone down by then, and you'll be able to go without the bandage, using makeup to cover any temporary redness or bruising. A month from tomorrow no one will be able to guess that you've had the procedure."

He told her the price. "That includes your recovery and all follow-up visits. The entire fee is payable today."

She agreed.

"Just give your check or credit card to the receptionist," he said, "and we'll expect you at one o'clock tomorrow for prep for the two o'clock surgery."

She thanked him, then gave her credit card to the receptionist. Twenty minutes later she was back in her room, watching a movie on TV and ordering lunch from room service.

26

Herbie Fisher was sitting in his Eames lounge chair with the plans of Mark Hayes's renovation in his lap. James Rutledge sat in a chair across the Mies van der Rohe Barcelona table.

"I wanted you to have a look at these, Herb, before I get final approval from Mark," James said.

Herbie looked at the floor plan of Mark's projected duplex penthouse, which had four bedrooms, as many baths, living room, dining room, kitchen, a large study with a utility room to one side, to hold unsightly equipment that Mark would need to work at home. "This looks wonderful, but I don't understand how Mark gets to his apartment," he said.

"Via a spiral staircase from his offices one floor below."

"It's going to be a bitch getting his furniture up a spiral staircase," Herbie pointed out.

"Oh, we're going to extend the freight elevator shaft up a floor, so he'll be able to get anything, up to and including a concert grand piano, in that way."

"So, let's say he's throwing a dinner party for a dozen friends. Are they going to take the freight elevator up to the executive floor, then walk up a flight? That's awkward. What I think you should do is make a street entrance that opens into a private lobby with an elevator going straight up to both floors of the apartment. You can build a new shaft inside the building. There's plenty of square footage for that without crowding the space, isn't there?"

"Great idea!" James said. "And he can lock the elevator electronically, if he's not expecting guests." He took the floor plan and drew in the lobby and elevator shaft. "And he'll still have the freight elevator for bringing up furniture."

"Just make the private elevator big enough for that," Herbie suggested. "That way, you won't have to extend the freight elevator shaft, and it will be in use all during the renovation."

"Herb, you should have been an architect," James said.

"I know, I know," Herbie said. "I'm such

a fucking design genius!" They both laughed.

"How long to do the whole job?" Herbie asked.

"We'll be done with the main building in a month," James said. "Because of the recession in the building business, I've got three shifts working on it, with a foreman for each shift. We'll be done with the executive floor next week. Right now, Mark and his people are working one floor down. When they move upstairs we can start construction on the penthouse. The lower floors will be finished, but without interior walls, until they're needed for new staff. The garage is being plastered and painted and is going to look great, and the outside will be stuccoed. Mark has some big paintings that he can hang in the garage. I'll make an entrance from the garage to the private lobby, so that his guests can park there before going upstairs." James was sketching very quickly now.

"You should get the finished building in *Architectural Digest*," Herbie said. James had been the executive art director for the magazine before going out on his own.

"Good idea," James said. "There won't be another building like it in the city. We'll be doing extensive planting on the roof, too, so

175

the apartment will have gardens on four sides."

Cookie buzzed Herbie. "Marshall Brennan on line one," she said.

Herbie pressed the button on the phone. "Hello, Marshall."

"Good morning, Herbie. I want to take you up on your offer to help me into a new wardrobe."

"I'd be delighted to help," Herbie said. "What time?"

"How about right after lunch?"

"All right. Meet me at two o'clock, and we'll get started." Herbie gave him an address on Lexington Avenue.

"What is this place? I don't know any stores in that block."

"It's my Chinese tailor. You'll like his work better than expensive off-the-rack stuff, and it's no more expensive."

"All right, I'll see you there at two. How long will this take?"

"We'll have a couple of other stops to make, so don't make any appointments for the rest of the day."

"Whatever you say." Marshall hung up.

Herbie had a sandwich at his desk, then took a cab to the tailor's shop. Marshall simultaneously got out of another cab, and they walked up the stairs together. Herbie introduced him to Sam, the tailor, and they went to a wall of fabric books and a rack of bolts.

"You like lightweight or heavier cloth?" Herbie asked.

"Lightweight. I'm always too hot."

"Yeah, me too. Let's look at the Loro Piana and Zegna fabrics. I love the Italian stuff." Herbie picked fabrics for a dozen suits, a tuxedo, cashmere for a blazer, and four tweeds for jackets and gabardines for trousers. Sam measured Marshall, and Herbie dictated the details of the suits and jackets. They were done in an hour.

"That was quick," Marshall said.

"You'll need to come back three times for fittings," Herbie said. "I know it's time-consuming, but after that, all you have to do is pick a swatch and Sam can go straight to the finished product, assuming you haven't gained or lost weight."

"I still weigh what I weighed when I graduated from Harvard," Marshall said. "It's arranged a little differently, though. What's next?"

"Shirts," Herbie said, hailing a cab.

"I have to have shirts made, too?"

"You don't want to let off-the-peg shirts make your suits look bad." They went into Turnbull & Asser on East Fifty-seventh

Street, and Marshall was measured, then Herbie helped him pick two dozen fabrics, then they went downstairs and Herbie picked out two dozen neckties.

"What about shoes?" Marshall said.

"Let's see if we can get away with ready-made shoes," Herbie said. They took a cab to Seventy-ninth and Madison, the Ralph Lauren store, where Marshall tried on a lot of shoes. "The workmanship is as good as with custom shoes," Herbie explained, "as long as they fit properly. And you don't have to wait for them." Marshall had ten pairs of shoes sent to his home.

"That's it," Herbie said, when they were back on the sidewalk. "In a couple of months you'll have everything in your closet. I want you to promise me that, after everything is delivered, you'll throw away every single suit, jacket, shirt, tie, and pair of shoes that you own. The Salvation Army will be glad to see them."

"I promise," Marshall said.

"I'll go with you to your final fitting at Sam's," Herbie said.

"Thanks, Herb," Marshall said. "Oh, I almost forgot: a friend of mine is looking for new legal representation." He handed Herbie a business card. "His name is Kent Holbrooke. He's an entrepreneur, into lots of things. Call him."

"First thing in the morning, Marshall." Herbie shook his hand and got a cab home, pleased with his day.

27

Shelley swam slowly into consciousness and found herself in what looked like the guest room in some tasteful person's home, except for the hospital bed she lay in and the equipment surrounding her, ticking and beeping. A nurse sat at her bedside reading a newspaper. She looked up. "Oh, you're awake!"

"I seem to be," Shelley said. "May I have a mirror?"

The nurse laughed. "Oh, you don't want that," she said, "at least not yet. You have a bandage across your nose and two black eyes. You look like a raccoon."

"Swell," Shelley said. "What do I do now?"

"The doctor will be in in a moment, then you can relax, read, watch TV, or just rest. He'll discharge you tomorrow morning."

The doctor came in, smiling. "Everything went perfectly," he said.

"I'm glad to hear it."

"You'll be out of here in the morning, and by that time I can minimize the dressing."

"And I'll look like someone who's just had a nose job," Shelley said.

"No, like someone who's had an accident, maybe in the car."

"Can I go to the hairdresser's tomorrow?"

"Of course, as long as you're feeling up to it."

"I'm feeling up to it now."

He patted her on the shoulder. "Just rest today. You'll feel fine tomorrow, and I'll give you something for the pain."

"Pain? You didn't mention pain!"

"There's always some pain associated with any surgery, but I'll give you some medication that will make it go away."

"Right now I just feel numb all over."

"That's normal. Now, if you need the nurse or me, just use your bedside buzzer, and we'll be here. In any case, I'll stop by to see you again before I leave the office, around seven."

"Thank you, Dr. Charles."

The doctor left, and Shelley drifted off to sleep again.

Herbie dialed the number, and a woman with a British accent answered. "The Holbrooke Group, good morning."

"Kent Holbrooke, please."

"And who may I say is calling?"

"Herbert Fisher, of Woodman and Weld."

A moment later, Holbrooke came on the line. "Herb Fisher?"

"That's me."

"Marshall Brennan says good things about you."

"Marshall is my smartest client."

"We need to get together. Where do you want to do it?"

"If you want to see what we look like, you can come here, otherwise I'm happy to come there or meet you somewhere."

"There's nothing to see here except a lot of steel furniture and grubby offices. You're in the Seagram Building, right?"

"Right." Herbie gave him the floor number.

"I'll come over just as soon as the market closes. See ya." He hung up.

Herbie pressed a button. "Cookie, a Mr. Kent Holbrooke is coming over around four-thirty or five."

"I'll stay until we've got him settled," Cookie replied.

"You can ask him if he wants a drink," Herbie said.

At five sharp, Cookie ushered Kent Holbrooke into Herbie's office, and they shook hands. Holbrooke settled into the sofa.

"Can I get you something to drink?" Cookie asked.

"You got a single-malt scotch?"

"How about Laphroaig?"

"Perfect. No ice, just a splash."

Cookie made the drink and poured Herbie a Knob Creek, then made her escape.

"Nice office," Kent said, looking around.

"Thank you."

"You're pretty young, Herb. How long have you been a partner at Woodman and Weld?"

"I'm a senior associate, one rung below partner."

"Oh, right, Marshall mentioned that. I've never dealt with a lawyer who wasn't a partner in his firm."

"You'll get more attention and faster results from a hungry senior associate," Herbie said.

"Good point."

"Tell me about your business," Herbie said.

"Businesses. I'm involved in a dozen or fifteen, I keep losing track of how many."

"How are you typically involved?"

"Sometimes just as a venture capitalist. I prefer that with tech stuff that I don't have a deep understanding of. Sometimes in partnerships, and sometimes I own the business."

"Are they all techs?"

"Oh, no. I don't care what the business is, just as long as it produces profits. For instance, I own a little group of three fancy dry cleaners and laundries called Jasper's."

"Then I am your customer," Herbie said. "You do all my suits and shirts."

"And they're all running full blast," Kent said. "I'm thinking of opening on the Upper West Side."

"Why don't you centralize the work and put on a second shift?"

"That's a thought."

"And if it's working so well, why don't you franchise?" Herbie asked.

Kent looked at him thoughtfully. "I don't know anything about franchising," he said.

"All you need is a law firm that does."

"Are you a franchising specialist?"

"I'm a generalist. My job is to put together a team of the right people in the firm and liaise between you and them."

"All right, I'll put you to work," Kent said.

"Would you like me to put together a presentation on franchising Jasper's?"

"Sure, that's a good start. I understand you're representing one of Marshall's startups. I've got a couple of those that could use some legal and accounting structuring. The techies know everything about tech, and nothing about business."

Herbie handed him a legal pad. "Give me some names and numbers, and I'll go see them. Nothing that will conflict with Marshall's start-up, though."

Kent took the pad and began writing.

There was a knock at the door, and Bill Eggers walked in. "I'm sorry, am I disturbing you?"

"No, come in, Bill, and meet Kent Holbrooke, of the Holbrooke Group."

They shook hands.

"We're going to put together a presentation on franchising a group of high-end laundry/dry cleaners called Jasper's that Kent owns."

"Of course," Eggers said. "My wife and I are your clients."

"I'm liking Woodman and Weld better and better," Kent said.

28

Dink Brennan sat in a circle of chairs and gazed at the seven other people occupying them. They were a mixed bag of people, but they were all well dressed and carefully groomed. Dink's guess was that this place didn't take Medicaid.

The psychiatrist ended the session, and an orderly came in and whispered to Dink, "You have a visitor in the main lounge."

Finally, Dink thought. He had been there a week and was clean of any drug, but they weren't going to let him out of there so easily, so he was going to have to keep doing business from there.

He walked into the main lounge, which looked more like the lobby of a chic SoHo hotel, and saw Parker Mosely, his roommate at Yale, waiting for him. They shook hands and sat down.

"How they treating you, Dink?" Parker asked.

"About how you'd expect. I've blinded them with cooperation. They make us clean our own rooms, and you should see mine: neat as a pin."

"That doesn't sound like you."

"I can do it when I want to. Anyway, they seem to look at a neat room as proof of character, so I've had a head start since day one."

"You got a shave and a haircut, too."

"Yeah, more proof of character. All I had in my blood when they tested it was a little grass. My plan is to make them think my old man overreacted by sending me here, that I don't really belong. In fact, I've already started working on the psychiatrist to get him thinking that the old man is the problem, not me."

"Smart." Parker looked around the room casually, then slipped a small book envelope to Dink. "Here's the cell phone you wanted, and a charger, too. I gave the number to Carson, and she knows not to expect an answer when she calls, just voice mail. I told her you'd get back to her."

Dink tucked it into his belt, under his shirttail. "Tell her I want to see her here tomorrow. I've got something I want her to do."

"She'll be here within the hour. She's

driving over from her folks' house in Washington."

"Great!"

"How long do you think you'll be here?"

"My guess is that they're not going to let me out in less than a month, because they want to make some money before they release me. However, that doesn't mean we're out of business. You need to recruit a couple more sellers. I don't want you selling direct — you're management, and I don't want you getting busted. Don't tell the people you hire your real name, either. I'll call my connection and set up a delivery for another six kilos."

"Coke, too?"

"Nah, we're doing fine with grass."

"Gotcha," Parker said. "What else?"

"I want you to call the lawyer that Dad sent to get me in here. His name is Herbert Fisher, at Woodman and Weld. Tell him how well I'm doing and that I expressed a wish to have him visit me as soon as he can manage it."

"What do you want to see a lawyer for?"

"He's the key to squaring things with the old man. If I can convince Fisher I'm on the road to a complete recovery, he'll convince Dad, who would never believe *me*."

"Smart move."

Dink looked up to see Carson walking into the room and looking around. She was wearing a dress her mother must have picked out for her. Her hair was freshly done and she was carrying a Chanel handbag. The girl was the complete actress. He stood up and waved her over.

"Hello, sweetheart," Carson said, kissing him on the cheek as if she were his sister. "You look wonderful!"

"Sit down, baby," Dink said, and sat down on the sofa with her. "Parker, you get out of here now, and there's something else I want you to do."

"Name it."

"First of all, I want you to bring my car up here. There's a gas station at the bottom of the hill, on the outskirts of the village."

"I saw it."

"Take the car there and ask them to keep it for me. Pay whatever they want. Leave one key with them, and then bring the other key to me. This is just in case I have to effect an early release from this place."

"Gotcha," Parker said. "It'll be here tomorrow."

"You can get the car service to pick you up at the filling station and take you back to New Haven."

"Right." The two shook hands, and Parker left.

"Come on," Dink said to Carson, "I want to appear to be giving you the tour." He led her out of the main lounge into the garden, then showed her the pool, aware that various staff members were keeping an eye on them. They sat in the garden for a while.

"The dress was a nice touch," Dink said. "The handbag, too."

"They're both my mother's," Carson said. "Is there somewhere we can go?"

"Yeah, I think the heat's off for the moment. Come with me." He walked her slowly toward his cottage, chatting along the way, careful not to seem to be hurrying. He walked her through the living room of the cottage, then into his room, closing the door behind him.

"Does it lock?" Carson asked, pulling the dress over her head. She was naked under it.

Dink put a chair under the doorknob. "We're okay," he said, dropping his jeans and pulling the polo shirt over his head. In a flash they were in bed, and for the next half hour Dink devoted himself to pleasing her. When they were done she used the bathroom, then came back and lay down beside him.

"Man, you look good to me," Dink said.

"I meant to. I've been so horny I couldn't stand it." She took him in her mouth and got him started, then pulled him on top of her.

Half an hour later they lay together, catching their breath. "Are you going to the city anytime soon?" Dink asked.

"I can if you like," she said. "I can go directly from here and stay at our apartment tonight. The folks will be away for the weekend."

He wrote down a name and number for her and gave her the slip of paper. "This is the lawyer who Dad got to put me in here. I want you to call him and get together with him. Tell him how well I'm doing and how grateful you are to him for helping me and tell him I'm grateful, too. Then fuck him."

"Am I going to enjoy this?" she asked.

"He's a decent-looking guy, about thirty, dresses well, smart."

"Okay, then I'll fuck him. What then?"

"See him a couple of times. Get him hooked on you, because I've got plans for him. I'll tell you more later."

"I'd *better* enjoy this," she said.

"Sweetheart, you enjoy sex more than any girl I've ever known."

191

"You have a point there," she said.

"You'd better get dressed and get out of here. Try not to be noticed until you're back at the main lounge. If anybody asks about me, say that I went back to my room for a nap."

"Okay, baby," she said, planting a big kiss on him. She slipped the dress over her head, zipped it, fluffed her hair, picked up her bag, and was gone.

Dink hid his new cell phone, then fell asleep.

29

Herbie finished up his meeting with the franchise group and asked to see a copy of their presentation before his new client did. Cookie buzzed him.

"Allison on line one," she said. Allison was Stone's Woodman & Weld associate who worked out of his house. He had been seeing her for the better part of a year.

"Hey, there," Herbie said.

"Hey. Where are we having dinner tonight?"

"The Park Avenue Café all right?"

"That's fine. I can't be there before eight," she said.

"Eight is good. You want me to pick you up?"

"No, I'll meet you." She said goodbye and hung up.

That was unusual, Herbie thought. Allison liked being called for. Cookie buzzed again. "Mike Freeman on one."

"Good morning, Mike."

"Good morning, Herb. I'm going downtown to take a look at the work my people are doing on the High Cotton Ideas building. Would you like to come along?"

"Yeah, sure. I've got time for that. I haven't seen it since the work began."

"I'll pick you up in front of your building in fifteen minutes, then."

"I'll be there."

Bobby Bentley knocked on the door. He had been at the franchise meeting and had asked some good questions Herbie hadn't thought of.

"Come in, Bobby, and take a seat."

Bobby sat down. "I had dinner with Dad last night, and he asked me to give you his best regards."

"That was good of him."

"He said he wasn't far from having some business for you."

"For us, Bobby. The firm wouldn't be getting this business if it weren't for you, and Bill Eggers will hear about that, believe me."

Bobby looked relieved, but now he looked worried again. "Dad ran a background check on you," he said.

"Oh? I'm sure he found the report very interesting."

"He didn't know you killed that guy in

194

Little Italy a few years ago."

"It was in the papers — it's no secret. Does he know that the initial charges were dropped?"

"I'm not sure."

"Next time you speak with him, tell him to ask me about it. I'll be happy to tell him the whole story."

"I think that's a good idea, Herb. Dad is a very conservative guy, a real straight arrow, and the idea that you have an arrest record is alarming to him."

"That's why I want him to talk to me about it personally. I'll answer all his questions."

"Good, I'll pass that on to him." Bobby went back to his cubicle.

Herbie was standing at the curb when Mike Freeman's car pulled up. He got in, and they headed downtown to High Cotton Ideas.

"How's the new business thing going?" Mike asked.

"Wonderful! Thank you so much for sending me Joshua Hook!"

"Josh is a hard-ass but a good guy. He told me you advised him to ease off the boot camp atmosphere, and I agreed. He's even having the accommodations done up a bit to make them more hotel-like, and nobody will be bunking with anybody else."

"My guess is, he was a Marine before he joined the Agency."

"Close — he was a Navy SEAL."

"He asked me how far I could run without passing out. I told him I don't run."

"Are you going up there next week?"

"I'm already booked in," Herbie said.

They arrived at the High Cotton Ideas building, and Herbie was struck by the transformation the stucco had made to the exterior. The lobby entrance to the new penthouse was under construction, and there was a crane in the street, lifting pallets of construction material to the roof.

James Rutledge came over and joined them. "The elevator to the roof will be operating in another ten days or so, then we can run materials up there and get rid of the crane."

"Sounds good," Herbie said.

They walked through the open door of the garage and the difference from before was striking.

"We're installing a new steel garage door that will be veneered in mahogany but will be very secure. We can thank Mike's people for that suggestion."

"I'm glad they've been of help to you,"

Mike said.

"The security systems are in, and, miracle of miracles, they actually work!"

"That's what we aim for," Mike replied.

They rode up in the elevator to the floor where Mark Hayes and his people were temporarily working.

"This is pretty much what the lower floors will look like," James said. "Open plan, unless there's a need to divide the areas. Now come on up one floor and see what the executive offices are going to look like." They got back onto the freight elevator and rode up, then exited into a coolly decorated reception room with the High Cotton Ideas logo painted large on one wall.

"We're creating an elevator stop from the private lobby to the executive floor," James said, as they walked through the main doors. The floor was plush, compared to the lower floors, but decorated in bright colors, almost like a series of children's rooms. The office furniture was handsome but spare, of light wood, with small conference tables and sofas in the larger offices. At the rear of the floor was a more open area of low-walled cubicles. "This is programmer country," James said. "They'll be in here next week, as soon as the computer wiring installation is complete and tested."

"Is there anything to see on the roof?" Herbie asked.

"Right now, it's just a roof," James said, "and it's dangerous for us to be up there. Give me a month, and we'll have something for you to look at."

Mark Hayes entered the area and took them to his corner office, near the new elevator shaft. Men were carrying pieces of furniture through a set of double doors into the big room.

"The conference table will go there," Mark said, pointing, "and each seat will have a workstation so that all the people in a meeting can view the same screen."

As they left the room, Mark stopped them. "Herb, Mike, I'm very impressed with everything you've done to help us get this thing up and running, and I want to invite both of you to join the High Cotton Ideas board of directors. Marshall Brennan is joining, and he'll be our financial guru."

"I'd be delighted," Herbie said.

"So would I, Mark," Mike said.

Mark rode down to the street with them. "The next time you see this place, it's going to look like an important place of work." He shook their hands and went back upstairs.

Herbie and Mike thanked James for the tour and rode uptown together.

30

Herbie got back to his office and had a message to return a call to Parker Mosely, Dink Brennan's roommate at Yale. He dialed the number.

"Hi, Mr. Fisher," Parker said. "Thanks for returning my call."

"How can I help you, Parker?"

"I just wanted to relay a message from Dink. He wants you to know how grateful he is to you for getting him into rehab. I saw him yesterday, and he's doing really well."

"I'm glad to hear it, Parker."

"He asked me to tell you that if you're anywhere near there, to please visit him. He'd like to see you and thank you personally."

"If I get up that way I'll stop in for a visit," Herbie said. "Thanks for calling, Parker, and give Dink my best." He hung up and tried to imagine Dink Brennan as a reformed character. He failed.

Parker put away his cell phone and turned to Carson Cullers, on whose parents' living room sofa they were sitting, smoking a joint. "Okay," he said, "that should prime the pump." He handed Carson a small package wrapped in brown paper. "Now, here's what Dink wants you to do," he said. When he had finished he waved away a puff of her smoke. "Now, have you got that? He wants it done exactly that way."

"Got it," Carson said. "You know, this could be fun."

"Okay, I gotta run," Parker said. "There's a car waiting, and I've got a shipment to get back to New Haven." He said goodbye and left.

Carson went into her mother's dressing room and pressed the button that started the moving closet, which resembled the sort of long, electric rack in dry-cleaning establishments. She let it run for a few seconds, then stopped it and removed a sheer, silk minidress. "Perfect," she said. "He'll never know what hit him."

Herbie waited at the bar of the Park Avenue Café, since he knew Allison would be a little late; she was always a little late. She hurried in after a ten-minute wait, gave him a peck on the cheek, and they were seated in the dining room. He ordered her a drink, and they took a look at the menus.

"I'm not staying for dinner," she said. "You order."

Herbie closed the menu. "All right," he said, "tell me what's wrong."

"Nothing is wrong," she replied. "I just have to talk to you."

She took a swig of her drink, as if she needed it.

"I'm listening," Herbie said.

"I don't think we should go on seeing each other," she said.

"Do you want to tell me why?"

"You've been promoted at the firm, and I want to be promoted. I don't think it would help my chances if we became an item of office gossip."

"I don't think anyone knows," he said.

"Joan knows, and that means Stone knows, and that may mean that Eggers knows."

"Stone wouldn't mention it to Eggers."

"I hope you're right. I just don't think it does either of us any good for *anyone* at the firm to know we're seeing each other."

Herbie shrugged. "Well, as far as I know, there's no rule against it."

"Still," she said, "you must see that it's not good for either of us."

"I won't argue with you," Herbie said gently. "Now, let's order some dinner."

"There's probably somebody from the firm in this restaurant right now," she said, tossing off the rest of her drink and standing up. She put a hand on his shoulder. "I'm sorry, Herbie," she said.

"Please don't be concerned," he said, and then he watched her leave.

He waved at a waiter and ordered the veal chop. He didn't have a girlfriend anymore, but it didn't seem to have hurt his appetite.

Herbie got a cab home, and as he walked into his apartment, the phone was ringing. He sat down in the living room and picked up. "Hello?"

"Is this Herbert Fisher?" a low female voice said.

"Speaking."

"My name is Carson Cullers," she said. "I don't know if that means anything to you."

Herbie thought for a moment; the name sounded familiar. "Dink Brennan's friend," he said. "Washington, Connecticut."

"That's right. New York, really, Washington is just a weekend place. I live at Park and Seventy-first."

"Then we're neighbors. I'm just a couple blocks away."

"I wonder if we could have a drink sometime?" she said. "I'd like to talk to you about Dink."

"Sure," Herbie said. "Would you like to come here now?"

"That would be great," she said.

He gave her the address. "It's the penthouse," he said.

"I'll be there shortly," she replied, and hung up.

This was interesting, Herbie thought. Why would Dink Brennan's girlfriend be calling him? He'd already had a call from Parker Mosely, Dink's roommate, and now this? Was this some sort of campaign to persuade him that Dink should be released?

He got up and walked around the living room, straightening up a bit. Ten minutes later, the doorman rang, and Herbie asked that she be sent up. He answered the door to find a tall, slender, elegantly dressed young woman standing in the foyer, in a nearly sheer dress, looking a little nervous. "Come in, Carson," he said, and showed her into the living room. "Have a seat. What can I get you to drink?"

"Can you make a vodka martini?" she asked.

"Of course." Herbie went to the bar and began to put that together. Since Allison had opted out of his life earlier in the evening, he felt glad to have someone there.

Then he brought himself up short. Hang on, this was his client's son's girlfriend, he thought. Better be careful.

He returned to the sofa with her martini and his cognac on a tray and started to take a chair.

"Please," she said, patting the sofa next to her. "Sit here."

Herbie had already had a drink and half a bottle of wine, and the girl was looking very good. What the hell, he thought. "Give me a minute, will you? I have to go to the powder room."

"Of course," she said.

Herbie got up and left.

Carson opened her purse, took out a prescription bottle, and shook two small pills into her hand. She put them on the glass coffee table, took a razor blade from her purse, and chopped them into powder, then held Herbie's brandy snifter at the edge of the table and raked the powder into his glass. She stirred it with a finger, watching it dissolve, then licked her finger and put the glass back on the table.

Herbie came back from the powder room,

sat down beside her, and raised his glass. "Cheers," he said.

Carson smiled. "Cheers, indeed!" She took a gulp of her martini and rested her hand on his thigh.

"So, tell me about Dink," Herbie said, taking a sip of brandy.

"As far as I'm concerned, Dink is history," Carson said. "I'm sick of his behavior. I'm here because he told me about you, and I thought you sounded interesting." She moved her hand up his thigh a bit.

"Well, that's flattering," Herbie replied, taking another sip. He rested his head on the back of the sofa cushion and felt her hand move up farther.

"What are you looking for there?" he asked, sipping more brandy.

She moved her hand up to his crotch. "This," she said.

"Well, now that you've found it, what's next?"

She unzipped his fly and took out his penis.

Herbie felt drowsy. He took another pull on the brandy and set the glass on the coffee table.

She teased him erect, then took him into her mouth.

31

Detective third grade Vivian DeCarlo walked into the emergency room at Lenox Hill Hospital and looked around for her partner, Rose Mahon, who was supposed to meet her there to interview a hit-and-run victim. No sign of Rosie.

"Hey, Viv," a young female resident in green scrubs said to her.

"Hey, Liz," Viv replied. "How's it going?"

"Now that you mention it, I've just examined a rape victim, and you might want to talk to her. She's behind the curtain, there, in exam one."

"What's her story?"

"She says some guy got her drunk and raped her. She wasn't wearing any panties, but there was no bruising, either internal or external, and she didn't seem all that drunk, either."

"You think she's lying?"

"I've seen a couple of dozen rape victims

in here, and she doesn't fit the mold. She's not crying, not even looking upset, and, like I said, not a mark on her. Her first name is Carson."

"Did you do a rape kit?"

"Yep. I found no semen in her vagina, but there was some on what pubic hair she has left after a major wax job. I'll get you the kit."

Viv walked over and pulled the curtain back a few inches. "Carson?"

The girl was stretched out on the exam table, and she lifted her head a bit. "Yes?"

Viv walked into the cubicle and pulled the curtain closed behind her. "I'm Detective DeCarlo. Dr. Edwards tells me you've been hurt."

Carson put her head back onto the table. "I'm not hurt, just raped, that's all."

Viv pulled up a chair, sat down, and got out her notebook. "Tell me what happened."

"I went over to this guy's apartment for a drink and had a martini. He was doing coke and drinking brandy. He made a move, but I wasn't into it and I told him so. He slapped me across the mouth, pulled up my dress, and ripped off my panties, and he raped me."

Viv looked at the woman's mouth — no

sign of swelling. "What's the man's name?"

"Herbert Fisher. He's a lawyer at some big-time firm."

"Address?"

She rattled off the address. "The penthouse."

"Did anyone see you go to his apartment?"

"Just the doorman."

"What's your last name and your address and phone number?" She jotted down the information. "Do you want to make a formal complaint?"

"Maybe. Or maybe I'll just go to the newspapers and TV. If I sign a complaint, what are the chances of anything being done about it?"

"Frankly, based on what you've told me, not very good. It's a he-said-she-said situation. He'll likely maintain that the sex was consensual, and since you have no injuries, the DA would probably not go forward with the case."

"Let me think about it," Carson said.

Viv gave her a business card. "You can reach me at both of those numbers."

Carson suddenly sat up and hopped off the table. She was at least four inches taller than Viv. "I'm going home," she said.

"You should speak to the doctor first."

The curtain was pulled back and Dr. Edwards entered and handed Viv a paper bag. "Here's the kit. Where are you going, sweetheart?" she asked Carson.

"Home."

"You're sure you're okay to travel?"

"Yeah, sure."

Edwards took a form from her clipboard and handed it to Carson. "Give this to the cashier on your way out. She takes credit cards."

"Okay, thanks." And she was gone.

"That was not like any rape victim I've ever seen," Edwards said.

Viv found her partner in the waiting room. "Sorry, I was interviewing a rape victim."

"I spoke to the hit-and-run victim. She had nothing useful. Didn't see a thing, didn't remember anything."

"Let's go talk to the alleged rapist," Viv said. "He lives near here."

They got into their unmarked car and drove to the building. The doorman buzzed the penthouse repeatedly. "I don't get it," he said. "Mr. Fisher always answers immediately."

"You think he could be ill or hurt?" Viv asked.

"I don't know — there was nobody up

there but a woman, and she left in a hurry."

Viv flashed her badge. "Can you let us in? We just want to be sure he's all right."

"Sure, give me a minute." He picked up the phone and asked for somebody to spell him at the desk, then he led them to the elevator and pressed the PH button. "Actually, he doesn't usually lock the elevator door when he's home. It opens directly into his foyer."

The elevator stopped, and the two women stepped off.

"You want me to wait?"

"No, that's all right. We won't be long."

The elevator door closed behind them.

"Mr. Fisher?" Viv called. "NYPD. Anybody home?"

Nothing.

Viv led the way into the living room, which was lit by lamps at either end of the sofa. A man was sitting on the sofa, his head back and lolling to one side. His fly was open and his penis exposed.

Viv walked over to him and shook him by the shoulder. "Mr. Fisher? Wake up. We're the police." There was no response. Viv peeled back an eyelid and the pupil contracted. "Well, he's not dead." She pinched his cheek, hard. Still no response.

"I think we need an ambulance," Rosie

said. "He could have OD'd. Look." She pointed at a pile of white powder on a piece of brown paper on the coffee table. "There's at least an ounce here."

"It's a neat little pile," Viv said. "It hasn't been cut into lines, and I don't see a straw or rolled-up bill that he could snort with. I wonder how much he's had to drink." She tapped the brandy snifter on the table. "Most of at least one drink."

Rosie walked across the room to a bar and lifted a bottle of Rémy Martin cognac. "Looks like a fresh bottle. One drink missing, maybe."

"I'll call it in," Viv said, reaching for her phone. "We don't want him to die on us."

Rosie came back to the sofa, pulled the man's pants up until the penis fell back inside, then zipped it up. "We don't want to embarrass the EMTs, do we?" She looked toward the end of the sofa, then walked over and picked up a pair of torn panties. "Looka here."

Viv ended her call. "They're on the way." She looked carefully at the panties. "There's a tear, but not the sort of tear that would get made when somebody ripped them off. You know, this situation is off. I'm going to get somebody up here to take prints." She dialed another number.

32

Dino was getting ready for bed when his phone rang. "Bacchetti."

"Lieutenant, this is Viv DeCarlo."

"What's up, Viv?"

"I've got ahold of an alleged rape case, but everything's a little off. Guy named Fisher, has a penthouse on Park Avenue. A young woman named Carson Cullers says he raped her, but there are no marks on her and no semen inside her. There's other stuff that doesn't add up, too."

"What's Fisher's first name?"

"Herbert. Cullers says he's a lawyer with a big firm."

"Let me speak to Fisher."

"I'm in his apartment, but he's out like a light, and I can't wake him up. I think there might be something in the drink he was drinking. I've called an ambulance."

"Have them take him to Lenox Hill, and send your partner with him. I'm coming over to the apartment, and we'll look at the scene together. Fifteen minutes."

"Right." She gave him the address.

Dino hung up and called Stone.

"Hello?"

"It's Dino. I just got a call — some woman claims Herbie raped her, but my detective on the scene says her story looks hinky. Herbie's unconscious in his apartment, and she can't wake him. She's called an ambulance to take him to Lenox Hill. I'm going to the apartment now."

"I'll meet you there shortly," Stone said, then hung up.

Dino reached for his pants.

Stone walked into the apartment and found Dino there with his detective. There was a technician dusting surfaces for prints, but no sign of Herbie.

"Stone Barrington, Viv DeCarlo," Dino said. "Stone and I were partners in the squad about two hundred years ago."

The two shook hands.

"Where's Herbie?" Stone asked.

"On his way to Lenox Hill," she replied. "You know him?"

"We're with the same law firm. Give me the tour."

"We couldn't raise anybody, so the door-

man took us up. We found Fisher unconscious on the sofa with his fly undone and
his penis out. I couldn't wake him, so we
called an ambulance."

"Did you talk to the girl?"

"Yes, that's how I got into this. She was in
the ER at Lenox Hill, complaining of being
raped, but the doctor thought she might be
lying."

"What's her name?"

"Carson Cullers. Lives a few blocks up
Park."

Stone nodded. "Getting any prints?" he
asked the tech.

"Two sets on the glass," he said.

Stone turned back to DeCarlo. "Fisher
has an arrest record, so you can pull his
prints. Might be a good idea to see if the
girl's prints are on file. It would save you a
trip to her place."

The tech opened a laptop and went to
work feeding the prints through a scanner.
"Okay, I've got hits on both," he said. "They
match the ones on the snifter, and they're
both on the martini glass, too."

"Herbie makes her a martini and pours
himself a brandy," Dino said. "He hands
her the martini glass, so both their prints
are on it. But why are both their prints on
Herbie's snifter?"

"What was the girl arrested for?"

"Possession of a controlled substance — cocaine," he replied. "She got a suspended sentence and rehab."

"We got cocaine here," Dino said, pointing at the coffee table, "but it looks undisturbed."

"Well," Stone said, "we know Ms. Cullers knows how to buy the stuff."

"That's quite a lot to leave behind," Viv said. "I wonder why she didn't take it with her."

"Because she wanted us to find it," Dino said.

Viv showed them the panties in an evidence bag and explained her theory about them.

"I want to know what's in that brandy glass," Dino said.

The tech opened another briefcase and went to work on a computer analysis of the liquid in the glass.

"How the hell did Herbie get mixed up in this?" Stone asked.

"Who knows?"

"She is a very beautiful girl," Viv said. "Lots of guys would have gotten mixed up with her."

"Hey," the tech said, "I've got a hit on the analysis. There's Ambien mixed with the

216

brandy. It's a sleeping pill, and it looks like a hefty dose. He drank most of it, too."

"I'm going to the hospital," Stone said.

"Me too," Dino replied. "Viv, you pick up the girl on suspicion of filing a false report. Take her back to the precinct and milk her dry before she can lawyer up. I'll be over there later."

"Yes, boss," Viv replied, then left.

Dino and Stone took a good look around the apartment.

"Nice place," Dino said. "I didn't know Herbie had taste, except maybe in clothes."

"Herbie packs a lot of surprises," Stone said. "He made senior associate at the firm in two years. Never been done before."

"Come on, we'll take my car," Dino said.

At Lenox Hill they found Herbie in an ER cubicle, being attended by a young female resident. Dino made the introductions. "How's he doing?"

"He's still out. We've sent blood and urine to the lab, but we may not have results for a while."

"He was drinking brandy, heavily laced with Ambien," Dino said.

"Are you sure about that?"

"We can run that test on the scene these days."

"In that case, I know what to give him. I'll be right back." She left the cubicle.

Dino peered at Herbie. "Sleeping like a baby," he said.

"Drooling like one, too," Stone said. He picked up a tissue from a box at bedside and wiped Herbie's mouth.

The resident returned with a hypodermic. She unbuttoned Herbie's sleeve, swabbed a vein, uncapped the hypo, and injected it. "Watch this," she said, recapping the hypo and tossing it into a disposal unit.

Herbie's eyelids began to flutter, and in a moment he opened his eyes and looked around. "Holy shit," he said. "This looks like a hospital."

"That's because it is," the resident said. "You're in the ER at Lenox Hill."

"How are you feeling, Herbie?" Dino asked.

"A little fuzzy around the edges," he said. "Last thing I remember, a beautiful girl had her face in my lap."

Even the resident had to laugh.

33

Herbie sat in the backseat of Dino's car. "Okay," he said, "what the hell happened? How'd I go from getting a blow job to the ER?"

"The girl drugged you," Stone said. "She put more than one Ambien in your brandy glass, then she went to the ER and said she'd been raped." Stone told him the rest of the story. "Who is Carson Cullers?"

"She's Dink Brennan's girlfriend," Herbie said. He told Stone and Dino how she came to be in his apartment.

"Dink had to have sent her," Stone said. He explained to Dino who Dink was.

They parked in Herbie's garage and went upstairs.

"There was an ounce or so of cocaine on the coffee table," Dino said. "My tech took it into evidence."

"I don't remember anything about cocaine," Herbie said. "I never touch the stuff."

"You were set up, pure and simple," Stone said.

"Listen, Herbie," Dino said, "you get some sleep. Stone and I are going to the precinct and see what the girl is saying."

Herbie showed them out. He was starting to undress for bed when he remembered something. He got dressed again.

Stone and Dino were sitting in an observation room, watching through a one-way mirror while Viv DeCarlo questioned Carson Cullers.

"I told you, he hit me in the mouth, and he ripped off my panties and raped me."

"Let me tell you the problems I have with your story," Viv said. "First of all, there isn't a mark on you anywhere, including your mouth. There was no semen inside you. Fisher was drugged with Ambien. Nobody believes you, Carson, not the doctor who examined you, not my boss, and not me. Now, you're looking at some serious charges here, and if you want to walk away from this without doing time, you'd better start telling me the truth. Let's take it from the top: why did you go to Herbert Fisher's apartment?"

The door to the observation room opened, and Herbie walked in.

"I told you to go to bed," Dino said. "Let us handle this."

"Has she told you anything?" Herbie asked.

"Yes, a lot of lies."

"Have you got a VCR in this joint?" Herbie asked.

"Right over there," Dino said, "under the TV screen."

Herbie walked over to the machine, inserted a tape into it, and pressed the play button. They all watched as a split screen came up.

"I forgot about this: Mike Freeman's people installed cameras when they did my security system. It's motion-activated."

Each screen displayed a different view of the living room, so they could see two different angles. "I've cued it from when she arrived," Herbie said, "and I've got a tape of her phone call, too." He turned up the volume, and they watched and listened as Carson arrived. Herbie waited until she had left the apartment, then the screen went dark. A moment later it came up again as Viv DeCarlo and her partner entered the apartment.

"She's nailed," Dino said. "Rewind that, and we'll show it to her." He picked up the phone and pressed a button. In the interrogation room Viv picked up the phone. "Yes?"

"Watch the TV," Dino said. "We've got the whole thing on tape." He walked over to the equipment and fiddled with it, then the screen in the interrogation room came alive. They watched Carson's face dissolve from anger to fear to tears.

"Time for bad cop," Dino said. He left the room and appeared on the other side of the one-way mirror and sat down at the table.

"I'm Lieutenant Bacchetti," he said to the woman. "I'm the detective's boss. You're in deep shit, young lady. We've got you cold on filing a false report, obstructing justice, drugging Fisher, and lying to the police. You're going to do hard time."

"I want a lawyer," Carson said, and she was trembling.

"We'll be glad to get you a lawyer," Dino said, "and the minute he walks into this room, you're cooked. He'll tell you to shut up, and we'll file the charges. Then we'll show him the tape, and he'll tell you to do a deal. But I'll tell you what: you give us the truth in writing — the whole story about who put you up to this, agree to testify in court, and you can go home tonight, and your parents won't know where you've

222

been. Otherwise, you'll sleep in a cell for a couple of nights, until your folks can post bail, and you'll be convicted on the evidence you've already seen. Now what's it going to be?"

"Can I have a drink of water?" Carson asked.

Viv went to a cooler and came back with a cupful. Carson sipped it and seemed to be thinking hard about her position.

"No charges?" she asked.

"Not if you tell us the absolute truth, sign the statement, and agree to testify. If you tell us even one lie, the deal is out the window, and your life as you know it will be over."

Carson took a deep breath. "Dink made me do it," she said.

"Dink who?" Viv asked.

"Dink Brennan, my boyfriend. His roommate at Yale, Parker Mosely, came to my apartment this afternoon, gave me the cocaine, and told me exactly what Dink said for me to do."

Viv was taking notes. "And where does Parker live?"

"His parents live at 580 Park Avenue, but he went back to Yale. He lives in a dorm there."

Dino ripped her notes from the pad and

stood up. "You finish up here," he said to Viv, "and get it all. Explain to her that her statement is being videotaped and recorded, and don't let her leave until she signs the typed statement."

"Yes, sir," Viv said.

Dino left the interrogation room and went back to the observation room. Herbie took the paper from his hand and began to write. "Here's the address and room number of his dorm," he said, handing it back to Dino. "Tell your people they might get a disease if they touch anything in the place."

"They'll go in with a search warrant," Dino said, "and I'll bet we find drugs."

Stone spoke up. "You know you don't have anything on Dink yet. She didn't get her instructions from him. You're going to have to turn Parker, too."

"Stone," Herbie said, "can I talk to you alone for a minute?"

"I'll go away," Dino said, and left the room.

"What is it, Herb?"

"I've got a problem here, and so have you."

"Marshall Brennan?"

"Exactly. He's the firm's client, and a very important one, and since you and I are both heavily invested with him, we don't want to cause him any more pain than can possibly be avoided."

"By having his son arrested and charged?"

"That's it. Look, nobody's been hurt here so far. She's not going to charge me with rape, so it's not going to make the papers and I'm not going to be fired from Woodman and Weld, and Marshall is not going to fire the firm, and my career won't be over tomorrow."

"You have a point," Stone said. "How do you want to handle this?"

"Let's do it a different way," Herbie said, and began to explain.

34

Herbie awoke the following morning, still feeling fuzzy. He'd had only about four hours of sleep, but that would be enough. He called the rehab farm in Connecticut and made an appointment to see Dink, then he had a long conversation with the director of the farm. He showered, shaved, had a good breakfast, then transferred his security tape to his iPad and put it into his briefcase, along with a copy of Carson Cullers's signed statement. He inserted a tiny recorder into the breast pocket of his tweed jacket, then he called Cookie and told her to clear his morning, that he had to see a client, which was true. He got out the Maybach and drove up to New Haven, thinking that, maybe, he should be driving something less ostentatious.

He drove through the gates of the farm and presented himself at the reception desk, then waited in a comfortable lounge that reminded him of a hotel he had once stayed in.

Dink appeared a few minutes later, dressed in khakis and a polo shirt, clean-shaven and finely barbered. "Hello, Herb," he said cheerfully, offering his hand. "I'm sorry to keep you waiting. I had to wrap up a group therapy session. I'm glad you could come to see me."

"Oh, I was in the neighborhood," Herbie replied, shaking the hand. "Have a seat, Dink. We need to talk."

Dink sat down, crossed his legs, and smiled broadly. "I want to thank you personally for getting me into this place. It has really changed my life, and they tell me I'll be ready for release in a week or two."

"You're entirely welcome, Dink. But what I'm about to tell you is going to change your life again — and again for the better."

"Well, that sounds great, Herb."

"Of course, there's an alternative scenario, but we'll get to that later. Right now you should know that you're not getting out of here in a couple of weeks. In fact, I think you're probably going to be here for the remainder of this year and maybe for the year after, too."

Dink's face took on a scowl.

"What are you talking about?"

Herbie took the small recorder from his pocket. "I want you to listen to what Carson Cullers had to say last night." He switched it on. "She said it to the police, and then she put it in writing." As Carson began to speak, Herbie switched on his iPad, which began to play his security tape.

Dink listened and watched. "This is bullshit, Herb," he said.

"Shut up and listen," Herbie said. When the two tapes had played, he switched on the recorder and put it back into his pocket. "Now, what you've just seen and heard is enough to get you five to seven years at a very uncomfortable state institution, a place not nearly as nice as this one."

"That's ridiculous," Dink said. "Carson is making this up. She's crazy, you know — she has spells where she doesn't know who or where she is."

"Those probably come during sessions with the drugs you supply her," Herbie said.

"And it's her word against mine. You have no evidence tying me to this."

"Your old roommate, Parker Mosely, is at this moment having a very long conversation with an NYPD detective lieutenant. I'll have the recordings of that session for you in a day or two. And your stash of drugs has been located, so we can add another ten years to your sentence for that. You're going to be well into your middle years before you see the light of day, Dink."

"I want a lawyer," Dink said sullenly.

"I'm the only lawyer you're going to get, Dink. Have you forgotten that you signed a document making me your only legal representative for the foreseeable future? You also made me your legal guardian, upon your self-admission to this facility. Add while you are a patient here, you are, ipso facto, incompetent to change those agreements."

"My old man won't let you get away with this," Dink said. He was looking very worried now.

"Your father has already had a long conversation with my associate, who is his good friend, and he has wholeheartedly approved of everything I'm telling you."

"And if I don't do what you want me to?"

"Oh, yes, the alternative scenario. In that case this facility will declare you competent, and you will be arrested and tried for your crimes. Carson and Parker will testify in court that you supplied her, through Parker, with drugs, then instructed her to entrap your attorney into a rape charge. You will be convicted and, when all charges are taken into account, sentenced to a term of fifteen to twenty years in a hard-core, non-country-club prison. Oh, and your father will wash his hands of you and disinherit you, as well. When you are finally released you will have to rely on the criminal and sexual skills you learned in prison to support yourself. Are you beginning to get the picture, Dink?"

"Now look, Herb," Dink said, tears appearing in his eyes, "I want to apologize for this whole thing. It was just a big practical joke that went wrong, and I'll do whatever I possibly can to make it up to you, really I will."

"Well, Dink, that's a great start on the new attitude you're going to have to adopt if you want to be a free man before you're forty."

"I'll do whatever you tell me, Herb. Trust me, I will."

"Trust you?" Herbie laughed at that one. "You're a junkie and a drug dealer, two of the most untrustworthy beings on the planet. You've just put the girl you supposedly love and your best friend, perhaps your only friend, in jeopardy of long prison sentences, and you've gravely endangered your relationship with the father who loves you and, not incidentally, with his very considerable fortune, and for what? You should start asking yourself that today."

"I'll do whatever you say, Herb," Dink

said, and he sounded truly contrite.

"You can start by stopping trying to use the people in this place who want to help you. The general consensus among them, you might like to know, is that you are a liar, a narcissist, a con man, and a sociopath who is a danger to himself and to others. You see, they are accustomed to being lied to by people like you, and they know how to deal with you.

"By the way, while we've been having this conversation, the staff have taken apart your very comfortable quarters and removed all of your personal possessions and confiscated them. For the foreseeable future you'll be wearing the orange hospital gown that you already know identifies the least trustworthy patients of this facility, and you are being moved to a room that is very much like the prison cell you will be occupying, if you should give your father or me the slightest difficulty. He and I are the only people authorized to contact you, and you may not contact anyone, especially Carson and Parker. Have you grasped your situation yet?"

Dink looked out of breath. "Yes," he said. "I'll be good." He sounded like a small child who had been chastened.

"Ah, here come your escorts to your new quarters," Herbie said. "They'll give you your new gown after they've strip-searched you and given you today's medications."

Herbie got up to leave as the two large men in white approached. "Enjoy your stay on the farm, Dink. I'll be in touch from time to time, when I feel like it."

The two men took Dink's arms and marched him away.

Herbie went back to the Maybach and turned it toward the city. He thought he might do a little car shopping on the way home.

35

When Herbie got back to his office, Stone Barrington was seated on his sofa, drinking a cup of coffee. "How did it go?" he asked.

"Pretty much as we expected," Herbie said "He started with bluster and finished with blubbering. How did it go with Marshall?"

"I think we've underestimated Marshall," Stone replied. "Not only did he take it very well, but I think he had been dreading something like this situation. He seemed, at first, relieved, then determined to leave Dink in your hands, without interference."

"It's a responsibility I don't want, but I've got it, and I'll handle it as best I can," Herbie said, pouring himself a cup of coffee.

"Dino called. His people found Parker Mosely at his parents' home in the city, so he didn't have to involve the Connecticut authorities. He reduced Parker to a quivering mass of jelly and got a signed statement from him. Both he and Carson will be in rehab facilities before the day is out."

"I'm very grateful to you and Dino, Stone."

"Oh, I don't think you would have been convicted on her evidence alone, Herb."

"No, but my career would be in ruins."

"Put that behind you," Stone said. "If anything, you're in better shape today than you were this time yesterday. You've certainly earned Marshall's trust, and I wouldn't be surprised if he sends more business your way."

Herbie shrugged. "The really bad thing about all this is, I don't know if it's going to help Dink. I'm not at all sure that a year at the farm can make a decent human being out of him, and I'm very much afraid that Marshall will end up having to do all the things I told Dink he would."

"If that happens, Herb, it won't be your fault. You've done everything you possibly could to help him."

Cookie knocked at the door. "Josh Hook is on his way up," she said.

"God, I forgot about him," Herbie said.

"Who's Josh Hook?"

"He's the guy who's running Strategic Defense's new training camp for armed bodyguards," Herbie replied. "I said I'd spend a few days up there learning to do whatever it is that they do."

"It'll be good for you," Stone said. "Take your mind off Dink Brennan." He got up. "I'll leave you to your client."

Josh Hook arrived, and Herbie introduced him to Stone.

"I've heard about you from Mike Freeman," Hook said.

"Mike is a good man," Stone replied. "You'll enjoy working with him."

"He says the same about you," Hook replied.

Stone took his leave.

"So," Josh said, settling into a chair, "what have you been up to, Herb?"

"If I told you, you wouldn't believe me," Herbie said.

Dink sat on his bed and looked around his new quarters. It was a room of about nine by twelve, furnished with a bed and a chair. There was a small bathroom with a shower, but no closet and no chest of drawers. They were unnecessary, since its occupants had no clothes. There was no TV, either, and the overhead light was controlled by the staff.

Dink had recovered from the shock of what Herb Fisher had said to him, and now he was angry. He got up and walked around the room, looking for something of interest.

There was nothing. Well above his head was a single window, of about one by two feet, covered with a heavy wire mesh that let little sunlight through.

He sat back down on the bed, since the single chair looked very uncomfortable. He reflected on what he had going for him, and it wasn't much. He knew he was not going to be beaten up or raped, and that was a start. He took a few deep breaths and tried to relax.

He had more assets on the outside, of course, but at the moment, he had no access to that world. There were clothes out there and money, and he was going to need those things.

The door opened and the two men who had escorted him to the room stepped inside.

"Medication time," one of them said, holding up a small paper cup and a cup of water.

"What kind of medication?" Dink asked.

"Just something to relax you," the man said.

"I'm perfectly relaxed," Dink said. "Please tell the doctor I don't need to be medicated. Tell him I'll be cooperative."

"I'll be sure and mention that to him," the man said, "but right now, you have to take your medication."

"I really don't —"

"You want us to help you get it down?" the man said. Apparently, the other one never spoke.

"All right," Dink said, "I'll take it."

"That's a good boy," the man said, handing him both cups.

Dink looked at the large pill inside. He swallowed it, and chased it with the water.

"Good boy!" the man said. "Everything's going to be fine now. The doctor will be here in a few minutes." They left.

Dink immediately put to work a skill that had served him well in the past. He went into the bathroom, stuck a finger down his throat, and vomited the pill into the toilet.

"Fuck you all," he said aloud, then he went and sat down on the bed again.

The door opened, and a middle-aged man in a white coat carrying a clipboard came into the room. "Good afternoon," he said, "I'm Dr. Morton."

"Good afternoon, Doctor," Dink replied.

The doctor pulled up the chair and sat down. "Now, let's have a little orientation," he said. "Oh, are you feeling the medication yet?"

"I'm feeling relaxed," Dink replied.

"Good. Now first of all, you are no longer

a patient in the facility where you've been living and were treated. It was deemed by the people who were working with you that you were pretending to cooperate, just so that you could get out."

Dink nodded. "I'm afraid that's true," he said. "But I want you to know that I understand that I'm not a well person, and I want to do everything I can to get well."

"That's a good attitude, if you're not lying," the doctor said. "The first thing that you're going to have to learn is to be scrupulously honest with the people who treat you. They all have a great deal of experience with being lied to, so do yourself a favor and don't lie to them."

"Do you mind if I lie down, Doctor?" Dink asked.

"Yes, I mind, I'm not through yet. When I'm through, you can lie down if you want to."

"All right." Dink decided to be polite but not to try to sell this guy anything, just appear to go along. Only going along could get him the things he needed to get out of there, and he had no intention of spending one more day there than necessary.

36

Stone sat on his kitchen sofa and waited for Marla to appear from across the garden. It was to be their first evening together since her show had opened, and she seemed to prefer dining at his house to going out.

She rapped on the garden door and let herself in. He rose to greet her and got a kiss on the corner of his mouth for his effort.

"What can I get you to drink?" he asked.

"I think I'll try some of your bourbon."

Stone poured two Knob Creeks, and they sat down on the sofa. "So, is the show finally wrinkle-free?"

"There will always be ironing to do, but I had to make myself stop going to performances. I think we're in for a good run. The advance ticket sales were light, but that's picked up a lot since the reviews came in."

"You look more relaxed," Stone said.

"Relieved is more like it. Also, there's

always a letdown after a show opens and there's nothing else for me to do." She took a sip of her bourbon. "This is good," she said.

"Were you going to say something else?"

"Well . . ."

This is where she's going to tell me there's another man, he thought.

"I have something of a problem."

"Can I help?"

"I need some advice, that's all."

"Advice is what I do, mostly."

"There's this man."

"Uh-oh. I was afraid of that."

"No, I'm not dumping you."

"Now *I'm* relieved."

"I had a few dates with this guy a while back. It was nothing serious — at least, not to me."

"But he took it seriously?"

"He seemed to. Then I started rehearsals for the show, and I used that as an excuse not to accept any more dates with him. Then, without my knowledge, he sought out our producer and invested some money in the show, apparently so he could attend some rehearsals and see me."

"Sounds like it was a good investment. He should be pleased."

"Yes, but now that the show has opened,

he's started a new campaign to see me. Flowers and gifts arrive, and the gifts were embarrassingly expensive, so I sent them back to him. I also wrote him a tactful letter explaining that, while I thought he was a nice fellow, I didn't want to see him anymore."

"That would have been my first piece of advice," Stone said. "How did he take it?"

"Badly," she said. "He called this afternoon and was very angry. How could I string him along? I didn't. I finally said I wasn't listening anymore, and not to call me anymore, then I hung up — right after he threatened me."

"Tell me exactly what he said."

"He said that I would soon learn that women don't get away with ill-treating him, that I would regret it."

"All right," Stone said, "it's time for your attorney to write the next letter."

"I don't have an attorney."

"You do now," Stone said. He picked up a pad and got out his pen. "What's his name?"

"Ed Abney."

"What does he do?"

"He has a publicity agency, specializing in Broadway and off-Broadway shows and theater people. He seems to be pretty

241

successful."

"What's the name of the agency?"

"Bright Lights, Ink. He has offices on Eighth Avenue — I don't know the number."

"I'll get the address and have a letter hand-delivered tomorrow morning."

"What are you going to say in the letter?"

"That Ms. Marla Rocker would not like to see him or hear from him again, and that any further advances or gifts from him would be unwelcome, and that any further communication must be through your attorney."

"And what if it doesn't work?"

"Then we go to a TRO, a temporary restraining order."

"Will that work?"

"If he ignores it I'll haul him in front of a judge, and if he continues after that, he could end up in jail."

"What's to keep him from killing me?"

Stone put down his pad and turned toward her. "What reason do you have to think that he might become violent?"

"I didn't tell you about this, but he was at our opening party, at Sardi's. I saw him across the room with a woman who looked familiar, and when I went to the ladies' she followed me. She told me that I should be

242

careful with him, because he has a history of violence with women. I asked if that was the case, why was she seeing him? She said because she was afraid not to, and that she was leaving town, moving away from New York to get away from him, and she wasn't telling anybody where."

"Do you know her name?"

"Annette Redfield. She's an actress. I looked her up and it seems that she has been working regularly for the past ten years or so, in supporting roles on and off Broadway. I suppose that's why she looked familiar."

Stone got up. "I'll be right back," he said. He walked down the hall to his office, then into Joan's office, where he found a copy of that afternoon's *New York Post*. He went back to the kitchen and leafed through the paper until he found the article he was looking for, then handed it to her.

ACTRESS FOUND DEAD

A popular supporting actress on Broadway was found late last night by a neighbor, dead on the kitchen floor of her apartment. Annette Redfield, 38, had been strangled, according to police sources, and it appeared that she had been trying to defend herself with a kitchen knife.

"Don't read any more," Stone said, taking the paper from her.

Marla's face had drained of color. She took a pull on her drink and sat back on the sofa. "Now what? Am I going to have to leave town?"

"No," Stone said, "and I'm going to see that he doesn't bother you again. Do I have your permission to do that?"

"Whatever it takes," Marla said, "short of killing him."

"Don't worry," Stone said, "nobody is going to die."

Marla sighed. "Someone already has."

37

Herbie stood in a gymnasium that smelled of fresh paint and listened to Josh Hook, who was standing on a mat, teaching a self-defense class.

"Welcome to Strategic Defense," Josh said. "You'll begin your training here by taking a class that is incorrectly named. This is not a class in defensive measures, it is a class in offensive tactics. If, in protecting your client, you find yourself in a defensive posture, it is already too late to defuse the situation quickly. If you do this, or this, or this" — he assumed the postures of boxing, karate, and judo — "you are wasting time. All you're doing is getting yourself into a fight, and while you are fighting, your client is unprotected — at least, by you."

He took a large student by the wrist and led him in front of the class. "Assume a fighting position, any kind of fighting position," he said to the young man, who turned his left side toward Josh and made two fists. Josh kicked him hard in the left shin. The victim grabbed his shin and hopped around on one foot, swearing. Josh kicked him in the ass, and he fell down.

"I did what women are taught to do in anti-rape classes," Josh said. "I kicked him in the shin, and his response was to grab where it hurt and put all his weight on his other foot, making it easy for me to kick him to the ground. I could have pushed him with one finger, and he'd have gone down, but he has a big ass, and it was an inviting target." That got a laugh from his audience. "Now he's on the ground and at a disadvantage. If he looks like he wants to continue fighting, then I can kick him in the balls and put the thought right out of his head." Josh helped the young man up. "I know that hurt, and I'm sorry, but I had to make a point. Get yourself an ice bag from the little freezer over there and apply it to your shin. It'll stop hurting in a minute." The young man limped away and did as he was told.

"My point is, when confronted with a threat, don't wait, take action. Don't tell him to get out of your way, don't push him, don't yell at him. Put him on the ground in a suitably painful way so that he won't want to get up and take you on. By the time he's decided he's mad enough to fight, your client will be in the car and on his way, and so will you, and you won't be the one in pain.

"That's how to deal with a physical threat. The threat of a man with a weapon — a knife or a baseball bat, say — requires even quicker action. You have to act before he assumes an offensive posture, like holding the knife in front of him or backswinging the bat. A very good technique is a straight punch to the nose with either hand, while he's still thinking about what he's going to do to you. Don't make your punch short — that might not stop him. Punch right through his head to a point six inches behind him. You'll knock him on his ass, it will hurt him like hell, and he'll be confronted with the sight of his own blood all over his shirt, which is very disturbing to almost anybody. And he will be afraid of you, giving you time to get your client into the building. By the way, when encountering that kind of opposition on the way into a building, always leave the building by another exit because the man you humiliated might be waiting outside for you, and you don't want an angry man with a knife or a baseball bat waiting for you because next time, he'll be ready to use his weapon."

"What happens if he has a gun in his

hand?" somebody asked.

"Not now, in a few minutes," Josh said. "Other weak points." Josh took Herbie by the wrist and led him forward. "Don't worry, Herb, I'm not going to hurt you. This time." Another laugh. "The knee is a very good place to kick a man, especially if he's larger than you are." He aimed a kick at Herbie's knee, but stopped short of contact. "The only problem with the knee is, if you really connect, you may do serious damage, requiring a trip to the ER, surgery, physical therapy, and a personal injury lawsuit. But that's what your client's liability insurance is for. Also, you should have your own liability insurance, which is cheap as long as you don't list your occupation on the application as 'bodyguard.' " Another laugh.

"The throat is good for a punch," Josh said, again demonstrating on Herbie, "but carries the same dangers as the knee, with the additional risk of death. Then there's the solar plexus. If he's drawing back with a baseball bat, his abdomen will be wide open for a hook to the solar plexus. If you already have your hands on your attacker's upper arms or shoulders, the two-handed ear slap is a good shock tactic." He brought both his open hands to Herbie's ears. "The noise is stunning, and it's painful enough to persuade him to be somewhere else. Cupping your hands increases the effect on the eardrums.

"You may find yourself in a situation where carrying a weapon is illegal — and you never want to break the law. If you can possibly help it. Then another kind of weapon can be useful. Not a knife or a blackjack, which is likely to get you into more trouble than your assailant, but something innocuous, like a very tightly rolled newspaper." He picked up a *Wall Street Journal* from a table and began rolling it. "Nobody's going to arrest you for carrying a newspaper, especially the *Wall Street Journal,* and it would be tough to sue you for it, too. But swing it across a man's jaw, and you'll knock him silly, and ramming it into the solar plexus will disable him for a few minutes."

Josh picked up an umbrella from the table. "In rainy weather, the handle of an umbrella upside the head will divert an assailant's attention from your client, same to the solar plexus, but don't use the pointed end for that. Always use an expensive umbrella, because its handle will be heavy enough to hurt. A ten-dollar umbrella from a street vendor won't be of much use." He put down the umbrella and picked up a short, thick object in a plastic sleeve. "The folding umbrella — again, a high-quality one — makes a fine club, with just enough padding to keep from splitting somebody's head open. Also, it's a good puncher, and especially effective on the back of the neck, if you have that opportunity."

Josh allowed Herbie to return to his place, then he sat on the table and addressed the group. "Now, let's talk about guns. If you're pursuing a career in protection because it allows you to shoot people legally, you're in the wrong line of work. Join the army. Here are the rules about guns. One, never carry a gun. If it's absolutely necessary to carry a gun, don't, unless you're licensed to carry a concealed weapon *in the jurisdiction where you're working.* You are going to have a long class on how to become licensed almost anywhere, complete with the forms and fingerprinting necessary. Two, if you are carrying a gun, never withdraw the weapon from its holster. Three, if you ignore two, due to circumstances beyond your control, and withdraw the weapon from its holster, never point it at anyone. Four, if you should foolishly point it at someone, never touch the trigger. It is very good if eyewitnesses to a gun in your hand see your trigger finger laid along the barrel, instead of on the trigger. Five, if you should accidentally touch the trigger, never pull or squeeze it, unless during this whole process you have become absolutely convinced that the loss of your own life is imminent if you do not pull the trigger. Six — and this is the second most important rule, after number one — if you make the decision to pull the trigger, *DO NOT MISS!* We will be conducting classes in not missing every day of your visit with us."

Josh hopped down from the table. "Now we'll take a fifteen-minute break so that you can pee in your pants. After that, one of my associates, an expert with the fighting knife, will demonstrate to you how to introduce an assailant to his own intestines. Bring something to throw up in." He walked out of the gym, leaving his students to mill about.

38

Stone and Dino met for lunch at P.J. Clarke's.

"Okay, what's going on?" Dino asked. "You sounded funny on the phone."

"Funny ha ha or funny queer?"

"Funny queer. Ha ha."

"You're right. Marla Rocker has a problem, maybe a very serious problem. I've moved her into my house for a few days while we sort this out."

"You mean, while *I* sort it out."

"I mean, I'll sort out her problems, but you can make the arrest."

"Gee, who do I get to arrest?"

"A man named Ed Abney."

"And who the fuck is Ed Abney?"

"He runs a publicity agency called Bright Lights, Ink, with a 'k.'"

"Cute. Did he issue an illegal press release?"

"You know the actress found dead in the

apartment in your precinct a couple of days ago?"

"You're just wondering if I know what goes on in my precinct, aren't you?"

"Well, yes."

"Annette Redfield."

"You win this," Stone said, handing him a French fry.

Dino ate the French fry. "I want to thank everybody who voted for me."

"Ed Abney scared Annette Redfield enough so that she was about to flee the city to get away from him."

"And you know this how?"

"Remember the other night at Marla's opening-night party?"

"Yes."

"She saw Abney there with Redfield. Abney has been sort of stalking Marla, in spite of her asking him to go away. Redfield followed her into the ladies' john and told her to watch out for him, that he has a history of violence with women. Apparently, she was talking about herself, since she was about to make a run for it."

Dino got out his cell phone and pressed a speed dial button. "Viv? Bacchetti. We've got a suspect in the Annette Redfield strangling, name of Ed Abney." He gave her the name of Abney's agency and told her about

Marla's conversation with Redfield at Sardi's. "No, don't pick him up just yet. I want to know if Abney has an arrest record and if he has any TROs out on him. Call me back with results before you make an arrest. Thanks, kiddo." Dino hung up.

"So you've got DeCarlo on speed dial now?"

"It makes it easier to dial her."

"I'll bet. How many of your other detectives do you have on speed dial?"

Dino ignored that one. "What are you doing about Marla?"

"I'm keeping her at my house, and I sent Allison to court to get a TRO against Abney."

Dino looked at his watch. "How long ago?"

"Around ten this morning."

"See if you can stop her," Dino said.

"Why?"

"Because I don't want to rattle the guy's cage just yet. We'll have a moment later when we can use the TRO to piss him off."

Stone pressed Allison's speed dial number. "Allison here."

"It's Stone. Have you made the application for the TRO yet?"

"No, not yet."

"Get it but don't serve it yet. Dino wants

to wait a bit."

"What's Dino got to do with it?"

"Dino is the police, remember? He feels that he should do some investigation before we slap Abney with the TRO."

"Whatever you say. Who do I bill for this on my time sheet?"

"Call it pro bono."

"Sounds more like pro boner to me," she said, then hung up.

Stone laughed and put his phone away. "She said it sounds more like 'pro boner.'"

Dino laughed. "Smart girl, Allison."

"Smart-ass," Stone said.

When Stone got back to his office he found Marla, Joan, and Allison sitting in his office, giggling.

"Did you ladies get into the cooking sherry?" he asked.

"No, it was your bourbon," Joan replied, getting up. "Come on, Allison, Simon Legree has returned." The two women went back to their own offices.

"So," Stone said, "what's happened that made the three of you need a drink in the early afternoon?"

"It's not all that early," Marla said.

"Two-thirty is early. I'm going to have to

start marking the bottle. Now come on, give."

"Oh, all right. I went over to my house to get a few things."

"Marla . . ."

"I know, I know, you told me not to go over there without you. It's all right, I took Joan." She took a sip of her bourbon. "And she took her gun."

"Swell," Stone said. "What will the neighbors think? The two of you traipsing around Turtle Bay Gardens with a gun."

"Who cares?"

"You still haven't told me what rattled you. And don't tell me you're not rattled. I know when Joan is rattled, and she doesn't rattle easily, and if she's rattled, you're rattled."

Marla took another sip of her bourbon. "The house had been ransacked."

"Ransacked?"

"Well, not the whole house, just the living room and my bedroom."

"Ransacked?"

"Stop saying that — you know what it means."

"What, exactly, does it mean in the context of your house?"

"Things had been upset in the living room, thrown around."

"And in your bedroom?"

"The same. And some of the drawers had been pulled out."

"Which drawers?"

"The ones with my drawers in them."

"Did your visitor leave any, ah, message?"

"You mean like the semen on my drawers?"

"Exactly."

"You could say he made his presence known."

"How do you know it was semen?"

She rolled her eyes. "Really, Stone."

"All right, all right. What did you do?"

"I grabbed a few things, and we got the hell out of there."

"What did you do with the semen stains?"

"Do with them? Yuck!"

"I mean, are they still there?"

"Well, I wanted to put the garments in question in the garbage, but Joan stopped me."

"Good," Stone said, picking up the phone. "That's evidence. I'll get Dino to send somebody over there."

"They'd better come here first and get my key."

"Right." Stone started dialing.

39

Dink Brennan was playing some one-on-one in the fenced-in exercise court of his unit with Otto, the large man who was his watchdog and only companion. Dink let him score, and then they sat down at a picnic table nearby to cool off.

"You're doing okay, Dink," Otto said. "I'm proud of you."

"It's important to me to do well here," Dink replied. "And I want to thank you for helping me."

"That's my job," Otto said.

"Tell me about you, Otto. You married? Kids?"

"Married fifteen years, a thirteen-year-old daughter."

"What's her name?"

"The wife is Betty, the daughter is Caroline. She's something, Caroline — smartest kid you ever saw. Won a scholarship to Choate Rosemary Hall!"

"Funny, I went there," Dink said. "Good thing she won a scholarship. It's an expensive school."

"Well, the scholarship pays only half. I've got to come up with the rest."

"Jeez, that's what, twenty grand?"

"Twenty-one," Otto said. "I can manage the one. Betty wants to get a job to help, but she's not well — really bad asthma."

"Do me a favor, Otto," Dink said. "Let me use your cell phone."

"What for?" Otto said. "And you're not allowed to have a cell phone. I'd get in trouble."

"Okay, you dial a number for me. Don't worry, it's just my bank — you won't get into trouble."

Otto picked up his jacket and came up with his phone.

Dink gave Otto the number. "What's your last name?"

"Krieger." Otto tapped in the number and listened. "Whaddaya know?" he said. "It's your bank." He handed Dink the phone.

"Lora Trenkle, please," Dink said. "Hello, Lora? Dink Brennan. Just fine. I assume you've made the necessary adjustments to my accounts since I have access to my trust. Good. I'd like to send a wire transfer to the bursar at Choate Rosemary Hall School.

You'll have to call them for the account information. Twenty-one thousand, for the tuition of Caroline Krieger. Can you still get that out today? Great, and please deposit one hundred thousand from my trust into my checking account. Thanks so much." Dink handed the phone back to Otto. "Done."

Otto stared at him in disbelief. "That was a joke, right?"

"Call the bursar in an hour," Dink said.

"Dink, why would you do that?"

"It is for a worthy cause. Caroline sounds like a great kid."

"I'm overwhelmed," Otto said. He looked at Dink suspiciously. "You want something from me?"

Dink got up and grabbed the basketball. "Just another game. I'll spot you two points." He threw the ball to Otto.

During the next few days, Otto became Dink's manservant. He brought burgers from a fast-food place, books from the library — self-help books, mostly. He couldn't do enough.

"I've spoken to the director," Otto said one day, "and told him I think you should be returned to your old quarters. I talked to Dr. Morton, too, and he seemed to agree with me. It'll probably be tomorrow. I'll get your things out of storage."

"Gee, thanks, Otto," Dink said.

The following day, Dink walked into his old room and found his civilian clothes on his bed and an envelope containing his wallet. There were no credit cards, of course — Herb Fisher had cut those in half — but his driver's license was there, and a little over a hundred dollars. The next morning, Dink was having coffee with Otto in the rec room. "There's a terrific movie on in town," he said. "I saw it in the local paper. I hear the management allows trips to the village. Why don't we go this afternoon?"

"They'll sometimes let us take a day trip," Otto said. "I'll see what I can do." He left and walked toward the administrative offices, then returned ten minutes later. "We're on," he said. "Starts at two-thirty."

Otto drove Dink into the village and parked on Main Street. The theater was two buildings from the corner gas station, as Dink had remembered. Otto bought him a ticket, and they went inside. Twenty minutes into the feature, Dink grabbed his gut and made a grunting sound. "I've got to go to the john," he whispered to Otto.

"Okay."

Dink left the theater and walked quickly down to the gas station, where he found the owner reading a newspaper. "Hi," Dink said. "My name's Brennan. You've got my car stored here."

"Right," the man said. "Can I see some ID?"

Dink showed him his driver's license.

"Take me a minute," the man said. "I gassed it up when it came in." Ten minutes later, the man was back with Dink's BMW convertible. "You're all paid up," the man said, handing him the keys.

Dink gave him a twenty and pulled out of the station. It felt good to be out and behind the wheel. He headed for New Haven. He drove to his dorm and found the custodian.

"Hi, Paul. Can you let me into my room? I've lost the key."

"Hey, Mr. Brennan. The boss said you'd left school, so I boxed up your stuff."

"I'll save you the trouble of getting rid of it," Dink said.

The man unlocked the door. "There's some mail, too. It's on your desk, and there's a package."

Dink had thought there might be mail. He riffled through the envelopes and found three he wanted. They contained the new credit cards and an ATM card that Parker

Mosely had ordered to replace the ones Herb Fisher had destroyed.

Then he turned his attention to the larger package. He opened it with a box cutter. Inside was a beautiful leather briefcase, one that matched his luggage. He opened the case and found a card inside: "Happy Birthday! You're a man now. Love, Dad." *The old man didn't forget,* he thought. *How about that?*

He packed his suitcases with some clothes, then he found his passport and checkbook in a desk drawer and put them into the briefcase with his Mac Air. He carried the cases out to his car, stowed them in the trunk, and headed for New York City. Once in the city he visited the Apple store and bought a new iPhone. His old one had disappeared. His first call was to the Lowell, a small, elegant hotel on East Sixty-third Street, near Madison. He booked himself a suite, then retrieved his car from the garage, drove there, and checked in.

Herbie was in his room at the Strategic Defense training center, sore from exertion and with tired arms from firing a pistol — something he discovered he did very accurately. His cell phone rang.

"Herb Fisher."

"Mr. Fisher, this is the director at the farm," a male voice said. "I'm afraid I have some bad news."

Oh, God, Herbie thought, the kid has died, or something.

"What's happened?"

"We allowed young Mr. Brennan to make a day trip into the village with a staff member, and he managed to get away from him. We haven't been able to locate the boy."

"Have you called the police?"

"No, he hasn't committed a crime, and he was here voluntarily."

"But he committed himself."

"He agreed to that under your guardianship, but that's no longer in effect."

"Why not?"

"Because he had his twenty-first birthday the day before yesterday."

"Shit," Herbie said.

"Well, yes. I'm afraid there's nothing more we can do for him, unless you can persuade him to return voluntarily."

"Thank you," Herbie said, then hung up. Now what?

40

Shelley Bach sat at the dressing table in her room at the Carlyle and regarded her image in the mirror. She used a hand mirror to look at her profile and liked what she saw, even without makeup. There were still a few red places, but as she sponged on her makeup, they magically went away. She liked her new auburn hair, too; it went beautifully with her natural, pale skin color. She dressed and left the hotel.

Now she made her third visit to her new dentist for the fitting of her new smile. The veneers from the dental lab corrected small irregularities in her front teeth, and they were whiter than the originals. She had approved them on her second visit, when they had been affixed to a mold of her teeth. Now they were put permanently in place. She gave the receptionist her credit card and regarded herself in the mirror. She was exactly what she had wanted to be: a different person. No one who knew her would recognize her with her new profile, her new teeth, and her new clothes. She looked ten years younger, and she was no longer the government drone she had been at the FBI; she was a New York woman.

Now all she wanted was to go shopping. Oh, and one other thing: she wanted a man. She stepped out onto Madison Avenue and swung her long legs toward Seventy-second Street and the Ralph Lauren store.

Dino looked up from his desk to see Viv DeCarlo standing at his office door. She looked great, he thought: slim, but busty, black hair as thick as fur, nice clothes. She seemed to be dressing better these days. "Yeah, Viv? What have you got?"

"I've got two TROs on Ed Abney," she said, "but a few years back. I have a theory about that."

"Have a seat. What's your theory?"

Viv sat down and crossed her legs. "I think he's never stopped abusing women," she said, "but I think he's gotten better at intimidating them. I think that's the only reason there are no recent TROs."

"Makes sense to me," Dino said. "Are you ready to make an arrest?"

"I'm not sure about that," she said. "All

we've got are the old TROs and Marla Rocker's statement about what Annette said to her in the john at Sardi's."

"What sort of job did the crime-scene guys do on Annette's apartment?"

"We didn't get lucky there. He seems to have wiped everything down, and get this: they found an empty chemical douche in her kitchen garbage can. He probably flushed out her vagina, too."

Dino frowned. "If he's that careful, he's going to be hard to nail. Do we know of any other women he's been out with?"

"No, but I'd like to tail him and see who we can turn up. Any chance of a wiretap?"

"You can talk to the DA, but I doubt it. And we're short of manpower. We couldn't manage a proper tail team right now, unless we suspected he was about to hurt some-body again."

"I've checked back on unsolved murders of women with theatrical backgrounds. There are two that might be a fit, but we've no evidence to connect him with them."

"It's all too nebulous," Dino said.

"I have an idea about how to make it less nebulous," she said, "but you're not going to like it."

"Why am I not going to like it?"

"Because it involves Rosie and me getting

to know Mr. Abney."

"Wait a minute, you're not talking about —"

"Of course not. Neither of us is going to sleep with him and certainly not a threesome. You don't think I'm crazy, do you?"

"Not entirely. What do you have in mind?"

"I thought we'd give Abney a choice, see which of us he likes. If he bites, the other can run the tail, if you'll give us one more team."

Dino thought about it. It was a bold move, he had to admit. "You're never to be alone with him," he said. "Never."

"I had a thought about that, too. We'll wire an apartment and take him there. He'll always be on camera, and there'll be a team next door, watching. We won't be alone that way, and we'll have a record of what happens."

"Where would you do this?"

"I've got a girlfriend who's going to Europe for three weeks. She has a nice place, and I think she'll let us use it. It has a romantic look to it — soft furniture, lots of pillows."

"If you can set it up properly, I'll give you two teams," Dino said.

Viv rewarded him with a broad smile.

■ ■ ■ ■

Shelley Bach cut a swath through the new Ralph Lauren women's store, across the street from the old Rhinelander mansion, which now housed the men's store. Lauren's designs fit her beautifully, and there was a new line just in. She picked half a dozen things and ordered them delivered to the Carlyle. The sales assistants couldn't do enough for her.

Dink Brennan put on a suit, left the hotel, and took a cab the few blocks to his father's office. He had thought of calling first, but he didn't think he could pull this off on the phone. What he was going to do now needed to be done face-to-face.

He hadn't been to his father's offices for a couple of years, and the firm had moved to a new building on East Sixty-seventh Street since then. He found the name in the building's directory and took the elevator to the top floor.

He was impressed with the decor in the new place — cool and modern, obviously designed by a top architect. He walked to the reception desk.

"Good morning. May I help you?" the

269

young woman said.

"Yes, I'd like to see Marshall Brennan. My name is Dink Brennan."

"Is he expecting you?"

"No, I thought I'd surprise him."

"Surprise him?"

"I'm his son."

The woman made the call, then hung up. "Someone will be right with you," she said.

Dink took a seat, but only a moment passed before his father's secretary appeared in the reception room. He stood up. "Hello, Anne," he said. "Long time."

She shook his hand. "You're looking very well, Dink," she said.

"I hope Dad will think so, too. Will he see me?"

"Of course. Follow me."

Dink followed her down the long hall and into the lion's den.

41

Marshall Brennan stood up as his son walked into his office, and Dink thought his face registered surprise.

Marshall came around the desk with his hand out. "Hello, Dink," he said.

"Hello, Dad," Dink replied, shaking his hand warmly. "It's good to see you." He followed his father to the sofa, and they both sat down.

"They told me at the farm that you had . . . checked yourself out."

Dink smiled. "I thought I'd save them the paperwork. And by the way, thank you for the handsome briefcase. I'll try and put it to good use."

"I hope you will."

"Dad, I have some things to say to you, and I hope you'll hear me out before you start asking questions."

"I do have a way of interrupting, don't I?"

"Sometimes. First of all, I want to apolo-

271

gize for the way I've behaved for the past couple of years. I did some stupid things: I was smoking a lot of grass, gambling, and then I started selling the stuff. That's over now. I was never addicted to anything, thank God. During my stay at the farm I had time to do a lot of thinking, and I want to get my life back on track."

"I'm glad to hear it," Marshall said, warily.

"I'm going back to Yale in the fall and finish my degree, and I should be able to graduate with my class next year."

"You were a good student once," Marshall said.

"And I will be again. I'm thinking about law school."

Marshall nodded. "You might make a good lawyer."

"We'll see. I have to tell you about some recent events, too. You'll remember Parker Mosely and my former girlfriend Carson Cullers."

"Of course."

"They're both in rehab now, and it's where they belong. Something went really wrong with Parker. He went to Carson and told her that I wanted her to meet Herb Fisher, then claim he tried to rape her and ruin his career. I want you to know that I knew nothing about all this until Herb came to see me at the farm. I'm sure he still thinks I was involved, but honestly, I wasn't. Parker and Carson are lucky they aren't in jail, and they could have dragged me down with them."

Marshall said nothing.

"In any case, once they're out of rehab they can resume their lives, and I hope it won't be their old ones."

"I hope so, too."

"As you know, I now have access to my trust, so I won't be needing financial help from you. You've done more than enough for me. I went online and looked at the statements, and I see that you've trebled the principal with your investing skills, and I'm grateful to you for that."

"I would suggest that you continue to let me invest the bulk of your funds," Marshall said.

"Thank you, I'd like that."

"I'll have Anne get the paperwork done for your new account."

"Thank you."

"Where are you staying?"

"I've got a room at the Lowell, on East Sixty-third. I haven't thought beyond that."

Marshall went to his desk and wrote down something, then took a key from a drawer and returned to the sofa. "The firm has a couple of apartments that we use to house out-of-town clients once in a while. If you like, you're welcome to stay in one until you go back to Yale." He handed Dink the address and key.

Dink accepted both. "Thank you, Dad, that's very kind of you. I'll move in tomorrow."

"The house in East Hampton is still there, too. I don't get out there as much as I used to, but the staff is still there. They'd be glad to see you whenever you like."

"Thank you again, Dad. I'd enjoy that."

"Have you spoken to Herb Fisher?"

"Not since he came to the farm. He was, understandably, angry."

"You might go and see him," Marshall said. "I think Herb is someone you'd profit from knowing, and anyway, you'll need a lawyer."

"I called his office, but he's away this week."

"Oh, that's right, he went up to Mike Freeman's new training facility."

"Mike Freeman?"

"I'm sorry, he's the CEO of a firm called Strategic Services. They've opened a new school for security people."

"I'll call him next week," Dink said, then he got to his feet. "Thank you for seeing me, Dad. I'll try to do a better job of living up to your expectations."

Marshall, uncharacteristically, hugged his son. "Just live up to your own expectations, son."

Dink signed the documents for his new investment account, said goodbye to Anne, and left.

Anne came into Marshall's office. "You seem to have a new son," she said.

"It appears I do," Marshall replied. "I hope it lasts."

42

Herbie came out of a class on defense strategy and ran, head-on, into Mike Freeman.

"Hi there, Mike. I didn't know you were coming up."

"I'm giving some prospective clients a tour. Are you enjoying yourself?"

"Very much."

"Well, cut your next class and come with me," Mike said, "and you'll learn a lot more. I'm giving these folks an overview of what we do."

Herbie followed Mike and his party of half a dozen into a conference room, where they all sat down and Mike switched on a projector. "Gentlemen, this young man in camouflage is Herb Fisher, the corporate counsel for our new division, Strategic Defense." Everybody waved, and Herbie waved back.

"Now, I'm going to give you an overview of our operations as a company, so you can see the breadth and depth of what we offer." He put a chart on the screen. "As you can see, we have a number of subsidiaries: vehicle armoring, communication electronics, security and surveillance systems, computer security and software, and our latest subsidiary, Strategic Defense, which is devoted to the training of security personnel. As you have seen around our new site, we offer a number of kinds of training: personal defense, client defense, firearms, high-performance driving, client relations, emergency medical treatment, and penetration and rescue — more about which later.

"All of you use some of these services now, albeit with our competitors, but I want to show you what full-service security looks like." He switched to a schematic of an office building. "Let's say you're planning a new company headquarters or a large branch, and you're constructing your own building. Our services begin at the design stage. Our architects help yours lay out your floor space in such a way as to make it difficult to penetrate and easy to defend. Our electrical engineers help design a wiring loom for the building that incorporates wiring for the security system and an abundance of high-definition color cameras and recording systems. We place check-in and check-out areas in the street lobby and on each floor, and each of these desks is able to communicate instantly with your security personnel.

"Those personnel would be trained by us, of course, and we would train your employees to work seamlessly with them to protect your premises, your personnel, and your intellectual property. We divide your parking garage into public and corporate areas and screen every vehicle and driver entering either area.

"Executive personnel would be able to arrive and depart from a secure area, since walking from a car to a building is a vulnerable time. The local police would be invited to cooperate with your on-site security personnel. You'll get along better with them in an emergency if they know your people and their practices ahead of an emergency.

"By the time your new offices open we would have brought your security officers to this facility and trained them in a standardized program, so that if they are transferred from one office to another anywhere in the world, their training and operation will be consistent.

"For your highest-level personnel, we will design protective transportation for their use, ranging from a lightly armored SUV to a vehicle very nearly presidential in its strength, and your drivers will be trained in the appropriate vehicles. We will also offer security planning and equipment for top management residences and vacation homes.

"Our flight services division will consult with your people on the selection and purchase of the best aircraft for your needs, whether it be short-hop visits to branches and plants, or ocean-spanning flights to international venues. We can build a hangar for you and establish your corporate flight department for the piloting and maintenance of your aircraft and to oversee the training, both initial and recurrent, for your pilots and airframe, engine, and avionics technicians.

"Our international department can smooth the way for important executives who are relocating, helping them to find suitable, secure housing and schools, as well as furnishing personal protection for the whole family.

"In locations where kidnapping is practiced by local criminals or terrorist groups, we can send in specialists in penetration and recovery, and when that is not possible, we send personnel to negotiate the freedom of personnel being held. Our insurance associate, Steele, offers insurance packages for personnel sent abroad, which can include kidnapping insurance, making large sums immediately available for negotiation and recovery.

"We are pleased to offer services that none of us has even thought of yet — invented or improvised, as the situation calls for. All our personnel are thoroughly trained for the environment in which they work, at home or abroad. We draw people from the armed services, particularly Special Forces and Navy SEAL veterans, as well as from the FBI, the treasury department, the CIA and NSA, and from police departments in many countries. They are trained to always operate legally in any setting, especially with regard to local weapons laws.

"Finally, when we have designed a top-to-bottom security plan for your company, we will make a comprehensive presentation to your board of directors, demonstrating the cost-effectiveness of each part of our plan."

Mike then took questions for nearly an hour, then invited the group to lunch in the company mess. Herbie excused himself to take a phone call on his cell.

"Hello?"

"Hi, it's Cookie."

"What's up?"

"You had a call from Dink Brennan a few minutes ago."

"You're kidding."

"I'm not. He asked for an appointment to come and see you when you get back."

Herbie thought about that for a moment. "Make the appointment," he said, "and make it early."

"All right. When are you coming back?"

"I'll be there Monday morning, first thing."

"Then that's when I'll make the appointment for Dink."

"Good. Let's see if he can get up that early. Anything else?"

"I think I'm going to need some help around here," she said.

"I've been thinking about that," Herbie said. "I don't want you spread too thin."

"There's a woman I know who works here in Accounting that I think would be very good for the things we do. Her name is RoseAnn Faber."

"I'll see what I can do," Herbie said. "See ya." He hung up and called Bill Eggers.

"Having fun at camp, Herbert?"

"I'm having a lot more than fun, Bill. I just watched Mike Freeman give a presentation to prospective clients that taught me more about Strategic Services than I thought I'd ever know. I think you would enjoy watching, next time he gives it."

"I'll figure that out," Eggers said. "What's up?"

"I need another secretary," Herbie said. "Cookie is beginning to drown in the work."

"That's not an unreasonable request, given the work you've created for yourself. I'll speak to Personnel."

"Speak to Accounting, instead," Herbie said. "There's a woman working in that department named RoseAnn Faber. Cookie knows her and thinks she'd be good in the job. Then Accounting can speak to Personnel about replacing her."

"I'll look into it," Eggers said. "Are you ever coming back to work here?"

"I never stopped, but I'll be in my actual office Monday morning."

"See you then." Eggers hung up, and Herbie went to lunch.

43

Stone woke from a deep sleep with somebody shaking him. "What?" he said.

Marla laughed. "You were having a nightmare," she said, "and talking in your sleep."

"I remember," Stone said. "I dreamed you were a Republican."

She laughed. "I *am* a Republican," she said. "Didn't you know?"

"Apparently not, I let you in the house."

"I take it you're a Democrat?"

"I'm a Yellow Dog Democrat."

"What's that?"

"That's a Democrat who would vote for a Yellow Dog before he would vote for a Republican."

She laughed again. "Well, I'm not that dyed-in-the-wool a Republican. I just grew up in a Republican family."

"You poor girl." He rolled over and pulled her to him. "I think we have to begin your reeducation now."

She kissed him. "You mean we're going to have Democrat sex?"

"Democrat-*ic* sex," Stone said. "Don't insult it by mispronouncing the name. That's the first step in your reeducation."

"What's the second step?"

He kissed her. "That's step two."

"I can't wait for step three."

He gently pinched a nipple.

"I think you've just found the start button," she said. "Can we skip to the final step?"

He rolled on top of her.

Half an hour later, they lay, panting and sweating, holding hands. "Does that complete my reeducation?" she asked.

"That's only the first lesson," Stone said. "We have a lot to work through yet."

"Such as?"

"You'll see, lesson by lesson."

"I guess it's good that I seem to have relocated to your house. It saves all those trips through the garden and in the back door."

"It is good, isn't it? Even difficult situations can have their bright side." He rolled over and kissed her. "Where's that start button again?"

■ ■ ■ ■

Herbie was at his desk by seven on Monday morning, and Cookie came into his office, leading another young woman, taller than she and dark-haired.

"Herb, this is RoseAnn Faber," Cookie said. "She's going to be working with us."

"Wow, that was fast," Herbie said, standing up and shaking her hand.

"It all happened Friday afternoon," Cookie said.

"Are you glad to be out of Accounting, RoseAnn?" Herbie asked.

"You bet your ass . . . Excuse me, yes, I'm very glad to be out of Accounting." The accent had a tinge of Brooklyn.

"And we're glad to have you," Herbie said. "I've been working Cookie too hard."

"So she tells me," RoseAnn said.

"RoseAnn!" Cookie said, blushing. "I haven't been complaining, Herb. I love my job."

"I know you do, Cookie, because I know how well you do it. RoseAnn, I hope you learn to love your job as well as Cookie does hers."

Cookie looked at her watch. "Your appointment is probably here now," she said.

"I'll go see if he's in reception."

Both women left, and Cookie came back a couple of minutes later, leading Dink Brennan, who was dressed in a suit.

Herbie shook his hand and sat him down. "I had a call from the director at the farm," he said.

Dink sat down and accepted coffee from Cookie. "Yes, well, I felt the farm had done all it could for me. You see, I was never an addict, and almost everybody at the farm was. I felt out of place."

"Have you spoken to your father?"

"We met last week, and I think we both went a long way toward patching things up."

"I've gotten to know him pretty well," Herbie said. "He deserves better from you than what you were giving him."

"I can't deny that," Dink said. "I'm going to do better by him."

"Why are you here, Dink?"

"Several reasons. First, I want to apologize to you for being such a handful."

"Apology accepted. Don't do it again."

"Secondly, I'm sufficiently impressed with you that I'm thinking of applying to law school."

Herbie shrugged. "There are worse ways to make a living, but, as with most careers, it's only really good when you love doing it.

286

A year in law school to find out if you could love it might be a good idea. Where are you thinking of?"

"Yale. I've always liked it there."

"What are your grades like?"

"Surprisingly good, considering. I have a three-point-eight average, and I might be able to improve on that in my final year. I want to graduate before going on to law school."

"Let me know if you need any advice."

"That brings me to my other reason for being here," Dink said. "I'd like you to represent me as my attorney."

"You're a college junior — why do you need an attorney?"

"Because I've just come into my inheritance from my mother, which is considerable."

"How considerable?"

"Thanks to my dad's brilliant investing over the years, my trust grew from around six million to just under twenty million," Dink said.

"Is your dad going to continue to invest for you?"

"I'd be crazy not to let him. He's the best there is. But I think I'm going to want to invest in other things, too."

"What sort of things?"

"Small businesses that can grow."

"I have another client — one your father sent me — who is that kind of entrepreneur," Herbie said. "I'll introduce you, if you like. You might learn a lot from him."

"I'd appreciate that," Dink said. He gave Herbie a card. "This is my address, until I go back to Yale in the autumn."

Herbie looked at the card. "Nice address."

"It's one of two apartments Dad's firm uses to house out-of-town investors."

"What are you going to do with your money besides invest it?" Herbie asked.

"I haven't decided."

"I once came into a lot of money all at once," Herbie said, "and I blew a third of it in a year. It'll take me five or six years to earn that back."

Dink shrugged. "I've already got a nice car. I may have some clothes made, and I'm thinking of buying an apartment in the city."

"That could be a good investment, Dink. Prices are lower than they were before the recession." Herbie took a card from a drawer and handed it to him. "This is a good agent, if you're looking to buy on the East Side or downtown. Those are her specialties."

"Downtown interests me," Dink said. "I'll give her a call."

"All right, Dink, I'll be your attorney. Just remember, you can fire me at any time, and I reserve the same right."

Dink stood up to go. "I hope it won't come to that on either side," he said. He shook hands and left.

Cookie came into the office. "So that's Dink Brennan? He looks awfully normal."

"Yes, he does, doesn't he? Let's see how that goes. Oh, he's our new client, so you can open a file for him." He handed her the card. "Here's his address, until he goes back to Yale in the fall."

Cookie started back to her desk.

"Oh, and, Cookie?"

She turned. "Yes?"

"Don't let RoseAnn talk to clients until she learns to watch her language."

"Gotcha."

44

Viv and Rosie stood in Viv's friend's apartment and looked around. "It's not obvious," Viv said to the tech guy.

"That's because they're wireless — we didn't have to hide a lot of wiring." He pointed. "You've got four cameras in here, one at roughly each corner of the living room. Nothing can happen here that we can't see." He led them into the bedroom. "We've got one in the light fixture here and one in that basket on the chest of drawers."

"Don't worry," Rosie said, "we're not going to get this far."

The techie shrugged. "Whatever. Each camera has a microphone, too. We'll be in the second bedroom, down the hall. There's a lock on the door, so he won't walk in on us by mistake. When are you guys going to start the ball rolling?"

"You may not have noticed this, Albie," Viv said, "but we're not guys."

"I hope your mark notices that," Albie said. He handed Rosie a wristwatch. "I've only got one of these, so you'll have to decide who wears it."

"What does it do?" Viv asked.

"Two things: it's got a GPS chip, so if we should lose you in the street, we can still keep track, and if you press the stem, it's a panic button. It sets off an alarm that flares your location on the screen and buzzes loud, in case somebody's in the john."

"You're going to have two cops in there with you, so don't all go to the john at the same time," Rosie said.

Viv and Rosie sat in an unmarked car on West Forty-fourth Street and watched the entrance to the building that housed the Bright Lights, Ink, agency. It was raining. Viv's cell rang. "DeCarlo."

"It's Bacchetti. I see you on West Forty-fourth on my laptop screen."

"Shall I wave?" Viv asked.

"Just watch your ass," Dino said. "I'm not up for wearing my uniform to your funeral."

"Don't worry, Lieutenant, there'll be three guys in the second bedroom, and when one of us is in the apartment with him, the other will be outside the door with a key. What could go wrong?"

"Are you armed?"

"One of us will be. If the one in the apartment is packing, it might be a tip-off. And Albie gave us a panic button, and the one who's doing the tailing will have the radio."

"I'll feel a lot better when this is over," Dino said. "Be careful, Viv, goddammit!" He hung up.

"I think Dino cares," Rosie said. "About you, I mean."

"Oh, stop it."

"He didn't tell *me* to be careful."

"That's because he wasn't talking to you."

"He didn't call me, either."

"He couldn't call both of us at the same time."

"I've seen him watching your ass," Rosie said. "Believe me, he wants your body."

"Rosie, if you don't shut up, I'm going to shoot you, I swear to God!"

"You're not going to have time to shoot me," Rosie said.

"What?"

"There's our boy."

Ed Abney came out of his office building, wearing a tan raincoat and a black hat, and hurried up West Forty-fourth, hunching his shoulders against the rain. It was a little before seven.

"He's headed for Sardi's, I bet," Rosie said.

"That's the intel we've got on him. He's old-school Broadway."

Abney turned into the restaurant, and they could see him taking off his raincoat.

"Let's go," Viv said. She started the car and drove slowly to within a few yards of Sardi's' door, then she flipped down the sun visor, which had an official-looking card attached to it, reading Physician On Call.

The two women got out of the car and hurried into Sardi's in time to see Abney walking up the steps to the upstairs bar. They checked their coats and followed.

"You got our story straight?" Viv asked.

"We're two girls fresh off the farm who want to be on the stage, right?"

"I don't know why I partner with you."

They climbed the steps, then stopped, looking around. Abney was talking with the bartender. A headwaiter appeared and told the couple sitting next to him that their table was ready.

"Lucky so far," Rosie said. They hurried to grab the seats.

Abney was served a martini as they sat down, and he took due notice of them. "Good evening, ladies," he said, raising his glass. "Can I get you two a drink?" He was a little over six feet, heavyset with pale red hair and a smooth, pink complexion, maybe fifty.

"Thank you, I'll have a Tom Collins," said Rosie, who was sitting next to him.

Abney turned to the bartender. "Eddie, is there still such a thing as a Tom Collins in the world?"

"There is," Eddie replied, then went to work.

"And you?" he said to Viv.

"I'll have a vodka martini, straight up," she said.

"Eddie? You heard that?"

"I did."

"Only one of them is from the sticks." Abney laughed at his own joke.

"We're both from the sticks," Viv said. "Cleveland."

"Ah, Cleveland," Abney said.

"Don't say it like that," Rosie said. "It's not nice."

"No insult intended," Abney said. "I haven't been there for twenty years. I stage-managed a national tour of *Charley's Aunt,* and we played a week there."

"Oh, you're in show business?" Viv asked.

"My dear, you're looking at the hottest press agent in the Big Apple."

"Wow," Rosie said without irony. "You

must know a lot of show business people."

"I'm afraid that, in my trade, I'm not able to avoid that." He was listening to Rosie, but he was looking at Viv. "I'm Ed," he said.

"This is Rosie, and I'm Viv."

"Short for Vivian?"

"You're psychic."

Abney laughed. "I like you," he said.

"Then let's switch seats," Rosie said, hopping off her stool. Viv moved over and gave her a glare when her back was turned to Abney.

"Anybody hungry?" Abney asked.

"I've got a date," Rosie said, "but Viv is free."

"Rosie!"

"Viv, I know an excellent French restaurant over on the East Side, and my car is waiting outside."

"What's wrong with eating here?" Viv asked.

"The food isn't so hot," Abney said. "Trust me on this."

Rosie tossed off her drink and got off her stool. "I gotta run," she said. "You two kids have a good time." She kissed Viv on the cheek and whispered, "Don't worry, I'll be right behind you." She stopped, took off the alarm wristwatch, and handed it to Viv. "Thanks for the loan of your watch. I'd have been late!"

Viv buckled the watch onto her wrist.

"Another martini before we go?" Abney asked.

"Not on your life. One's my limit before dinner. It's nice that you've got a car — it's nasty out tonight."

"Well, let's get started with the evening," Abney said. He signed their check, and they went downstairs and got their coats.

"Right this way," Abney said, opening the door for her.

A black Lincoln sat idling at the curb, and a driver in a black raincoat opened the door for them.

"Antoine's, please, Ricardo," Abney said, resting his hand on Viv's knee.

Her impulse was to break his wrist, but Viv sat still for it.

45

Rosie was at the wheel of the squad car, staying a little back from the black Lincoln, when the radio on the seat beside her came alive. "Viv? It's Bacchetti."

She picked it up. "It's Rosie, Lieutenant. Abney went for Viv, no surprise."

"Where is she?"

"In a chauffeured town car just ahead of me, going to a restaurant called Antoine's."

"Restaurant? That wasn't part of the deal!"

"I guess our man feels that he owes a girl a good dinner before molesting her."

"She won't be safe."

"Relax, boss, it's a public restaurant."

"I want you inside, where you can see them."

"I can't do that. He already knows what I look like, and I told him I had a date when I left Sardi's."

"Then you'll be on them when they leave

297

for the apartment."

"I will, boss, don't worry."

Viv walked into Antoine's with Abney and
looked around. *It must be good,* she thought,
because it's packed. "Looks like we're not
going to get a table," she said.

"Not to worry," Abney said, as a headwaiter approached.

"Good evening, Mr. Abney," the man said.
"Your usual table is ready upstairs."

Abney took Viv's arm and steered her
toward the stairs. "It's nicer up there," he
said.

"I need the ladies' room," Viv said, not
sure what to do.

"There's one upstairs."

At the top of the stairs they turned left,
and she could see a room ahead. They
walked into it, and it seemed to be a comfortable sitting room. Their table had been
set at the center, and behind it was a large
sofa. *Uh-oh,* she thought. "And where is the
ladies'?"

"Just over there," Abney said, pointing at
a door.

Viv let herself into the powder room and
locked the door behind her. She fished her
cell phone out of her bag and pressed the
speed dial button for Rosie's phone. Noth-

ing happened. "No signal," Viv muttered to herself. She stood on the toilet. Still no signal. No part of the small room would produce one. Well, she thought, she still had the panic button on her wristwatch. She peed, flushed the toilet, then looked at herself in the mirror.

"You dead in there?" Abney shouted.

Viv opened the door. Abney had opened a bottle of champagne and was holding out a flute to her.

"To new friends," Abney said. He sipped from his glass, then leaned over and kissed her on the cheek.

Viv tried not to flinch. "I'm starved," she said. She reached for her cell phone. "Mind if I make a quick call?"

"It won't work here," Abney said. "Antoine has the place electronically blocked. He hates cell phones."

"Well, I guess that makes for a quieter dinner," she said, wondering if it would block the panic button, too.

"Have a seat," Abney said. "I've already ordered for us."

"How nice of you," Viv said as he pushed her chair under her.

Dinner was three courses, and it was good. Abney kept filling her champagne glass.

"So, Viv, what brings you to the big city?"

"Just a vacation," she replied. "A friend of mine lent me her very nice apartment while she's on a European vacation."

"Sounds nice."

"It is. I'll give you a nightcap there when we've finished dinner."

"Maybe," Abney replied.

She had thought that he would jump at the opportunity. Maybe this was going nowhere.

They finished dessert, and Viv began to wonder if she had drunk too much. "You have a heavy hand with the champagne," she managed to say, but she slurred her words.

"You've had only one glass," Abney replied. "And half a martini at Sardi's."

"Then why am I so . . ." She couldn't seem to get the words out.

Abney got up, took her by her left wrist, and led her toward the sofa. "Let's get comfortable," he said, then he pushed her arm behind her, pulled her to him, and planted a big kiss on her lips, grinding his crotch into hers.

Viv could stand up, but she didn't seem able to resist him. Then she felt a hand under her dress, and, in one strong motion,

Abney ripped off her panties. She tried to protest, but the words wouldn't come. Then she was on her back on the sofa. He kept the grip on her left wrist, over the watch, and undid his trousers with the other hand. Viv's right hand was pinned under her own body, and she couldn't get it out. She wanted to scream.

In the car, Rosie got on the radio. "Lieutenant Bacchetti?"

"I'm here, Rosie. What's happening?"

"They've been in there a long time. Have you got a male detective nearby? I want to go in, but I ought to be with a date, in case Abney sees me. I don't want to blow this."

"I'm two blocks away, in my car, and I'm on the way."

"I read you," she said.

Viv's ankles were over Abney's shoulders, now, and he was fumbling to get inside her. She made a monumental effort to move and managed to get one foot against his shoulder and push.

"Hold still!" Abney snarled. "Don't worry, you're going to enjoy it." His face was flushed, and he was breathing hard.

Viv started to struggle again, and he put his free arm across her throat and pressed hard. She couldn't breathe, and she thought she felt something in her throat snap. Then she passed out.

Abney felt her go limp. "Shit!" he said aloud. He didn't want a rag doll; he liked the resistance. Then he froze. She wasn't moving, didn't seem to be breathing, either. He reached for her throat to get a pulse and found nothing. Swearing, he got up and pulled up his trousers, then went to the rear door of the room and looked down the stairs. It was clear.

He went back to the table, slung her handbag over his arm, then went to the sofa, pulled her up into a fireman's carry, and left through the back door, down the stairs to the alley.

Dino pulled up, and Rosie was out of the car, waiting for him.

"Let's go," Dino said.

"Don't rush," she said. "We don't want to call attention to ourselves."

They walked into the restaurant, and the headwaiter approached. "I'm afraid it's going to be another forty-five minutes before I'll have a table."

"We'll just have a drink at the bar," Dino said. They took two stools, and Dino looked around. "I don't see her," he said. "Do you see Abney?"

"No," she said. "They're not here."

Dino called the bartender over. "I was supposed to meet Ed Abney here. Have you seen him?"

"Sure, he's in the upstairs dining room," the bartender replied, nodding toward the stairway. "But he doesn't like to be disturbed when he's up there." He winked for emphasis. "Can I get you a drink? He won't be much longer, if he's true to form."

Dino grabbed Rosie's hand. "Come on!" he said, and ran for the stairs.

46

Dino ran down the upstairs hallway and tried the door: locked. He knocked. "Mr. Abney?"

"God knows what's going on in there," Rosie said from behind him.

Dino knocked again. "Mr. Abney, it's the police. Open the door." No response. Dino pulled his weapon, took a step back, and kicked the door open, splintering the jamb. Rosie followed him in. There were dishes and glasses on the table, but the room was empty.

Rosie opened one of the two other doors in the room. "Powder room," she said.

Dino opened the other door and found the back stairs. "Let's go!" He ran down the stairs, pushed open the fire door, and stepped outside. He found himself in an alley and it was raining. There was a dumpster and half a dozen trash cans scattered about.

"He's got a car," Rosie said. "The shortest way is back through the restaurant." She tried the door, but it had locked behind them. "Shit!" she yelled. "We'll have to go around!"

They started down the alley at a run, but as they ran, Rosie heard a sound like a car alarm, muffled as if from a garage, but there was no garage in the alley. "Wait!" she yelled at Dino, then she turned back, looking around.

"What is it?"

"I hear an alarm. Viv was wearing a wristwatch with a panic button." She ran to the dumpster and pushed up the lid. Viv was lying inside in a pile of garbage, her eyes glazed.

"Give me a hand," she said to Dino. Together, they lifted her out of the dumpster and laid her on the wet tarmac.

Rosie produced her cell phone and called 911.

"I can't get a pulse," Dino said, bending over Viv and gently moving her hair from over her face.

"We need an APB for Abney's town car," Rosie said.

Dino got on the radio. "License number?"

Rosie sighed. "I didn't get it, and there are a million black town cars in this fucking city."

■ ■ ■ ■

Dino paced up and down the hallway outside the ER, talking rapidly into his cell phone. "Rosie, do you know Abney's address?"

"He lives in a hotel on the West Side, the Broadway Savoy."

Dino got back on the phone. "Abney lives at the Broadway Savoy, on West Forty-sixth, west of Eighth Avenue. If he's not there, try his office." He made a beckoning motion to Rosie.

"West Forty-fourth, a couple of doors west of Sardi's."

Dino relayed the name and address. "The charge, for now, is assaulting a police officer." He hung up.

"I could kill myself, not getting the license plate," Rosie said. "That's rookie stuff."

"It might not have helped," Dino said. "There are too many town cars." He sat down on a steel chair in the hallway.

"What the fuck are they doing in there?"

A young doctor in green scrubs pushed through the doorway, followed by Viv on a gurney. "OR four," he said to the orderly. "I'm right behind you." He turned to Dino. "She's been drugged. We won't know what until the tox screen comes back, but it's probably some sort of date rape drug. They're everywhere. She's also got a partly crushed trachea, so she's headed for surgery. The drug may have saved her life. It slowed her respiration and heartbeat. If she'd been conscious and had panicked, she might not have been able to get enough air. OR four is on the third floor. I've got a reconstruction surgeon on the way in. She'll be okay in a couple of hours. Gotta go." He turned and ran down the hall after the gurney.

Dino sat down again. "I should never have let you two do this thing."

Rosie sat down beside him. "We didn't count on the restaurant, and once we knew about it, we didn't count on the upstairs room. From what the bartender said, it was a regular stop for Abney."

"He threw her in a fucking dumpster, like she was garbage," Dino said.

"He must have thought she was dead, or he would have finished her off."

Dino looked at her. "If you tell me she got lucky, I'll transfer you to the Bronx."

Three and a half hours later, a man in scrubs walked into the surgery waiting room. "Who's the lieutenant?"

Dino stood up, and so did Rosie.

"Detective DeCarlo is in recovery and out of the woods," the surgeon said. "I replaced about two inches of her trachea."

"Replaced?" Dino asked. "With what? A plastic tube?"

The surgeon shook his head. "The real thing, from a cadaver."

Dino's face fell. "From a *cadaver?*"

"Don't get all creeped out, Lieutenant, it's a standard procedure these days. We transplant bone, cartilage, all sorts of body parts. It works. Her injury was below her voice box, so her speech won't be affected. She'll be on her feet in the morning and out of here in a few days."

"Thank you," Dino said. "Send the bill to the police commissioner."

"There won't be a bill," the surgeon said.

Dino and Rosie were there when Viv came to. The nurse allowed them to stay long enough to speak to her, then threw them out.

Dino got on his cell phone. "Have we got Abney? Why the hell not? Hang on." He turned to Rosie. "Where does Abney hang out?"

"Sardi's upstairs, but I doubt if he's there this late. That's all we got on him."

Dino spoke into the phone again. "Check

the upstairs bar at Sardi's, if it's still open. Add to the APB that the suspect badly injured a female cop." He hung up. "Maybe somebody will shoot the son of a bitch," he said.

47

Dino and Rosie were at the Bright Lights, Ink, office at the stroke of nine A.M. He showed his badge to the receptionist. "Is Mr. Abney in?"

"No, he normally doesn't arrive until around ten," she replied.

"Who is his secretary?"

"Margie Quinn."

"Where does she sit?"

"Through the double doors, across the big room to the corner office. Her desk is just outside his door." She reached for the phone.

Dino put his hand on hers. "Don't," he said, "and when Abney arrives, act normal, you understand?"

"No, I don't understand," the woman said.

"I have a warrant for his arrest," Dino said. "There's room on it for your name, too."

"I understand," she said.

"Let's go, Rosie." Dino pushed open the double doors and entered a large room with more than a dozen cubicles. He walked around them and came to Margie Quinn's desk and showed her his badge. "Come with me," he said, and pushed open the door to Abney's office.

It was big enough to hold a large desk, a conference table, and a sitting area with a sofa and a pair of chairs.

"What is this about?" Quinn asked.

"It's about Mr. Abney," Dino said. "How long have you worked for him?"

"Twelve years," the woman replied.

"Then you know what this is about."

She bit her lip. "What do you want from me?"

"Sit down, Ms. Quinn," Dino said, pointing at the sofa.

She did as she was told. "Has Ed Abney ever put his hands on you?"

She looked away.

"How long ago and how often?"

"The last time was a week ago. A couple of times a month for the whole time I've been here."

"You must be very well paid," he said.

"I am, but at first, it was a love affair. I know now it was never that, but I'm single and I have a daughter in a good private

311

school. There aren't any other jobs this good out there."

"Last night, he tried to murder an NYPD detective," Dino said. "I have a warrant for his arrest and another to search this place."

"Good God," Quinn said, and buried her face in her hands.

"First I need information: Abney isn't at his residence, and he's not here. Where else would he go?"

"He has a place in the Hamptons," she said, getting up. "I'll write down the address." She went to the desk and came back with a slip of paper.

Dino handed it to Rosie. "Call it in," he said. "Tell them I want two detectives over here, in case Abney comes in, and I want a police helicopter on the West Side pad right *now,* fully fueled." Rosie left the room and went to Quinn's desk to use the phone. Dino turned back to Quinn. "Where else?"

She shrugged. "I can't imagine. His apartment, the office, and the house out there are his world, except at night."

"Where at night, besides Sardi's?"

She got a pad and wrote down a dozen restaurants and bars.

"Who's his number two here?" Dino asked.

"He doesn't have a number two. He

312

doesn't trust anybody else to help run the place."

"You know," Dino said, "off the record, if I were you, I'd put together a few people here and make Abney a lowball offer for the business. He's going to need the money for lawyers."

"That's not the worst idea I ever heard," she said.

"If Abney calls, everything is normal," Dino said.

"I get you."

"If he comes here, my people will take him in, but my guess is, since he didn't spend the night at his apartment, he's in East Hampton."

"I think that's likely," Quinn said. "If he is, he'll call in about ten and start giving orders. I'd better let everybody know to expect that, or they'll say the wrong thing when he calls."

"I'll leave that to your judgment," Dino said. He followed her out of Abney's office and helped her climb onto her desk.

"Listen up, everybody!" Quinn yelled. People stood up at their desks and looked over the partitions at her. "The police are here, and for good reason. I'll explain that later. In the meantime, if Ed calls in, everything is as usual, got that?"

Everybody nodded. "I want Pierce, Williams, and Cohen in Ed's office right now." She got down from the desk and went back to Abney's office. The three others came in, looking curious.

Dino stood in the door and listened.

"Listen to me carefully," she said. "Ed is going to be arrested before the day is out, and you can guess why. This time, he's not going to get away with it. I think the four of us can buy this business cheap, as soon as he realizes how much trouble he's in. He's going to need cash, and quick. Who's game?" Three hands went up. "All right, let's talk about your 401(k)s and mine," Quinn said.

Dino closed the door and went out to the reception room, just in time to meet the pair of detectives who were arriving. He gave them their instructions, then turned to Rosie. "Let's go. I'm taking you to the Hamptons."

"Why, boss," Rosie said, "I didn't know you cared."

"Pull over here," Dino said. They were at a map store at Forty-third and Sixth Avenue. "I want to get a map of East Hampton."

"Map?" Rosie said, looking at him askance. "A paper map? Didn't you ever hear of GPS, boss?"

"Have you ever tried using a cell phone map in a moving helicopter?" Dino asked. "Maintaining an Internet signal at a hundred knots?"

She shrugged.

"I'll be right back." Dino bought a map of East Hampton, then Rosie used the siren, while Dino found the street on the map. When they got to the West Side heliport, a police chopper was sitting on the pad, its rotors turning.

Dino opened the pilot's door, gave him the street map, and pointed out the house. "Put it down as close as you can get to the house." He got into the passenger compartment with Rosie, and they put on headsets.

The chopper rose from the pad, turned out over the river, and gained a couple of thousand feet, then turned and flew over lower Manhattan. The view was spectacular. They crossed Brooklyn, got past the Verrazano Bridge, then followed the south Long Island waterfront east, toward the Hamptons. There was an overcast a few hundred feet above them, but as they flew, the sky cleared and the ocean shone beneath them.

"He's going to be there, I know it," Dino said.

"I've never flown in a helicopter before,"

Rosie said.

Dino patted her on the knee. "They're very, *very* dangerous," he said.

48

Dink Brennan finished his breakfast, then went to his computer address books and began making calls. It took three before he got lucky.

"Hello?"

"Hey, Vanessa, it's Dink."

"Hey, Dink, how are you doing?" Her voice was bright and inviting.

"I'm doing great," he said. "I don't know if you heard about Parker and Carson, but they're in rehab."

"Yeah, I heard last night."

"Best thing for them, really."

"I can believe it. Last time I saw Carson she was mucho strung out."

"What's the name of that place they're in?"

"I can't think of it, but it's that place up in Westchester."

"Oh, yeah, The Refuge."

"That's it. When are you coming to town?"

"I'm in town. You want some dinner to-night?"

"Love to."

"Come over here, and we'll order in." He gave her the address. "Say, seven?"

"See you then."

Dink hung up and googled The Refuge, got the address and a map, then he put on a suit and tie, got his new briefcase, and went down to the garage for his car.

An hour later, Dink pulled into the parking lot next to a large colonial house set in several acres of meadow and woodland. There was no fence, as there had been at the farm, and only the windows on the third floor had security screens. He wondered if Parker and Carson were up there.

Dink walked into the marble-floored lobby and presented himself at the front desk. "Good morning," he said, handing her Herb Fisher's business card. "I'm Herbert Fisher, attorney for Parker Mosely, who is a guest here. I have an appointment to see him."

The woman checked her computer. "I'm sorry, Mr. Fisher, but I don't see an appointment here."

"My secretary would have made it for eleven o'clock."

"Perhaps she didn't call."

"I'm going to have to speak to her about that," Dink said. "May I see him without an appointment? I've driven up here from the city."

"Let me make a call," the woman said. She dialed a number and explained the situation to her boss, then she held out the phone to Dink. "Mrs. Elliott would like to speak with you."

"Certainly." Dink took the phone. "Good morning, Mrs. Elliott."

"Good morning, Mr. Fisher. I just wanted to confirm: You're Mr. Mosely's attorney?"

"Attorney for his family," Dink replied. "His father asked me to come and see him."

"Is this about getting Mr. Mosely discharged?"

"Not per se," Dink said, "but his father did ask me to inquire about that while I'm here. Do you feel that Mr. Mosely is ready for release?"

"It's funny you should turn up here today, Mr. Fisher, because his case is up for review this morning, and I was about to go to the meeting. Tell you what, I'll give instructions to have Mr. Mosely brought to the library, and if there are any developments, I'll contact you there before noon."

"Thank you, that's very kind of you." He

319

gave the phone back to the receptionist.

"Yes?" she said into the phone. "Yes, he gave me his business card. All right." She hung up. "Mr. Fisher, would you please go down this hallway to the end, where the double doors are? That's the library, and Mr. Mosely will be brought to see you there."

"Thank you," Dink said. He reached for the business card. "Oh, do you mind if I keep this? It's my last one."

"Not at all," she said.

Dink walked down the hall and let himself into a handsome, walnut-paneled room filled with leather-bound volumes. He took a seat in one of a pair of wing chairs at a front window overlooking the grounds.

A couple of minutes passed, then a middle-aged woman in whites entered the room, followed by Parker Mosely, who was dressed in his own clothes — a blue blazer and khaki trousers.

"Mr. Fisher?" the woman asked.

"Yes, Parker's father asked me to come and see him."

Parker looked at him questioningly, then caught on.

"When you're done, if you'll just pick up the phone by the door and dial zero and let us know, I'll come back for Mr. Mosely."

She left the room.

Dink and Parker shook hands, half embracing.

"What the fuck are you doing here?" Parker asked.

"Sit down, and I'll tell you."

They took the wing chairs by the window. "How are they treating you?" Dink asked.

"They're about finished treating me, I think," Parker said. "I pretty much snowed them from day one."

"Have you seen Carson?"

"She's in the women's wing, but I see her at meals. We've had lunch together a couple of times."

"How's she doing?"

"She doesn't look so hot. Coming down off a cocaine habit is a little raw, if you know what I mean. I'm glad I never used it much."

"Carson has an addictive personality," Dink said. "Some people are just made that way."

"Yeah, I know. How the hell did you get out of that farm place?"

"Two ways. I snowed my keeper, and I turned twenty-one. The keeper took me to a movie in the village, and I took a hike and picked up my car from the place you left it. Thanks, by the way."

"Yeah, sure."

"I came into my trust from my mother when I turned twenty-one," Dink said, "and I'm well set up now. I snowed my dad, and he let me use a really nice apartment his firm owns. And guess who I'm having dinner with tonight?"

"Who?"

"Vanessa."

"You dog. Fuck her once for me, will you?"

"I'd be delighted. If you see Carson, better not mention Vanessa."

"Yeah, they're, like, second-best friends, or something. Why did you come up here? It could be dangerous for you, you know. That cop that questioned me acted like he was going to make the world fall on you."

"I figured that out," Dink said. "They're going to do nothing to any of us, because it would get Herb Fisher's name in the papers, and his clients wouldn't like it if their lawyer got charged with rape. It's not dangerous, believe me, and I've got plans, sort of, for Mr. Fisher."

Parker smiled. "Tell me."

Dink leaned in. "Here's what I need from you." He had just finished telling Parker what he wanted when there was a knock at the door, and a woman came in. Dink and Parker stood.

"Mr. Fisher? I'm Mrs. Elliott. We spoke on the phone."

"Of course, Mrs. Elliott. Do you have news for us?"

"Yes, I do. Mr. Mosely has been approved for discharge, just as soon as his father can come to sign him out."

"That's wonderful news, Mrs. Elliott. Congratulations, Parker, on completing your treatment. Mrs. Elliott, it occurs to me that I can give Parker a lift back to New York and save his father the trouble of a drive out here."

"I'm afraid a parent will have to give written authorization," she said.

"That's all right, I have his father's power of attorney, so I can sign him out. Isn't this great, Parker? We can surprise your dad."

"Oh, it's great," Parker said.

"Well, all right," Mrs. Elliott said. "Parker, why don't I walk you back to your room, and your can pack your things. Mr. Fisher, you may wait here, if you like, for Mr. Mosely to come back."

"Thank you so much, Mrs. Elliott, for everything." Dink shook hands with her, and she left with Parker.

Half an hour later, they were driving back to the city. "You can bunk with me for a

323

while," Dink said. "There are two bedrooms."

"Great," Parker replied. "I'm looking forward to this."

49

The chopper slowed as it reached East Hampton and ran along the beach. The pilot looked back at Dino and Rosie. "It's the smallest one," he said over the intercom, while pointing down. "There's a guy on the front porch. I'll fly past and approach from the landward side. There's a backyard."

Dino looked down and from their height of about two hundred feet saw a man sitting at a table on the front porch of the house; he seemed to be eating breakfast. Dino gave the pilot a thumbs-up. "I see him," he said. "There's a hedge behind the house that separates it from what looks like a park. Can you put it down on that side of the hedge?"

"Sure thing," the pilot said. Well past the house now, he swung inland.

Dino felt the deceleration and heard the chopper's noise decline. "They must have some sort of quiet mode," he said to Rosie.

"That's right," the pilot said, "we do. With the house and the hedge between us, he probably won't hear us land."

"Perfect," Dino said. He looked out the window at the enormous beach houses. "Abney must have a very old house," he said to Rosie. "His is a lot smaller than the others, and on less land."

The chopper slowed again and Dino could look over the pilot's shoulder through the windshield and see their landing spot coming. "Tighten your seat belt," he said to Rosie.

"Can I take the train back?" Rosie asked. She was looking a little pale.

"Sissy!" Dino said, and he heard the pilot chuckle.

"Fifty feet and descending," the pilot said. "How long will you be?"

"Just long enough to drag the bastard back here by his ears," Dino said. "Keep it running." The machine touched down and Dino opened the door and jumped out, followed closely by Rosie.

"Solid ground!" Rosie yelled, gleefully.

"Come on, we've got to find a break in this hedge," Dino said, trotting along the twelve-foot-high thicket. "There's no going through the thing." They came to a road and turned toward the beach. The hedge turned, too. "The driveway's gotta be along here somewhere," Dino muttered, slowing down.

"Just ahead," Rosie said. "You want to go in the back door?"

Dino got to the driveway and peeked around the hedge. A silver BMW was parked in the driveway. "Nah, I want to ruin the guy's breakfast. Let's go around." He unholstered his weapon and held it at his side, as did Rosie, as they walked around the house. At the edge of the porch railing they stopped and looked around the corner. The table, chair, and some dishes were there, but no Abney.

"Which way, boss?"

"I'll take the front, you go around back. He might be in the kitchen, so watch yourself. Yell out if you have trouble."

The two parted company, and Dino walked casually around the corner of the porch and up the steps. The front door was open, but the screen door was closed. He tried it: latched. Dino took a credit card from his pocket, slipped it past the jamb, and moved it up, flipping the latch off. The gun at his side, he slipped through the screen door, closing it quietly behind him, then stopped and listened. Nothing. "Yoo-hoo, Mr. Abney," he called out. "It's your neighbor. Are you decent?"

He heard the rear screen door slam and heavy footsteps running. "Stop! Police!" he heard Rosie shout, then the footsteps were climbing stairs. "Mr. Abney, it's the police!" Dino yelled. "Come downstairs with your hands up, or we'll come up after you!" There was more running upstairs, then the noise stopped in what sounded like the front corner of the house.

Dino walked through the dining room and saw Rosie standing in the kitchen a yard or two from the stairs. She pointed upward, and he nodded. He walked to the stairs, and she joined him. "Follow me up, and walk near the wall. The steps will squeak less there."

Rosie nodded. "Gotcha, boss."

Dino started up the stairs slowly, his back to the wall and his gun pointed upward. At the top of the stairs, he stuck his head out for a second, then snatched it back. "Hallway," he said to Rosie. "Mr. Abney! NYPD! Step into the hall, and let me see your hands in the air!"

"Go away!" a voice yelled back. "You can't come into my home!"

"Mr. Abney, I've got a warrant for your arrest for murder, attempted murder, and assault on a police officer! I can do anything

I want, and your house is surrounded by a SWAT team. Would you rather have them come in after you?"

Silence.

Dino stepped up the last step and into the hallway. Staying close to the wall, he moved quietly along toward an open doorway, perhaps twelve feet away.

"Ready?" he whispered to Rosie.

She nodded.

Dino swung around and charged through the door, his weapon extended. Abney was standing near a window, a gun pointed at his temple.

"Put the gun down, Abney, or I'll shoot you where you stand," Dino said.

Abney didn't move. "Go ahead, shoot me."

"Now, why would you want me to do that?" Dino asked. "You've got years of life ahead of you, all of them in prison. You'll love it — lots of sex."

"I'll shoot myself before I'll let you take me," Abney said.

"Go ahead, you son of a bitch!" Dino shouted. "Do us all a favor!"

Abney pulled the trigger, and simultaneously with the noise, the window behind him shattered and blood and brains sprayed all over the wall and the remaining window.

Abney collapsed like a felled ox.

Dino walked carefully over to him and kicked the gun away from his body. Dino holstered his weapon and turned to Rosie. "You didn't hear what I said to him."

"I didn't hear anything but the gunshot," she replied.

"I'll go call this in," Dino said. "You go tell the chopper pilot we're going to be an hour or two. Tell him to call his dispatcher and see if he can wait. If he can't, he can go, and we'll take the train back."

Rosie nodded and headed for the stairs.

Dino looked around the bedroom. It was sweetly decorated, frilly, even. There was nothing remarkable about it: a couple of department-store prints, some yellow curtains, now bloodstained, a bed, unmade.

He walked back down the stairs, got out his cell phone, and called his precinct, then asked for the captain.

"Egan," a gruff voice said.

"It's Bacchetti," he said. "I'm at Ed Abney's house in East Hampton." He read him the address. "Abney blew his brains out while we watched."

"Saves us a lot of trouble," the captain said. "You want me to get the locals to the house?"

"I don't see any way around it. I'll make

sure the scene is properly secured and lots of photographs taken, and Rosie and I will give them statements, then we'll chopper back to the city. My car is at the West Side helipad."

"Good work, Dino," the captain said. "You want me to get out a press release, or wait for you?"

"Go ahead. Just say that we gave him every opportunity to surrender, but he chose to end his life. And say that his death solves the murder of Annette Redfield."

"It will be done." The captain hung up.

So did Dino. He took a seat on the living room sofa and called Abney's office.

"Bright Lights, Ink," the receptionist said.

"This is Lieutenant Bacchetti. I was there earlier today."

"Yes, sir, I remember."

"Let me speak to Margie."

"One moment."

"This is Margie."

"It's Lieutenant Bacchetti. I'm at Abney's East Hampton house."

"Did you get him?"

"He got himself — blew half his head off to keep from going to jail."

She let out a long sigh. "I had a feeling," she said. "I've got his will right here. It was in my safe." She giggled. "He left me everything: the business, his apartment, the Hamptons house."

"Congratulations!"

"I won't be needing any partners. If you'll excuse me, Lieutenant, I need to get my people together and explain things to them before this breaks on the news."

"It'll be on the six o'clock shows."

"I'll have time to contact our clients before then," she said. "Goodbye, Lieutenant, and thanks!" She hung up.

Dino was still sitting on the living room sofa when the East Hampton cops arrived.

50

Stone put down the phone on his desk and walked back to the kitchen and into the garden, where Marla was relaxing on a chaise longue. There was a script in her lap and a bottle of gimlets and two glasses on the table next to her.

Stone sat down and kissed her, then poured them both a gimlet. "I'm sorry I took so long. I was talking on the phone with Dino."

"How is Dino?"

"Never better. He cleared Annette Redfield's murder this morning."

"What does 'cleared' mean?"

"Well, in this case, he didn't make an arrest."

"You mean, Ed Abney is still free?"

"Ed Abney is dead. He shot himself when Dino went to arrest him."

"Oh, God," she said, putting a hand to her face. "I'm never going to have to be afraid of him again."

"That's right, and it's a good thing, too. Abney nearly killed a female NYPD detective last night. She's recovering in the hospital, be out in a few days."

Joan came into the garden with some letters. "Marla, your neighbor dropped off your mail. There was something hand-delivered, too." She handed the packet to Marla.

Marla opened the hand-delivered envelope first. "It's from Bright Lights, Ink," she said.

"Are you their client?"

"They're publicists for the show I just finished."

"What does it say?"

"I'll read it to you:

Dear Marla,

We want to tell you about a big change at Bright Lights, Ink. Ed Abney is no longer in charge. As a matter of fact, it has been some years since Ed did any active publicity work for the company. Senior staff did the work, and Ed took the credit.

For our existing clients, like you, our work will continue as usual, but Ed is gone. Police went to his East Hampton home this morning to arrest him on charges of the murder of a woman and assault on a police officer. Rather than go to jail, Ed took his own life. The newspapers and TV will give you the details.

I have been with the agency for twelve years, and I am its new president. I will take great pleasure in seeing that your account is handled in an outstanding and personal fashion. If you have any questions or requests, please call me, day or night.

"It's signed by Margie, his secretary. She's a terrific lady, and I always thought she was the brains there."

"Then she still is," Stone said.

"I've got some news for you," she said.

"I hope it's good news."

"I hope it is, too. This morning I read your son Peter's play, the one he produced at Yale last winter." She tapped the script in her lap.

"Did you get the script from my study?"

"No, my agent had it hand-delivered to me this morning. It's coming to Broadway, and I've been asked if I have any interest in directing it."

"Do you?"

"Let me ask you a question first. Does Peter know that you and I are . . . friends?"

"No, that's such a recent event that I

haven't had time to tell him yet."

"Did you suggest to someone that I direct it?"

"No. Peter told me when the play opened at Yale that there was talk of a New York production, but I haven't heard anything about it since, until now."

"Do you want me to direct it?"

"Apparently Peter does, or they wouldn't have contacted you. My opinion doesn't enter into it. For my part, if you choose to direct it, I'll be happy for you both."

"Then I think I'd like to do it. It's charming, funny, and, in the end, very moving. I think a play like this — small cast, one set, put into a small theater like, say, the Music Box or the Helen Hayes — could have a long run."

"May I ask a favor of you?"

"You may."

"You didn't see the play at Yale?"

"No."

"Well, Peter played the lead, and he was very good in it."

"You want me to cast him again?"

"No, I'd rather you didn't. That's the favor I'm asking."

"Why don't you want him in the play?"

"Because of what you just said. I don't want him tied to the long run of a play, even if it's his play. I want him at Yale, finishing his degree, before he does something like that."

"I can understand that. All right, if I do it, I won't cast him. Will he be disappointed?"

"Maybe, I'm not sure. We haven't discussed it."

"Perhaps it's best if I don't use anyone from the original cast," Marla said. "They're all students, and what you've just said about Peter probably applies to them, too."

"I can't argue with that reasoning."

"Then I'll tell them I'm interested, and if the offer is right, I'll do it."

"That's great! Do you want me to tell Peter?"

"No, let him hear about it through channels, then he can have the thrill of telling you. There'll be time enough later to tell him about us."

"Peter's girlfriend wrote the incidental music, and it's very good."

"I'll hear it, and if I like it, I'll use it."

"That would make your playwright very happy. In fact, I think you should expect him to insist."

"Then I'll try very hard to like the music." She took a sip of her drink and sat back.

"Everything all right, now?" Stone asked.

"Everything seems just about perfect," she

said. "Ed Abney got what he deserved, I'm not out of work anymore, and, best of all, I'm here with you."

"Pilots have an expression," Stone said. " 'Severe clear.' "

"What does it mean?"

"It means that the way ahead is clear of foul weather and even clouds, the air is smooth, and visibility is unlimited."

"Severe clear," she repeated. "I like it." She squeezed his hand. "I feel it."

Herbie Fisher was clearing his desk at the end of the day when Cookie came in with a package.

"What's up?" he asked.

"A packet of invitations came for the grand opening of High Cotton Ideas' new building, and a housewarming for Mark Hayes's new apartment. It's a week from Friday. There was a note suggesting that you invite some of your clients."

"What a good idea," Herbie said. "Mark knows most of my clients, anyway. Invite them all. And Bill Eggers, Stone Barrington, and Dino Bacchetti. And invite RoseAnn."

"Dink Brennan, too?"

"Yes. Would you like a drink?" Herbie asked.

"Sure."

"Pour us both one and sit."

Cookie poured the drinks and took a chair. "Cheers." She raised her glass.

"Cheers."

"Is something wrong?" she asked.

"No, but I need to talk to you about something."

"All right."

"I know you find Dink Brennan attractive. He's young, handsome, charming, and rich."

"What a nice combination!" Cookie said, smiling.

"Normally, yes. The trouble is, I don't think there's anything normal about Dink."

"You mean, because he was at the funny farm?"

"No, I mean because he needed to be at the funny farm for a lot longer, and he didn't get the treatment he needed. He short-circuited the process."

"You think Dink is crazy?"

"I think, from what the director at the farm told me about him, that he might be a psychopath. At the very least, he's a sociopath. You know the difference?"

"A psychopath is crazy," Cookie said. "A sociopath has no conscience."

"Either one of them can appear to be a perfectly normal person," Herbie said.

"Handsome, charming, and rich."

"Which do you think Dink is?"

"I think that he's both. The psychiatrist thought Dink had violent tendencies."

Cookie gave a little shudder. "Eeww," she said.

"My thought exactly. I don't buy his reformed act, and I suspect his father doesn't, either. I think it would be a good idea if you treat him politely, but not warmly, and that you avoid seeing him outside this office."

"Herb," she said, tossing off her drink, "you talked me into it."

51

Stone and Dino were having dinner at P.J. Clarke's.

"Good job on the Abney guy," Stone said.

"You can thank Viv DeCarlo for that one," Dino said. "I nearly got her killed doing it." He told Stone about Viv's struggle with Abney in the restaurant. "She would have died in that dumpster if she hadn't been able to use the last of her strength to set off an alarm in her wristwatch."

"How is she now?"

"I saw her this afternoon at the hospital. She's walking and talking. She'll be discharged tomorrow."

"Is she going to be scarred?"

"A cosmetic surgeon closed her incision, and they tell me it won't show after it's healed."

"That's good." Stone looked up and saw Herbie Fisher come into the dining room and waved him over.

Herbie took a chair. "How are you guys?"

"Never better," Dino said.

"Same here," Stone echoed. "Got your invitation for the High Cotton event. I'll be there with my girl."

"Me too," Dino said.

"Why don't you invite Viv?" Stone said. "It's the least you can do."

Dino squirmed a little. "I don't know."

"There won't be anyone from the department there," Stone pointed out.

Dino shrugged. "Maybe. We'll see."

"What have you been up to, Herb?" Stone asked.

"I've got a new client I'm nervous about," Herbie said.

"Who's that, and why are you nervous?"

"Dink Brennan."

Dino put down his wineglass. "I thought we put him away for at least a year."

"He got himself out and convinced his father that he's a reformed character," Herbie said. "He didn't convince me."

"Then why is he your new client?"

"Because of his father. If there's any chance that the kid has turned a new leaf, I want to help him, for Marshall."

"How screwed up is he?" Dino asked.

"How about psychopathic sociopath with

violent tendencies? Or diseases to that effect."

"Is that your diagnosis?"

"It's what his shrink thinks."

"Herb," Stone said, "he's already tried to ruin you once. Why don't you just stay away from him? Marshall would understand your wanting to do that."

"I guess he would," Herbie said.

"Where are those two friends of his, Parker and Carson?" Dino asked.

"At a place called The Refuge, up in Westchester. Dink doesn't know where they are."

"Is he back in New Haven?" Stone asked.

"No, his father gave him the keys to a company apartment on the East Side. He says he's going back to Yale in the fall, then to law school after graduation."

"Well, he needs his father's goodwill to live, doesn't he?"

"Not really. A trust his mother left him became available to him last week, when he turned twenty-one. He's got the money to do whatever he wants without Marshall's help."

Dino shook his head. "If there's anything I hate worse than a violent psycho, it's a violent psycho with money."

"I know how you feel," Herbie said. "I

think the kid is a walking time bomb."

"How big is he?" Dino asked.

Herbie shrugged. "I don't know, six-three, two-twenty, maybe."

"And you're what? Five-seven, a hundred and sixty?"

"Good guess."

"Do you own a firearm?" Stone asked.

"No, but I got a carry permit from the city in today's mail, courtesy of Strategic Defense. And a very nice certificate that qualifies me to take a bullet for somebody else."

"There's a gun shop downtown, near headquarters," Dino said. "All the cops shop there. Now that you've got your permit, why don't you amble down there tomorrow and pick out something for yourself?"

"What do you recommend?"

"Nine millimeter, at least — something that won't make a bulge under that beautiful suit."

"That's not the worst idea I ever heard," Herbie said.

"You're the second person this week to say that to me," Dino replied. "I must give good advice."

"Not always," Stone said, "but this time, you're right."

"Gee, thanks."

"All right, I'll do that," Herbie said.

"Just remember," Stone said, "a gun is of no use to you unless you can put your hand on it in a hurry. Get yourself a nice holster, too. A dresser drawer isn't close enough."

"That's good advice."

"Yeah," Dino said, "even Stone gives good advice once in a great while. When it agrees with mine."

"Listen, fellas," Herbie said, "if anything bad happens to me, it won't be an accident. Please remember that."

Stone and Dino exchanged glances.

"Sure, kid," Dino said, "we'll mention it at your funeral."

52

Shelley Bach leafed through the *New York Post.* She was bored, horny, and getting annoyed about it. Then a name leapt out at her:

DETECTIVES BACCHETTI & MAHON WITNESS MURDERER'S SUICIDE

Shelley read the account of Abney's demise avidly. She had tried to put Dino out of her mind, but now he was back, and in a good way. She let her mind roam back to their time in the suite at the Hay-Adams Hotel in Washington, then she reached for her vibrator. Batteries dead. She threw it across the room, got out of bed, and ran a hot tub. She needed to relax.

Later, fresh, with her hair done, she surveyed her new image in the mirror once again. Such a difference! Dino wouldn't know her from Eve, but he would like her, she was sure of that. She had an idea but dismissed it — too dangerous — then she thought again. She found her prepaid cell phone and called the 19th Precinct. "Lieutenant Bacchetti," she said to the sergeant who answered.

"Bacchetti."

"Hi, Dino," she said in a low voice.

There was a silence, then, "Shelley?"

"I saw the write-up in the *Post*," she said. "Good work."

"Can you hang on just a moment, please?" He put her on hold.

Damn, she thought. *He's tracing the call.* She glanced at the second hand on her wristwatch. She'd give him sixty seconds of her time.

"I'm back," he said. "Where are you?"

"Oh, I'm at an available distance," she said. "Why don't we meet this evening for a drink?"

"Okay," Dino replied. "Where and when?"

"How about Bemelmans Bar at the Carlyle, ten o'clock? That close enough to your bedtime?"

"See you there," Dino said.

She hung up and made another call, this one to an escort service.

■ ■ ■ ■

Dino went to his office door and shouted, "Any luck?"

Rosie stood up in her cubicle. "Nope, not long enough."

"Shit! Come in here, Rosie." He went back to his desk.

Rosie came in and sat down. "What's up, boss? Who was on the call?"

"When's Viv getting out?"

"Tomorrow, if she doesn't have a temperature. They held her an extra day because of that."

Dino felt the wrestling match between his duty and his dick. "It would be nice to have this cleared up by then," he said.

"Have what cleared up? The phone call? Who was it from?"

"You ever heard of an FBI assistant director named Shelley Bach?"

"Heard of her? Are you kidding? She was big news last year. Was that Bach on the phone?"

Dino nodded. "I knew her when Stone and I were on that D.C. thing."

"I'm not going to ask what you mean by 'knew,' even though I want to know."

"I've got a shot at busting her tonight,"

Dino said.

"That would be quite a bust," Rosie said.

"She's asked me to meet her for a drink at the Carlyle."

"I expect the Bureau would like to know about that," Rosie pointed out.

Dino shook his head. "They're so desperate to nail her they'd flood the area with agents. She'd spot the setup from a mile away. You think she doesn't know how they think?"

"She doesn't know how *I* think," Rosie said.

"That's what I was thinking."

"Then let's do it."

"Who around here doesn't look like a cop?" Dino asked.

"Viv," Rosie replied.

"Viv isn't up to this yet."

"She'd hate to miss it."

"We'll have to live with that." He thought about it. "Shelley wouldn't be expecting two women, though."

"Who would?"

"Come with me," Dino said, checking his watch. "It's nearly nine o'clock."

Viv was sitting up in the hospital bed, flipping impatiently through a magazine when Dino and Rosie walked in.

"Have you two come to liberate me?" she asked.

Dino and Rosie pulled up chairs. "How are you feeling?" he asked, then he held up a hand. "No, how are you *really* feeling?"

"I was ready to go back to work the day before yesterday," Viv replied. "What's going on?"

"I'm reluctant to let you do this," Dino said.

Viv threw the magazine at him. "I don't care what it is," she said, "just get me out of here."

Dino looked at Rosie and nodded. Rosie set a shopping bag on the bed. "I picked up some of your stuff."

"Get dressed," Dino said. "I'll go find somebody to sign off on this." He got up and left.

"What's up?" Viv asked, swinging her legs over the side of the bed and reaching for the shopping bag.

"You're going to like it," Rosie said, grinning.

53

Shelley heard the doorbell and went to answer it. She opened the door and silently surveyed the man who stood there, to see if her wishes had been followed. He was in his mid-thirties, well over six feet, slim, wearing an expensive suit, expensive shoes, and an expensive haircut. "You'll do," she said. "Come in for a minute."

She stood back and let him enter. "I'm Brenda," she said.

He smiled, revealing expensive dental work. "I'm Steve."

"Hello, Steve," she said, offering her hand. "I think you're going to work out just fine."

"Thank you," Steve replied. "And speaking of work . . ."

"Of course," she said. She went to her handbag and retrieved the money, already counted out and in a hotel envelope. "Here you are."

"You'll get your money's worth," he said.

"Whatever you want."

"Right now, I want a drink and some dinner," she said. "I've booked a table in Bemelmans Bar, downstairs. It's in a corner with a good view of the bar and the entertainment. I'll take the gunfighter's seat, facing the room. Got it?"

"Whatever you want," Steve said.

"I may decide to leave suddenly. If I do, your first job is to get out of my way. Your second job is to follow close behind me. Your third job is to get in the way of anybody who follows me."

"Whatever you want."

"A jealous ex-husband could show up. Can you handle that?"

"I can handle whatever you want."

She looked at her watch. "Let's go."

Dino's driver stopped on Seventy-fifth Street, half a block short of Madison Avenue, as instructed.

"Okay, listen up," Dino said from the front passenger seat.

"We're listening," Viv said from the backseat.

"This is not going to be as easy as it sounds," he said.

"It doesn't sound easy," Rosie replied.

"It's even harder than that. Shelley Bach

is a very, very smart woman."

"She doesn't have a monopoly," Viv said.

"You start thinking like that, and she'll have you for dinner."

"All right, all right."

"Shelley will be armed."

"How do you know that?" Rosie asked.

"She was an FBI agent for twenty-odd years. She got used to packing, and she likes it."

"Does she take it off in bed?" Viv asked.

"Goddammit, will you two take this seriously?"

"We're listening, boss," Viv said contritely.

"She will suspect that I'm going to try to take her, and she will act accordingly. She will suspect that I will have help, and she'll act accordingly." Dino handed them the photograph he had printed from the FBI website. "This is what she looks like, sort of."

"What do you mean, sort of?"

"Last time I saw her, she was a flaming redhead. She will have done what she can to alter her appearance. What she can't alter is that she's tall — taller than I am, in heels."

Rosie put her hand over her mouth, then took it away. "So we're looking for a tall woman who isn't a blonde or a redhead?"

"That's a start. She dresses well, and I

don't think that will change. I want you two to go in first and sit at the bar. If you order booze, don't drink it. Order some food, a salad or something. It will give you something to do. I don't want you getting bored."

"What do we do if we spot her?"

"You're not going to spot her. I don't even want you looking around the room after you get there. Got that?"

"Got it, boss," Viv said.

"Start a conversation with each other — talk about something that absorbs your attention."

"Who's going to look for Shelley?"

"I am, dummy. I'm the only one who's got a shot at recognizing her. If I see her, I'll make a noise, or do something to attract your attention. Again, don't look around the room. When I attract your attention, look at me. I'll make a move, then you back me up. There may be a struggle, even a fight, but there will be *no shots fired.* You both got that?"

"Yes, boss," Rosie said.

"I don't want to be reading in tomorrow's *Post* that there was a shoot-out at the Carlyle Hotel, you understand?"

"Yes, boss," Viv said.

"I may want to go back to the Carlyle someday, and you may, too. We don't want to get eighty-sixed from the joint."

"Yes, boss," Rosie said.

"You're taking turns saying that," Dino said.

"Yes, boss," Viv said.

"It's like watching Ping-Pong."

"Yes, boss," Rosie said.

"Stop that!"

"Yes, boss," they said in unison.

"All right, go in there and get established. I'll be in in a few minutes. Don't notice me when I arrive."

"Yes, boss," they said in unison.

The two detectives got out of the car and started toward the hotel.

Shelley stopped at the door and checked out the room. Dino wasn't there yet, as she had suspected, and nobody looked like the FBI or a cop. There were two women at the bar, but they were looking at each other, not the room. Probably lesbians, she thought. The headwaiter seated them at the corner table she had booked, and Steve dutifully pulled out the table and gave her the gunfighter's seat.

Dino checked his watch for the fifth time. He didn't like letting them go in first, but it was for the best. They'd already be there when Shelley arrived, and maybe that would make her less nervous. On the other hand, maybe it would make her more nervous, who knew? All he could do was the best he could do.

Ten o'clock. "Take me around to the Madison Avenue entrance," he said to his driver.

In front of the hotel, he got out of the car and took a look through the glass door of the bar, then he walked inside. The place was packed, and a girl singer was working with a trio, doing Gershwin. He waited for the headwaiter to ask, then said, "I'll sit at the bar."

The man retreated, and Dino walked slowly behind the musicians, turned a corner, and spotted Viv and Rosie to his left, at the far end of the bar. He didn't check the crowd, not yet.

He found a stool at the other end of the bar. "Johnnie Walker Black on the rocks, fizzy water on the side," he said to the bartender, who gave him a quick nod and produced the drink in a flash. Dino sat on the stool, turned, and rested his back against the bar. The whole room was before him, now, and he began checking things out, face by face, left to right.

By the time his head had swiveled all the

way to the right, he had checked every table, looking for a single woman. There wasn't an unescorted woman in the place. Shelley was not in the room, he was sure of it.

54

Herbie was working late. It was after nine, and Cookie was long gone. He was just closing folders and his briefcase, when there was a sudden movement at the door of his office. Herbie instinctively leapt to his feet. Dink Brennan was standing in the doorway.

"Hey, I didn't mean to scare you," Dink said.

Herbie sank back into his chair. "I wasn't expecting you, Dink."

"If you're all done here, let me buy you a drink."

"I'll buy you one," Herbie said, getting up again and going to the bar. "You're legal now. What'll you have?"

"Whatever you're having," Dink said.

Herbie put some ice cubes into two glasses and poured Knob Creek over them, then handed one to Dink and sat down.

Dink sipped it tentatively. "Bourbon. I like it."

"You're a precocious drinker," Herbie said. He was still a little nervous about being there at night, alone with Dink.

Dink took a drag on his drink. "What do you think of me, Herb?"

"I think you should have been an actor."

Dink looked at him. "Funny you should mention that, I considered it once."

"You should consider it again," Herbie said. "Instead of law school."

"Why?"

"Because you're good at it. You'll get lots of attention from girls, and you won't have to sweat the work that goes with law school, and especially with practicing law. And I think you'd enjoy being famous."

"Somehow I get the impression that what you've just said is not exactly a compliment."

"Not exactly, no."

"You avoided my question about what you think of me by saying I should be something else."

"That's what I think."

"You think I'm acting now?"

"I think you've been acting at least since you made your exit from the farm — with me, with your dad."

Dink regarded him for a slow count of about five. "I don't like that much."

"I don't much care whether you like it or not."

"You want to be careful, Herb. I'm a lot bigger than you, and I can be mean."

"Both those things are obviously true," Herbie said, "but let me give you some very good advice. Never pick a fight with someone you don't know well. You won't know what you're getting into."

"What would I be getting into if I got into a fight with you, Herb?"

"It's time you knew a few things about me, Dink. Knowing them will save you a lot of grief."

"What should I know about you, Herb?"

"You should know that, in my time, I've killed three men."

"You were in the army?"

Herbie chuckled. "No, I wasn't cut out for that."

"Under what circumstances did you kill three men, Herb?"

"Have you ever heard of a man named Carmine Dattila? Also known as Dattila the Hun?"

Dink wrinkled his brow. "Mafia guy, maybe?"

"Mafia guy, certainly. I once owed some money to a bookie who worked for Dattila — oddly enough, the one I paid two hundred grand of your dad's money to to get out of your life."

"So, how did you handle that?"

"It's more about how Dattila handled it. He sent two men to beat me up, then kill me. Large men. They got into my apartment."

"And how did you handle that?"

"There was a fight. One of them came at me with a knife, so I took it away from him and killed him."

Dink seemed to be frozen.

"Then the other guy came after me, and I killed him, too."

"Why aren't you in jail?"

"I didn't commit a crime. I acted in self-defense. Dino Bacchetti and Stone Barrington saw that the whole business went away in a hurry."

"What about the third guy?"

"That was Dattila. I took a long walk, and I thought about it. I decided that Dattila was going to send more men to kill me, if he was still around to do it, so I went down to the coffeehouse in the village where he did his business. I walked into the place and shot him twice in the head."

"Why are you still alive?"

"Because a few minutes before my arrival, unbeknownst to me, the feds had raided the place, disarmed everybody, and taken half the people there away."

"And that was self-defense?"

"When Stone got through talking to the DA about it, it was self-defense."

"That's quite a story."

"My point is, it's a true story. Stone once said to me that I have a rat-like instinct for survival. You should remember that, Dink."

"I'll keep it in mind."

"There's something else," Herbie said. "I've just spent some time at a facility where people are trained to be expert with firearms and other weapons, and I excelled there." Herbie picked up a letter opener from a cup next to his chair and turned it over and over in his hand.

"So, when I came in here, you could have killed me with that?"

"With that or a couple of other innocuous objects in this room."

"Are you threatening me, Herb?"

"Certainly not. I'm advising you on your future behavior. I would not like to think of you as a threat, Dink. You should conduct yourself in such a manner so as not to make me think that of you."

"I see."

"I hope you do. You see, your physical size and your past behavior as a bully give you a false sense of confidence when dealing with other people. You should always remember that there are people who are smarter, tougher, and more lethal than you, and you never know who they are until you pick on the wrong person. Last week, I met people who could kill you with a thumb."

"I'll try to avoid people like that," Dink said.

"You can't avoid them, Dink, so you should make it a point not to be a threat to anyone you meet."

Dink nodded and tossed off his drink. "Thanks for the refreshment, Herb," he said, "and for the advice. I'd better run along."

"And," Herbie said, "you should give serious consideration to a career in acting. There's a very good drama school at Yale."

Dink got up and left. Herbie took another couple of minutes to finish his drink and calm himself.

55

He hadn't recognized her, Shelley was sure
of it. She could take her time now. Carefully, face by face, she checked the room
again. Nearly everybody was riveted on the
singer; the rest seemed absorbed with each
other, including the lesbians at the bar.
Dino had started to check the room again.

"Everything all right?" Shelley said to
Steve.

"I could use another drink. How about
you?" He looked over his shoulder and
waved at a waiter.

"I'm fine for the moment," she replied.

The waiter brought Steve another drink.

"I'll tell you this," Rosie was saying to Viv,
"even if I could afford it, I wouldn't wear
that designer shit — you know, Armani,
Ralph Lauren. It isn't cut for real women."

"If I had money, I'd wear nothing else,"
Viv replied. She flicked her eyes at the room.

"Don't do that," Rosie said. "The boss

said not to."

"I know, but it's driving me crazy."

"Look over my shoulder and tell me what the boss is doing," Rosie said.

Viv looked at Dino for half a second. "He's leaning on the bar, facing the room. Shelley isn't here yet."

"Why do you think that?"

"Because he's still looking for her, and he looks bored."

"Why would she not show up?"

"Maybe she couldn't get a table," Viv said. "The place is jammed."

"That would be a joke, wouldn't it? She couldn't get a table?"

"Wait a minute," Viv said. "Dino sees something."

"Stop looking."

"He didn't say don't look at *him*. Something's happening."

Shelley fixed her gaze on Dino now. His eyes were panning the room again, starting from her right. She looked directly into his eyes and flashed a little of her new cosmetic dentistry, which practically glowed in the dark. The eyes came to her and stopped.

Shelley turned back toward Steve. "In just a minute, I'm going to get up and walk toward the bar," she said.

"What would you like me to do?" he asked.

"If I stop at the bar and talk to a man standing there, pay the check and leave." She threw a couple of hundreds on the table. "If I keep going and leave the room, follow me upstairs. I'm going to want to fuck you."

"Anything you want," Steve said, waving for the waiter again.

Dino's moving gaze was stopped by half a smile and a pair of eyes. A woman he didn't recognize was staring directly at him. Then she turned back toward the man she was with. That couldn't be Shelley, he thought — or could it? He couldn't tell how tall she was, but the nose wasn't right. The hair was dark, though, maybe an auburn red. He continued to watch her. She glanced at him again.

Shelley took her handbag and stood up. Steve stood and pulled the table back for her, and she began picking her way slowly through the tables toward the bar. Then she was aware of another pair of eyes on her, in the mirror behind the bar. One of the two lesbians was watching her.

■ ■ ■ ■

Dino slipped off the bar stool and stood, unbuttoning his jacket. She was coming slowly, the tables being close together, but she was coming. He remembered he was supposed to give Viv and Rosie some sort of sign. He tilted his head back and let go with a loud sneeze.

Shelley saw the two women turn and look at Dino, but half the room was looking at him; he had sneezed in the middle of "Someone to Watch Over Me." Then she saw something that got her attention. As the women turned to look at Dino, Shelley looked in the mirror and saw something that looked like the butt of a pistol under one of the women's jackets. At the same time, she saw Dino unbutton his jacket. She reached into her purse and found her own weapon.

Viv hopped off the bar stool and put her hand under her jacket. Dino had sneezed, and he couldn't do that and watch the woman at the same time. She saw the woman's hand go into her purse and come out with what looked like a compact Glock. "Dino!" she yelled. "Gun!"

■ ■ ■ ■

Shelley saw the woman's hand go under her
jacket, heard her shout, then saw Dino's
hand go under his jacket. She didn't have
time to aim; she snapped a shot off at the
woman, then turned to see Dino's hand
coming up with a gun in it. Everything was
in slow motion. She saw the woman duck,
but she didn't think her shot had hit her.
The other woman was turning, and she was
coming up with a gun, but Dino was faster.
Shelley got a shot off at Dino and saw him
stagger, then she turned to her right and
ran for the door.

Viv got back on her feet and elbowed Rosie.
"Out of the way!" The woman had turned
and was sprinting toward the door, her back
to Viv. Viv fired once and saw, simultaneously, the woman struck and propelled
forward and the shattering of the heavy glass
door. Up until that moment she had heard
nothing, but now there was the sound of a
couple of women screaming and men shouting, and people all over the room were hit-
ting the floor. "Police!" Viv shouted. "Everybody stay down!" She started toward the
door, with her gun held out in front of her,

trained on the woman ahead of her. Rosie was right behind her.

Dino had been knocked back against the bar by the round, and his feet had slid from under him. Now he heard a shot from the direction of Viv and Rosie. Both women were walking past him, their attention ahead of them.

Viv had another eight feet to go, when the woman suddenly spun onto her back and got off another round. Viv fired, striking her full in the chest, and she didn't move again. "Rosie, check on Dino," she said, then continued toward the woman on the floor, her gun beside her. Viv kicked the weapon out of her reach, then got a hand on the woman's throat. Nothing. Her chest was a mess, and the floor was slippery with her blood. The screaming continued.

Rosie turned toward Dino. "Boss, are you hit?"

"Yes, goddammit!" Dino replied, taking a hand from under his jacket and holding it up, bloody. "Call this in and get these people quieted down!"

Rosie reached for her cell phone. "All right, everybody," she screamed at the crowd. "Police! Everybody sit down and shut up." To her surprise, they did.

56

Viv insisted on riding in the wagon with Dino. The EMTs had stripped off his jacket and shirt and were applying pressure to his wounds.

"You've got an entry wound and an exit wound," an EMT said to Dino.

"Fucking Armani suit!" Dino said. "Eighteen hundred bucks. I'm going to have to have it rewoven."

"Rinse it in cold water to get the blood out before you have it dry-cleaned," the EMT said.

"Everybody's an expert," Dino muttered. He looked up at Viv. "What are you doing here? You should be helping Rosie lock down Bemelmans."

"I'm where I need to be," Viv said. "Rosie's doing fine. The cavalry arrived as we were leaving."

"I hope she knows to get as many statements as she can," Dino said. "There's going to have to be a hearing before we're cleared."

"We did the right thing," Viv said.

"We didn't call the FBI," Dino pointed out.

"That was the right thing."

"We got Shelley off the street, anyway," Dino said. Then he threw up all over himself and passed out.

"Shock," the EMT said, elevating Dino's feet and starting an IV.

"Is he going to make it?" Viv asked.

"He'll be in surgery in ten minutes," the EMT replied. "We've already called it in. A team is standing by. We'll pass up the ER and go straight to the OR. Are you his girlfriend?"

"I'm a detective. I work for him."

"Oh, sorry, you look so concerned."

"I want to keep on working for him."

Stone was just getting into bed with Marla, and looking forward to it, when his phone rang. "Hello?"

"It's Rosie. I work for Dino."

"Hi, Rosie. Congratulations on the Ed Abney thing."

"Dino's been shot."

"Tell me."

"Dino, Viv, and I were in the bar at the

Carlyle Hotel, a setup to take down Shelley Bach."

"Go on."

"It was going fine, until it wasn't. Bach went into her handbag and came up with a Glock. She shot Dino, then Viv shot her. Twice. She's dead."

"Tell me about Dino."

"He took a round in the upper left chest — might have nicked a lung, I don't know. He was bleeding pretty good."

"Where did they take him?"

"Lenox Hill. He's in surgery. Viv is with him; I'm just finishing up at the Carlyle."

"Congratulations on taking down Shelley Bach. I know Dino didn't want to do it, but somebody had to."

"There's going to be hell to pay, because Dino didn't call the FBI."

"Dino knew what he was doing. They'd have had fifty agents there and the block cordoned off. Shelley would never have walked into the place. Any civilians hurt?"

"No, just Dino and Bach."

"That's going to make the hearing easier. The papers are going to like this, you watch. That'll help with the departmental brass."

"I'd better go," Rosie said. "I want to get to the hospital."

"I'll be there in fifteen minutes," Stone

said. "Thanks for the call." He hung up.

"Something wrong?" Marla asked.

"I'll give you the background later," Stone said, pulling on his pants, "but Dino's been shot and is in surgery. I'm going over to Lenox Hill."

"Is it bad?"

"Bad enough."

"Want company?"

"I'll want company when I get back," Stone said. "You get some sleep." He finished dressing and ran for a cab.

Viv sat in the recovery room and watched Dino as if she were afraid he'd flee. His color was good, she thought, and he was breathing normally. His eyelids fluttered, and he opened them and stared at her.

"Am I alive?" he asked.

"And kicking," she replied.

A doctor in scrubs walked over and examined Dino. "You are one lucky son of a bitch," he said. "Whoever shot you was firing hardball ammo, and it went straight through and out, along a path that avoided the heart, the lung, and the shoulder. Nicked the collarbone, but that's okay. You're lucky it wasn't a hollow-point slug, or we'd still be in the OR, trying to sort out the mess. You've also got the constitution of an ox. I've never seen anybody skate through gunshot surgery like that. You'll be back at work in a week, ten days, if we can keep you from getting an infection."

"Don't give me an infection," Dino said. "I don't need one."

"I'll keep that in mind," the doctor said. "Detective DeCarlo, there's a guy out there wants to see your lieutenant, name of Barrington. Only one at a time in here, so you go out and send him in."

"Right," Viv said. "I'll be back, boss."

Stone stood up when he saw Viv coming; so did Rosic.

Viv gave them a thumbs-up. "He's good and going to get better. You can go in, Stone."

Stone pushed through the door and saw Dino, his bed sitting him up. He went over and pulled up a stool. "We've got to stop meeting like this," he said.

"It's been a long time since we met like this," Dino said, "and last time, it was you here and me there."

"What happened?"

"I don't know exactly. Shelley was walking toward me, something spooked her, and she came up with a handgun. Mine never cleared the holster. Viv took her out."

"Did the denizens of Bemelmans Bar enjoy the experience?"

"You never heard such an uproar," Dino said, smiling weakly.

"You get some sleep, pal. There's no rush — you'll be telling me the gory details for years."

"You don't have any scotch on you, do you?"

"I'll buy you your first when you're out of here. Sleep tight."

Stone walked back to the waiting room and took a couple of deep breaths.

"You all right?" Viv asked.

"I'm not used to seeing him like that," Stone said. "I feel almost as if I took the bullet."

"I know how you feel," Viv said.

"He's got the hots for you, you know."

Her eyebrows went up. "What are you talking about?"

"You may have to take a transfer to deal with it. Dino will want to do the right thing."

"Whatever it takes," Viv said.

Stone gave her a hug. "You go home and get some sleep. That's what Dino is doing."

57

Stone was at his desk the following morning when Joan buzzed him. "FBI Deputy Director Kerry Smith to see you," she said.

"All right," Stone sighed, "send him in, and you'd better get him some coffee, too." He stood up and waited for Kerry to enter his office, then shook his hand and sat him down. "Good to see you, Kerry. What brings you to New York?"

"Was that supposed to be funny?" Kerry asked.

"It *was* funny," Stone replied. "To anybody but a DD of the Bureau."

"I'm going to see Dino, at the hospital, but first, I want to know what happened, and I'm sure you know."

"You didn't read the *Times* this morning?"

"Wasn't much in the *Times*."

"Well, it was right at their deadline, I guess. The *Post* will have a fuller account this afternoon."

"It won't have what I want to know."

"You mean, you want to know why Dino didn't call the Bureau before he met Shelley."

"A good place to start," Kerry said.

Joan brought in a small tray with a china coffeepot and a mug and set it on the coffee table, then left.

"He didn't call your people because they'd have had big black vans with flashing lights in the street and a SWAT team in the Carlyle lobby."

"Oh, come on!"

"You know that's true. The Bureau is incapable of doing anything small, even when the situation demands it. Also, Shelley probably knew three-quarters of the New York field office by sight."

"You have a point there," Kerry admitted.

"Dino was smart enough to take only two detectives with him — both of them women."

"I heard, and it was smart, I'll give Dino that."

"That's mighty white of you."

"I saw photos of Shelley's body. She was unrecognizable — nose job, hair color, lots of new dental work. I swear, I wouldn't have known her if I had been there, and I spent a couple of years in bed with her."

"Nobody ever said Shelley was stupid," Stone said.

"She was smart as a whip, and if she hadn't been a woman, she'd have been in my job, and I in hers."

"I expect that's what made her so hard to nail," Stone said. "I think her weakness was Dino."

"You're kidding me."

"Nope. The whole time we were in D.C. last year, she spent every night with Dino."

"Well, of course, she was crazy, or she couldn't have done what she did."

"You mean Dino?"

"I mean half a dozen murders."

"I'm sure the Bureau shrinks have had a wonderful time trying to figure that out."

"You should see the reports — you can't see the forest for the psychobabble."

"Yeah, I've read a few of those."

"Tell me about the DeCarlo girl."

"For a start, you'd better not call her a girl around Dino — or around her, for that matter."

"I guess not."

"She's probably a lot like a young Shelley," Stone said.

"Is Dino putting her in for the Medal of Honor?"

"That would be a little over the top, but

my guess is, he'll get her the Police Combat Cross, because it fits her conduct, and he'll probably get her kicked up to detective second class. Dino won't sign the orders himself, but he knows whose shell-like ear to whisper into."

"I expect he does."

"My advice to you, Kerry, is, when you see Dino, don't bring up your field office's noninvolvement, and I wouldn't mention it to anybody else in the department, either."

"I suppose that would be resented."

"All the way up to the commissioner. If you can't see Dino without avoiding that, then don't see him at all — just write him a nice note on your best stationery and copy the commissioner."

"I'll do both," Kerry said. "Now, tell me what happened in that bar."

"The girls went in first and established themselves at the bar. Dino came in a few minutes later and looked at every face in the room. He didn't spot her."

"I can understand why."

"Shelley must have felt comfortable with the situation, because she got up and started toward Dino. Something startled her — nobody knows what — and she started shooting, hit Dino with her first round. By that time, Viv DeCarlo was on her feet and firing. Put one into her chest and knocked her backward. Shelley played possum for a few seconds, and then tried to shoot again, so Viv fired a second time. Both her shots were expert quality. Then it was over, except to transport Dino and take witness statements. There'll be a hearing on the shooting, and if the Bureau is asked to send somebody, you might have a word with him about not making an ass of himself. Everybody on the panel will be NYPD, except somebody from the civilian review board."

"I guess we can live with that," Kerry said. "I'll have a word with the director about it. Maybe I'll testify myself, since I was Shelley's immediate superior."

"That would be the graceful thing to do," Stone said.

"Can I buy you dinner tonight?"

"I'm seeing a lady who is taking up all of my evenings, but next time you're in town, Dino and I will feed you."

"Deal," Kerry said, standing up. "Let me thank your girl for the coffee."

"Watch it, Kerry."

"Sorry." He excused himself and left.

Joan came in. "He was very nice," she said. "Thanked me for the coffee."

"He wasn't all that nice — he called you a girl."

Joan batted her eyes. "The man's a regular knight in shining armor."

58

Stone pulled his car up to the entrance of Lenox Hill Hospital and waited five minutes before Dino appeared in a wheelchair, his left arm in a sling.

Stone got out and opened the door for him. It was raining lightly, and the hospital orderly held an umbrella over Dino's head. Stone closed the car door and got in. "That's a very nice bullet hole through your suit," he said, "front and back."

"Yeah, I've got to have it rewoven. A nurse got the blood out, though."

"That's above and beyond the call," Stone said, driving away. "Does your shoulder hurt?"

"Not while there's enough Oxycontin in the world."

"If you run out, I'm sure there's plenty in the precinct evidence locker," Stone said.

"Thanks, I hadn't thought of that. Kerry Smith came to see me."

"Yeah, he came to see me, too."

"Is that why he didn't mention my not calling his agent-in-charge about Shelley?"

"I'm sure he was just trying to be a nice guy."

"A nice guy? In the Bureau?"

"Don't be too hard on him — he offered to testify at your hearing."

"Yeah, he mentioned that. The good thing is, the civilian review board will love him."

"You done anything about Viv?"

"What, exactly, do you mean by that?"

"Did you get her decorated?"

"Sure, I got her the Combat Cross. The sons of bitches downtown wanted to give it to *me*, but I told them I wasn't taking a medal for getting myself shot."

"Good for you. What else?"

"What do you mean, what else?"

"Come on, Dino."

"All right, I got her transferred to the Seventeenth Precinct. It's right next door, and it's closer to her apartment. And she'll be promoted."

Stone found a parking spot in front of Dino's building and flipped down his sun visor with the police emblem on it. "What, are you coming in?" Dino asked, as his doorman opened the car door.

"I'm walking you upstairs."

"The hell you say. I'm fine."

Stone walked around the car and caught Dino's right arm, just as he staggered a bit. He steered his friend through the front door and onto the elevator. "You're going to have to take it easy on the Oxycontin, unless you want to fall down in the street," Stone said.

The elevator arrived at Dino's floor, and Stone steered him to the front door, took his key from him, and opened the door.

"This is fine," Dino said.

"I'll walk you to the bedroom. You need a nap." They walked down the hall.

"I don't need a nap," Dino said, sitting on the bed.

Stone helped him off with his coat and shoes and took the sling from around his neck, then lifted his feet onto the bed and tucked a pillow under his knees.

"You should have been a nurse," Dino said.

Stone spread a blanket over him, and Dino closed his eyes.

"Don't get up until dinnertime," Stone said.

Dino made a gruff noise and let out a deep breath.

Stone bent over and kissed him on the forehead, then closed the bedroom door behind him. He got out his cell phone and called a number.

"DeCarlo," she said.

"Viv, it's Stone. I got him home, and he went right to sleep. I'm leaving his door unlocked for you, so bring him some dinner about seven. He'll be a lot better by tomorrow."

"Thanks, Stone," she said. "I'm on it."

"There are some things Dino won't tell you, so I will."

"Okay."

"You're going to get the Police Combat Cross."

"Wow."

"Is it your first commendation?"

"Yeah."

"It'll look good on your record. You made detective second, too."

"No shit?"

"No shit."

"That's great!"

"And you're getting transferred to the One Seven."

She was quiet. "He did that?" she said, finally.

"He did. And you know why."

"I didn't think he'd do that."

"You'll like it. You'll walk in there with a new rank and that nice, green ribbon, so you'll get some respect."

"That would make a nice change," she said. "Did he transfer Rosie, too?"

"He doesn't have the hots for Rosie. My guess is, if she requests it, Dino will get it done, but it might be a good thing to start in the One Seven with a new partner."

"Because she didn't get the medal and the promotion?"

"Let her get somewhere on her own — maybe you two can work together later."

"I guess that makes some sense. Does Dino know I'm coming over tonight?"

"No, but don't worry, he's not going to mind. Take his Oxycontin away from him and ration it. Don't tell Dino I told you so, but he's scared to death of being in pain."

She giggled. "I won't tell him."

"Congratulations on all counts, Viv, and have a good evening."

"Don't worry, I'll take good care of him."

"I know that." Stone hung up and told the doorman to expect Viv, then went home.

59

Marshall Brennan was working at his computer when his secretary buzzed. "Dink is here to see you. Do you want me to reschedule him? I know you're busy."

"No, send him in." Marshall turned away from his computer and rose to meet his son. "Hello, Dink." They shook hands.

"Good morning, Dad," Dink said. He was dressed in a tweed jacket, khakis, and a necktie. "I got your message, and here I am."

"Thanks for coming," Marshall said. He leafed through some papers on his desk and came up with a copy of Dink's brokerage account. "The computer flagged your account yesterday because of a large cash withdrawal, wired to your checking account. Mind telling me why you suddenly need half a million dollars?"

"Oh, this and that," Dink said, looking evasive. "I'm looking at apartments downtown."

"Find something you like?"

"Not yet, but . . ." Dink's voice trailed off, and he began to look irritated. "Mind telling me why you've flagged my account for withdrawals?"

"Just about every client's account is flagged for withdrawals over a predetermined amount," Marshall said. "It's a security precaution, designed to thwart someone who might have gained unauthorized access to an account."

"So I'm just like everyone else here?"

"As an account, yes. I just wanted to know if you made the withdrawal, and if so, why?"

"I think I just explained that," Dink said.

"I think you just avoided explaining it," Marshall replied. "Try again."

"I'm of age, Dad, and I don't have to explain things to you anymore."

"You do if you want my investment skills to remain at your disposal."

"What is it that so annoys you about my withdrawing half a million dollars?"

"It occurs to me that a sum that size might just be for a big drug buy." Marshall watched as beads of sweat appeared on his son's forehead.

"Nothing like that," Dink said.

Marshall swung back to his computer and brought up a new screen. "And I see that as soon as the funds were received in your checking account, they were wired to an offshore account in the Cayman Islands. Mind explaining that?"

"I just happen to be doing business with someone who has an offshore account."

"Well, you'd better be ready to explain that to the Internal Revenue Service, because you've flagged more than your account with me, you've flagged an automatic disclosure from your bank to the IRS about the transfer. That pretty much guarantees you an audit."

"An audit?" Dink asked weakly.

"Welcome to adulthood, son. It's a place where you are held responsible for your actions."

"Even private financial transactions?"

"*Especially* private financial transactions. Tell me, do you have an offshore bank account?"

"Well, ah . . ."

"I was afraid of that," Marshall said, rubbing his forehead. "You should have discussed all this with me before proceeding."

"You'd have just told me not to do it," Dink said.

"And in so doing, saved you tens of thousands of dollars in accounting bills. Who is your accountant?"

"I, ah, don't have one yet," Dink admitted.

"Would you like me to recommend one?"

"No, Dad."

"Then you should ask your private banker to recommend a good firm and schedule a meeting with them immediately. If they take swift action, they might be able to head off this thing at the pass, before you have IRS agents knocking on your door."

"It doesn't seem like all that big a problem. Anyway, how could an accountant help?"

"An accountant, having dealt with the IRS for his whole career, will know to call someone there quickly and explain that he has a young and inexperienced person for a client, and that he has done something foolish, but wants to clean up his mess."

"Oh. And that can happen?"

"Possibly. What won't happen is to get your name off a watch list for every sort of transaction you can dream of. You will now be known personally and permanently to agents of the Internal Revenue Service whose only task in life is to catch American citizens avoiding taxes by money laundering and hiding funds in offshore accounts. Even Swiss banks are now cooperating, in an attempt to save themselves millions of dollars in fines and accounting fees, and they are happy to throw a client overboard if that's what they have to do to please the IRS."

"I had no idea," Dink said, wiping his brow with a handkerchief and loosening his tie.

"By the simple act of turning twenty-one and gaining access to your trust, you have entered a whole new world, son, one with a complex set of rules and regulations that govern the way you will earn, spend, and pay taxes. You had better accustom yourself to playing by those rules, and an accountant, along with your private banker, can help you understand how to do that."

"I see."

"Moreover, any profit on the sale of the securities that was necessary to raise your half-million-dollar withdrawal will be subject to ordinary income tax at the full rate, whereas if you had sold something you'd owned for more than a year, you'd have paid the much lower capital gains tax, so you cost yourself some more money there."

Dink was sweating profusely now.

"Something else, Dink. If that money ended up in a drug dealer's account in the offshore bank, it is very likely that either the IRS or the FBI, perhaps both, has an informant in that bank who will, you should excuse the expression, rat you out. So there is another federal agency you'll be scrutinized by in the coming weeks and months. I strongly suggest that, in addition to an accountant, you call Herb Fisher and ask him to recommend a criminal lawyer."

"Dad, let me explain all this."

"Dink, it's very important that you *not* explain it to me, because communication between us is not subject to any kind of privilege, and I could be forced to testify against you before a grand jury or in a court of law. You can explain it to your criminal lawyer, with whom such communication is privileged. Do you understand?"

"Yes, sir."

"Well, is there anything else I can do for you today?"

"No, sir," Dink said, rising. "I'll go see Herb Fisher right now."

Marshall watched his son leave and tried not to weep.

60

The evening of Mark Hayes's party at High Cotton Ideas arrived, and Herbie hired a driver and picked up Marshall Brennan on his way there.

"No date tonight, Herb?" Marshall asked.

"You're my date tonight, Marshall. How are you?"

Marshall sighed. "I'm afraid Dink may have gotten himself into some new trouble. Did he call you?"

"No, I haven't heard from him since he stopped by my office for a drink last week."

"I was afraid of that. He's going to need a criminal lawyer."

"What has he done?"

Marshall explained about Dink's half-million-dollar error in judgment.

"That doesn't sound good," Herbie said.

"What scares me is that the money might already have been paid to a drug dealer, and that Dink may be taking delivery of something that could get him life in prison."

"I understand your concern, Marshall, but I can't pursue this with him unless it's his idea. I hope he'll call me, and if he does, I'll do everything I can to help him out of this mess."

"Thank you, Herb."

They arrived at the High Cotton building and drove into the garage, then took the elevator to the penthouse apartment. Herbie was stunned when the doors opened to a huge living room, beautifully designed and furnished. Everyone, even Mark's young colleagues, was in black tie, and the women were gorgeously dressed.

James Rutledge, the architect, came to greet them. "Good evening, Herb, Mr. Brennan. Your son arrived a few minutes ago."

"Thank you for telling me," Marshall replied.

"Jim, you've done a spectacular job on this place, in an amazingly short time," Herbie said.

"There are half a dozen design writers here tonight," Rutledge said. "*Architectural Digest* has already committed to a multipage spread on both the offices and the house. Be sure and see the upper floor."

"Will do," Herbie replied. He and Marshall got drinks and wandered around the room. Herbie spotted Dink, there with a beautiful girl, and so did Marshall, but neither made a move to speak to him.

Stone Barrington walked over with Marla Rocker in tow. "Hey, Herb." He swept an arm. "See what you have wrought."

"I'm terribly impressed with myself," Herbie said, and everybody laughed.

Mike Freeman joined them. "Hello, Herb."

"Mike, how are you?"

"Just great. Did you spot my security people around the place?"

"No, I didn't."

"Then I've done my work well. You'll probably run into Josh Hook, who is personally supervising the crew. All the cameras are in operation, too, so none of the guests had better lift anything."

Dino Bacchetti got off the elevator with a beautiful woman in what Herbie thought must be an Armani dress. Dino's arm was still in a sling, but he looked well. Greetings were exchanged, and drinks were snagged from passing waiters. He shook Herbie's hand. "I'd like you to meet Vivian DeCarlo," he said, and she offered her hand.

"I'm very pleased to meet you, and thank you for saving Dino's ass last week."

"It was my pleasure," Viv replied, smiling.

"No date tonight?" Stone asked.

"Just Marshall," Herbie replied.

"No Allison?"

"Allison bowed out," Herbie said, shrugging. "She felt that having an office relationship wasn't good for her career."

"She's probably right," Stone said.

A waiter passed, paging the guests to a large buffet dinner set up in the dining room. Everyone got a plate and a glass of wine and found seats.

Mark Hayes came by and welcomed everyone. "I want to thank you, Herb," he said, "for making this happen."

"It was more of a pleasure than I can tell you," Herbie replied. "And you're welcome. How's the software going?"

"We're out of beta and on the market," Mark said, "and the reviews have been amazing."

"I smell an IPO coming," Herbie said.

"You have a good nose — hang on to your stock."

"I certainly will."

"The IPO is going to be something," Marshall said. "There's great anticipation in the industry and in the investment world, too."

"Then maybe I'll hang on to my stock for

a few years, instead of dumping it on day one," Herbie said.

"Good idea."

After dinner, Herbie and Marshall climbed a broad staircase to the upper floor of the penthouse and wandered around. They found themselves alone in the master bedroom.

"I'm sure there's a john around here somewhere," Marshall said. "Excuse me while I find it."

Herbie stepped out onto the bedroom's terrace and was amazed at the view north. It was a cool night, clear of any haze, and the city's skyline looked like a gigantic movie set. He leaned on the railing and took it all in.

"Well, Herb," he heard a voice behind him say, so he turned around.

Dink Brennan was standing there, uncomfortably close to him. "Hello, Dink," he said. He put a hand on Dink's chest and pushed slightly. "Back off just a little, will you?"

Dink took hold of Herbie's wrist and twisted a little. "This is good," he said. "Did you take a look over the rail?"

"No, I didn't," Herbie said, trying to free his hand.

"Straight drop, seven or eight stories to

the alley," Dink said. "I've been waiting for a moment like this with you."

Herbie was backed up against the rail, with Dink only inches from him, so he didn't have much room to swing. He closed his free left hand and aimed a straight punch to Dink's nose, but Dink saw it coming and turned his head back, and the blow glanced off his cheek.

"Good," he said. "That makes this self-defense." Still holding the wrist, he hooked his other hand into Herbie's trousers and lifted him off his feet. Herbie swung his left again, to no great effect, and he found himself sitting, precariously, on the railing. He grabbed it with his left hand and hung on for dear life. It was clear that Dink was not kidding.

Then, with a push of both hands, Dink sent Herbie backward, off the railing. For a moment, Herbie clung with his left hand, but his body twisted from his momentum, and he lost his grip and started down.

"Bye-bye, Herb," Dink was saying.

A few feet down, Herbie flailed into a length of pipe jutting perhaps eighteen inches from the building. He had time to think that it must be a drain for the deck. He got one hand on it and dangled, trying to stop his yawing and get the other hand onto the pipe.

"Here, Herb," Dink said, throwing a leg over the railing, "let me help you." He put his foot on Herbie's hand and began to press his weight onto it.

Herbie got another hand on the pipe but couldn't free his other from Dink's foot. Then Dink drew back his leg for a kick.

"No stops this time," he said, "just straight down."

Herbie was looking up at Dink, and he saw a form behind him. Then, as Dink threw his kick, he seemed to lose his balance. The kick missed, and its momentum pulled him over the rail. "Oh, shit," Herbie heard him say as he fell.

Dink fell past Herbie and went straight down.

Herbie was still looking up, and Marshall Brennan filled his vision. Marshall had a hand reaching for him.

"Grab it," Marshall said, and Herbie did, then he heard a dull, crunching thud from below.

Showing surprising strength, Marshall hauled him upward until he could get both hands on the railing and a foot on the edge of the building. In a second, he was lying, panting, on the deck, and then Marshall was helping him up, aided by Stone, who had come onto the deck.

Herbie stood there trembling, leaning against Stone, who put a glass into his hand. "Take a big swig of this," Stone said, and Herbie did so.

Dino and Mike Freeman joined them. "What happened?" he asked.

Marshall Brennan turned toward him. "An unnatural act," he replied.

Later, Herbie sat on a sofa and talked to a police detective, remembering the things that Dino had told him and Marshall.

"Just tell me in your own words what happened," the detective said.

"I was on the deck outside the master bedroom, then all of a sudden, Dink Brennan was there. He was standing very close to me, and somehow I went over the railing, but I caught hold of a drainpipe that held my weight. Dink was trying to help me, then so was Marshall, but somehow Dink lost his footing and came over the railing and fell past me. Marshall was trying to hold on to him but couldn't. That's it."

"Were you having some sort of quarrel with Dink Brennan?"

"No, I just turned, and he was there. I tried to push him back, but he's a big guy, and I think I must have just pushed myself over the railing."

The detective closed his notebook, turned toward Dino, who was standing to one side. "We got a partial view from a security camera that backs everybody's story," he said, then he walked away.

Dino came over to Herbie. "How are you feeling?"

"I'm okay," Herbie replied, "but I'm not sure about Marshall."

"Stone is with him. He just needs a drink."

"Did you hear what he said?"

"Yes, he said 'an unnatural act.' "

"What did he mean?"

"It's an unnatural act when a man kills his son."

"I see."

"And we won't talk about this anymore," Dino said, "not with Marshall, and not with anybody else."

Stone and Marshall came over. "I think we've done enough for this party, and we should go," he said. "Do you and Marshall need a ride, Herb?"

"No," Herbie replied, getting to his feet, albeit a little unsteadily. "We're in my car."

A few minutes later they were headed up-town.

"I'm sorry, Marshall," Herbie said.

"Don't be. If it hadn't ended this way, it might have been much worse."

"You could be right," Herbie said.

AUTHOR'S NOTE

I am happy to hear from readers, but you should know that if you write to me in care of my publisher, three to six months will pass before I receive your letter, and when it finally arrives it will be one among many, and I will not be able to reply.

However, if you have access to the Internet, you may visit my website at www.stuart woods.com, where there is a button for sending me e-mail. So far, I have been able to reply to all my e-mail, and I will continue to try to do so.

If you send me an e-mail and do not receive a reply, it is probably because you are among an alarming number of people who have entered their e-mail address incorrectly in their mail software. I have many of my replies returned as undeliverable.

Remember: e-mail, reply; snail mail, no reply.

When you e-mail, please do not send attachments, as I never open these. They can take twenty minutes to download, and they often contain viruses.

Please do not place me on your mailing lists for funny stories, prayers, political causes, charitable fund-raising, petitions, or sentimental claptrap. I get enough of that from people I already know. Generally speaking, when I get e-mail addressed to a large number of people, I immediately delete it without reading it.

Please do not send me your ideas for a book, as I have a policy of writing only what I myself invent. If you send me story ideas, I will immediately delete them without reading them. If you have a good idea for a book, write it yourself, but I will not be able to advise you on how to get it published. Buy a copy of *Writer's Market* at any bookstore; that will tell you how.

Anyone with a request concerning events or appearances may e-mail it to me or send it to: Publicity Department, Penguin Group (USA) Inc., 375 Hudson Street, New York, NY 10014.

Those ambitious folk who wish to buy film, dramatic, or television rights to my books should contact Matthew Snyder, Creative Artists Agency, 9830 Wilshire Boulevard, Beverly Hills, CA 98212-1825.

Those who wish to make offers for rights of a literary nature should contact Anne Sibbald, Janklow & Nesbit, 445 Park Avenue, New York, NY 10022. (Note: This is not an invitation for you to send her your manuscript or to solicit her to be your agent.)

If you want to know if I will be signing books in your city, please visit my website, www.stuartwoods.com, where the tour schedule will be published a month or so in advance. If you wish me to do a book signing in your locality, ask your favorite bookseller to contact his Penguin representative or the Penguin publicity department with the request.

If you find typographical or editorial errors in my book and feel an irresistible urge to tell someone, please write to Rachel Kahan at Penguin's address above. Do not e-mail your discoveries to me, as I will already have learned about them from others.

A list of my published works appears in the front of this book and on my website. All the novels are still in print in paperback and can be found at or ordered from any bookstore. If you wish to obtain hardcover copies of earlier novels or of the two nonfiction books, a good used-book store or one of the online bookstores can help you find them. Otherwise, you will have to go to a great many garage sales.

ABOUT THE AUTHOR

Stuart Woods is the author of over forty-five novels, including the *New York Times*–bestselling Stone Barrington and Holly Barker series. An avid sailor and pilot, he lives in New York City, Florida, and Maine.

The employees of Thorndike Press hope you have enjoyed this Large Print book. All our Thorndike, Wheeler, and Kennebec Large Print titles are designed for easy reading, and all our books are made to last. Other Thorndike Press Large Print books are available at your library, through selected bookstores, or directly from us.

For information about titles, please call:
(800) 223-1244

or visit our Web site at:
http://gale.cengage.com/thorndike

To share your comments, please write:
Publisher
Thorndike Press
10 Water St., Suite 310
Waterville, ME 04901